# The Gifted

Elizabeth C. Bauer

Library of Congress Control Number: 2014918406
ISBN-10: 0692311548
ISBN-13: 978-0-692-31154-7

# DEDICATION

This book is dedicated to my late grandfather John, whose hugs always made me feel whole, and whose encouragement made me forget my fears. I would also like to dedicate it to those who struggle with self-worth. It's okay to be angry, depressed, and broken. Just remember you are not alone.

# CONTENTS

ACKNOWLEGDMENTS       i

CHAPTER ONE           1

CHAPTER TWO           22

CHAPTER THREE         35

CHAPTER FOUR          56

CHAPTER FIVE          69

CHAPTER SIX           80

CHAPTER SEVEN         93

CHAPTER EIGHT         111

CHAPTER NINE          131

CHAPTER TEN           139

CHAPTER ELEVEN        148

CHAPTER TWELVE        161

CHAPTER THIRTEEN      175

CHAPTER FOURTEEN      190

CHAPTER FIFTEEN       205

CHAPTER SIXTEEN       221

EPILOGUE              233

# ACKNOWLEDGMENTS

I would like to thank:

My parents, David and Jackie, for always pushing me to follow my dreams, and forming me into the person I am today.

My husband, Josh, who gives me more support and love than I could ever ask for.

My wonderful siblings, Addy, Kacie, and Eric, for always being there for me, but never being too easy on me, and telling me how it is.

All of my friends who allowed me to bounce my crazy ideas off them: Ryan, Tyler, Chris, Cassie, Ana, and many more.

Amy Farrar of Farrar Writing and Editing, for being patient with my constant questions and doing an incredible job editing my manuscript.

Juan Reyes, for the remarkable book cover, book trailer, and all the graphic designs for this book.

Kaira Lansing and Eduardo Suastegui for sharing their experiences with me, and helping me through the journey of becoming a published author.

# CHAPTER ONE

I live in the Inept Region, a land given to us by the gifted who are known as the Elite. This lovely land they so *graciously* gave us came with some pretty heavy strings attached. Besides being prisoners between two large walls that reach at least twenty feet high, we have the *privilege* of working in fields and factories to provide the Elite with their basic needs.

We believe that many years ago there was a nuclear war that destroyed everything in its wake and left a toxin in the air that seeped into the systems of the survivors. Our ancestors assume the toxin is what created the Elite gene we carry today. So now, once a year the children who turn fifteen get taken across the wall into the Elite Region, which the Inept Region completely surrounds, and are deemed either Elite or Inept. The ones who are determined to be Inept, or ungifted, are able to return home to their families, but the ones chosen as Elite, or gifted, are forced to stay behind and become a part of the Elite Core. The only time we see the Elite is when the Core walks our streets and takes to the towers along the walls.

The Inept don't have it all bad; we have homes, food, and get the medical treatment we need. Although the homes are small, the food is second-rate, and the medical treatment is just enough to keep us alive. Living in the Inept Region is a decent life. We know if an Inept gets out of line and forces the hand of the Elite that the penalty is not necessarily death. No matter how much they hate to admit it, the Elite need us. We tend to their fields providing them food, we man their factories providing them with all their supplies, and most of all we carry the Elite gene that can be passed on to the next generation. I'm not saying they never use death as a punishment, but it is frowned on. I have known a few Inept that have been sentenced to death for crossing the line.

One time it was during the homecoming of the children who were not considered Elite. A man named Benjamin was devastated to see that his one and only child, Wyatt, was taken by the Elite. Benjamin knew Wyatt would no longer know him, and that Wyatt would be trained to use his gifts against us. He could not bear to see his son turned into a stranger, so he ran for the gate, pushing and fighting any Elite that tried to stop him. Then suddenly he was still, and his feet were off the ground. Next we saw Benjamin being moved, though no one touched him, to face the crowd. Before anyone could say anything, defend him, or even turn away, Benjamin's head whipped to the side, breaking his neck, and his lifeless body fell to the ground.

The Elite that killed him is known by us all. His name is Titen, and the gift he possesses is the ability to move objects with his mind. Titen is a large man standing above six feet tall, and wide with muscle. His blond hair is shaggy but styled in such a way that it shows off the bone structure in his face. Titen would be a handsome man if it wasn't for his eyes.

When an Inept child is taken, their eyes change. Titen's eyes were dark green with a hint of blue when he lived in the Inept Region. Now that he is an Elite, his eyes are hazy like there is a cloud in front of them, blocking their true beauty. I knew Titen when he was still an Inept; he was no more than an acquaintance working in the fields with me, but I knew he was gifted. When he thought no one was looking, he would pick the field without lifting a finger. It was amazing to watch, to see him enjoying his gift, not harming people with it. Two years ago he turned that awful age of fifteen, and I knew he would be kept by the Elite. A gift like that is not taken lightly. I'm still trying to wrap my head around why anyone would call these abilities gifts; they seem more like a disease to me, yet for some reason whenever I come across the children who have one of these *gifts,* and I am always blown away by them.

As I lay in my bed I dream of a world where there are no walls, no one telling us what to do and where to be. In my dream, I hear someone calling my name: "Alexis!" over and over again.

To my surprise I am now being shaken, and I hear, "Alexis, get up! You're going to be late again." I open my eyes and see my mother standing next to me looking as disappointed as ever. "Alexis Mea Gander, get up and get dressed for a day in the fields."

"Alright, I'm getting up. I don't know what the big deal is, it's not like they're going to even notice that I'm late," I tell her. Then my mother turns away, storms down the stairs, and I can hear her arguing with my father about me and my tardiness.

My mother is a beautiful woman, she has long, wavy dark hair that reaches her waist. She has a very feminine build—short, slim, and lovely. Her eyes are a piercing blue that are like looking into the sky. My mother is one of the kindest souls I know, unless of course I'm running late.

Finally I roll out of bed and walk over to my dresser. There isn't much in it, just one nice dress and a couple of work outfits for the different jobs around the region. Today I get to work in the fields, one of my favorite places, so I put on the thinner pair of pants and the light grey t-shirt that indicates where I am working today. I walk over to my mirror and look at the ball of tangled hair that I have to try to comb out. My hair is light brown with hints of blonde that's wavy like my mothers, but doesn't fall to my back as gracefully. My features aren't as feminine as hers, but according to her I'm beautiful. It's hard to believe, especially if I am standing next to her—the way she holds herself alone is stunning. I think I'm a bit awkward, but she calls it unique. As I stare at myself in the mirror trying to pull my hair back, I try to convince myself I am just at a weird stage and someday I will look like my mother. Finally I wrestle my hair into a bun to keep it out of my face while I work.

I head downstairs to see my mother has packed me a lunch and my father is sitting in his usual spot at the table with a smile on his face. My father is a very handsome man. He has a muscular build with a jawline to match. He's a smart man who works hard, but isn't afraid to throw a joke at someone. When I see him and my mother around each other I can't help but think they are perfect together. When they stand side by side, it's hard to see where I fit in. Then he looks straight into my eyes with his caramel brown eyes and says, "Alexis, one of these days you're going to give your mother a heart attack. Being punctual isn't a bad thing, I know they may not care if you are late, but we do."

*Ugh, I knew it! My mother got to him like always.* "I just don't get the point, it's not like we get less food or necessities because I am running late," I rationalize. Then in as sarcastic of a voice I can muster I say, "They have to feed us because you never know, I might be *gifted* after all." Both my parents smile at me but I know it's hard for them to think about it considering my robot of a sister is located at one of the towers right now.

My sister Tara is a beauty just like my mother. Her lovely chocolate brown hair flows down her back, her features almost identical to my mothers. The only difference is her hazy eyes. My sister had the most beautiful caramel brown eyes just like my father.

Tara's ability was one we didn't think the Elite would care to have but apparently they take any and every gift we have to offer, even if it is just being able to jump high and land gracefully without making a sound. Tara used to show off by taking something of mine and jumping up to the roof to hide it.

My father replies, "Yes, you might be, but it still doesn't give you the right to be late!" I give my father a doubtful look, kiss him and my mother on the cheeks, grab my lunch, and head to the fields.

Today my group is working in the cornfields, which is always *fun* for the ones gifted with the short gene. As I get to the field I see my best friend waiting there for me at the edge of it. I yell out, "Hey Zander, you didn't have to wait for me, you know!" He hates when I'm late too, he takes pride in his work and I tend to slow him down.

I can see him shrug and then he yells back, "Sure, I did. Work isn't the same without you by my side."

I smile back at him and pick up my pace to meet him at the edge of the field. Zander is a little taller than I am, with light brown hair; he's thin but strong, and his eyes are my favorite part of him—they are a lush blue with hints of green in the center that stand out like no others I've ever seen. My plain blue eyes are nothing compared to his. I try to take in his eyes as much as possible each day while they are still his. Zander turned fifteen a few days ago, and unlike myself he is gifted. We both knew this year we would be taken over the wall to the testing facilities, but it didn't feel real until he was officially fifteen. I'm sure it will be even worse in a week when I turn fifteen too.

Finally I reach the spot where he is waiting for me, he turns to me and says, "It's about time, I thought I was going to have to come over there and make you move faster." I try to laugh but I can't, Zander knows I hate when he uses his ability, especially at work where the Elite watch us.

So I roll my eyes, teasing him, "Just because you're freakishly strong and can lift me like a feather, doesn't mean you move at light speed!" He laughs and then we both enter the field and begin to work.

Today in the field it's not so bad, I have my best friend a few rows down so we can still talk, and the corn is finally high enough to offer some shade. The only bad part is that we are pulling weeds, one of the worst jobs to do in the fields. I can pick, plant, and dig like no one else, but when they make me pull weeds it's a different story. The weeds have thorns, are thick, and are hard to pull out of the ground. As I struggle from weed to weed, I look to my left and see Zander pulling two at a time, one with each hand. It's a little annoying having a gifted friend, especially a strong one; work is so much easier for him and it rarely ever makes him exhausted. Finally I just sit on the ground defeated, knowing that the weeds won, and I start to eat my lunch.

Zander looks over at me and sulks, "Alexis... sometimes I wish you were gifted." I hang my mouth open. I'm about to storm off, but he grabs me before I can, knowing I won't be able to break loose of his grip. "Let me explain!" he says, looking at me with his wonderful eyes. "I only wish it because I see how much difference it makes to have a physical ability in the fields. On days like today, when I have to watch you struggle, I wish I could share my gift with you. I may be strong, but my biggest weakness is not being able to be strong enough to make your life easier." I see pain in his eyes and know there is more that he isn't telling me, but it doesn't matter because the anger I feel is melted by his words. I turn to face him, wrap my arms around his waist, and give him the strongest hug I can, which of course makes him laugh, it's so weak.

I shoot a look at him and say, "Hey now! I was just about to forgive you but now I'm not sure!"

Still laughing he says, "It's... just so... funny..." He notices the look I'm giving him, gives a small cough, and explains. "You somehow got a weed, some leaves, and dirt in your hair—how did you manage that?" I lift my hand to my bun, feel all the junk in my hair, and shrug, "I'm pretty sure it's from a half mile back when I got a weed with what seemed to have a never-ending root. Then to my surprise it ended and I was on my back." We both laugh for a while, finish our lunches, and get back to work.

Finally we get to the end of our rows and are done for the day. I am so exhausted I'm barely able to keep myself upright as Zander and I walk home. I look over to him and see that his forehead is creased and he is deep in thought. So I nudge him, which of course barely moves him, and I ask, "What's weighing on your mind so heavy?"

He looks up at me, erases the look on his face, and puts a smile on, claiming, "I don't know what you're talking about." Then he gives me a slight nudge that almost knocks me off my feet. We are almost to Zander's house when I decide it would be best for him to come to my home for a while, so he doesn't have to look at the sad faces of his family.

"Hey Zander, how do you feel about coming down the road to my place? I'm sure my parents would love to see you!" I tell him.

"Sure, I would love to," he says with a look of surprise, then with a joking tone continues, "Are you sure you just can't resist spending time with me?!" He winks and smiles at me, and I can't help thinking that might be true.

*He's your best friend, he is gifted, and he will be a stranger, pull yourself together.* I have always known what he said is true, but I have always somehow known he is gifted. *Hmm...I wonder if it's a gift to know others are gifted before they show signs... nah... probably not.* I shake my head trying to get rid of the thoughts. In a few short months we will go to the Elite Region, he will be turned into a stranger, be arranged to marry another Elite, and forget all about me. Just then I notice I had stopped walking, Zander's a couple feet in front of me looking at me confused.

"Did I say something wrong? Or did you just forget how to walk?" he teases me. Then he smiles and the next thing I know I'm off the ground and he's carrying me home.

The entire time he keeps his eyes forward looking toward our destination, while I am having a battle in my head that he knows nothing about. *I should tell him how I feel; no, no I shouldn't, he will be gone and never know me again. But maybe if he knows these next few months we can be together. That's just stupid, then it will be harder when he leaves! UGH!* Why do I need to feel this way, why can't he be Inept, or I be gifted?

We are about a block away when he says, "You should probably walk now, I don't want to freak out your parents and make them think you're hurt."

I sigh. "You're probably right, it wouldn't be the first time you carried me home with an injury." He puts me down and we both walk in silence toward my house. I can tell he is deep in thought again, and part of me wishes he would just tell me what's wrong, yet the other part of me knows he's probably upset that he doesn't have much time left with his family.

I open the door to my house to find my father at the table and my mother cooking. As I walk in my mom says, "Oh my! Look at what a mess you are!"

I shrug. "We had to weed the fields today...not my strong suit." Then I remember Zander coming in behind me, and I say, "I hope it's okay that I invited Zander over for dinner."

My mother smiles and greets Zander with, "Of course,

it's always a pleasure to have you here."

My father looks up at me with a worried look. I know exactly what he is thinking—my father is just concerned about how close Zander and I are; he knows Zander is gifted and knows in a few months we'll be separated. That I will lose my best friend.

We all sit around the table talking about the day when suddenly my mother says, "So Zander, how long have you fancied my daughter?"

Zander, my father, and I all look at her with open mouths, not sure how to react. So I quickly blurt out, "Zander is my best friend—just friends, Mom." Once Zander and my father remember how to close their mouths, Zander looks at me almost hurt, and then agrees.

*How can my mother of all people say something like that! She KNOWS the pain of losing someone to the Elite. She KNOWS we can never be together.* And then I remembered the look on Zander's face at what I said. It was almost like he has been having the same battle with himself as I have with myself. I make myself get rid of the thought immediately.

After dinner is cleaned up and the dishes are put away, Zander and I go outside. We sit on the grass and watch as the sun sets and the sky turns dark. After moments of silence, Zander finally looks at me and sighs. "Well, I better be getting home, my parents will be getting worried. I will see you tomorrow... friend." He gets up and starts to walk away. Shocked by his words, I sit motionless, then I get to my feet and start to run after him.

"Zander, wait," I yell out.

He turns and waits for me to catch up to him, commenting, "Alexis I get it, you don't need to explain."

When I'm finally done panting, I look straight into his eyes and explain what he doesn't know. "Zander, please give me a minute to figure out how to say this." He looks at me waiting patiently while I collect my thoughts, and then I decide to tell him everything. "You are my best friend, and..."

He interrupts me with, "Yeah, I know, I heard what you said, just a *friend*."

I put my hands on his face and look deep into his perfect eyes, pleading, "Please just let me finish, you are my best friend, so you deserve to know. I have been having a battle in my mind about how I do feel and about how I should feel. Zander, I've been afraid to tell you how I feel, because until right now I thought you believed we were nothing more than friends, also because I know in a few months you'll be an Elite and you'll be gone. Not only gone from here," I gesture to our surroundings, "but gone from here," I say, tapping his temple and then his heart. "Zander, I lost my sister to the Elite and I know how bad that hurts. I tried to convince myself it was better that you didn't know, that you could go without being worried about me." I finish my speech and turn to walk away, when he grabs my arm.

"Alexis...I...I had no idea you felt this way. I always thought I was the pathetic friend who wished he could be more. I know that I will most likely become an Elite, and I know they can control my mind, but they will never—" he pauses and pulls me close, running his fingers down my face to under my chin, then raises my head up to look at him. "They will never change my heart. They will never erase you from it." Before I can say anything, he leans down and kisses me. Then he hugs me, smiles, and walks away.

I stand in the street not being able to move, still weak from the kiss—the wonderful, perfect, amazing kiss. Then the panic sets in... *What did I just do?! I should have just let him walk away! Now when he is an Elite it will be worse, now that he knows what's in my heart.* And then the battle begins again. *But he feels the same, he has given me his heart in return. We will figure out something!*

I jump when my fathers' hand touches my shoulder. Just then I realize there are tears running down my face. As I turn to face him, he embraces me in his arms and says, "Just friends, huh?" I shake my head on his chest, and he continues, "Zander is your best friend, it's only natural to become more. Your mother and I were best friends many years ago, and we still are."

I bury my face in his chest more and mumble, "But neither of you were gifted."

He pats my back softly, saying, "No, we weren't, but you both are." I raise my head to look at him like he is crazy, and then he asks, "Alexis, do you really believe you are an Inept?" I shake my head *yes*, still looking at him, waiting for an explanation. My father sighs and begins to explain, "Do you remember when you were very little you came up to me and told me your sister Tara was special?" I shake my head *no* and he continues, "Of course you wouldn't, it was when you were very small. Before Tara jumped a great distance for the first time you *knew* she was gifted. Just like with Titen, you knew he could do amazing things before he even did. Even with Zander, you knew he was special before he had realized it... Alexis, you are gifted."

I pull back and huff, "Dad, having a feeling doesn't make me gifted! If I were to tell them what I think my ability is they would laugh me out of the Elite Region." He puts his arm around me and we begin to walk home.

"Alexis, your gift is more than that," he says, "Have you ever noticed that when an Elite is around you, if you are upset, for that brief moment their haze is gone? When you're with Zander, his grip is never too tight to hurt you, when I know for a fact he has not learned to control it yet." He pulls a tangled piece of metal out of his pocket, hands it to me, and says, "This is one of the silverware he was holding when you said you guys were just friends. Even when he hugs your mother and me, it's always too tight.

But with you it's not."

Still dumbfounded I ask, "What do you mean the haze goes away? How is that possible?" He smiles as we walk into the house, pulls out a chair for me, and answers.

"Alexis, your mother and I believe you have a very powerful gift of the mind, that you can sense other people's gifts, and you can even... hmm, how do I put this...you can even turn their gifts off in some way." Once my father finishes his sentence I get out of my chair, tears running down my face, walk to my room, shut the door, and sob.

I awake the next day still in the same work clothes, curled up in the same position I was in after I had that conversation with my father. It's not possible, I have never heard of a gift that can turn off other gifts.

As I try to wrap my thoughts around the possibility, I hear my mother call up the stairs, "Alexis, Zander is here to walk you to work today." Zander! If I am gifted I can be with Zander! I don't have to say goodbye! Obviously a Physical Elite and a Mental Elite would be people they would arrange to be together.

I quickly yell down, "I'll be right there... uhh... where are we working today?" and then I hear his voice.

"We will be in the corn fields again." I quickly shower out all the grime from my hair and put my field clothes back on. I throw my hair up in my typical bun and run down the stairs. As I reach the bottom of the stairs I see my parents and Zander sitting at the table. My father gestures for me to sit next to Zander. I take my seat, only to notice the sun isn't up yet, that there are hours until work starts.

I look at them all in confusion and then my father says, "Alexis, I told Zander about my thoughts of you being gifted." I quickly look at Zander and he smiles at me. My father clears his throat to draw my attention back to him. "Anyway, we wanted to test my theory to see if you truly are gifted, and are able to turn abilities off. I have already asked Zander to help and he has agreed. So first, Zander is going to hold something heavy, and Alexis, I want you to concentrate and see if you can turn off his gift. Just use however you feel when you and Zander are together that makes him gentle with you." As I sit here trying to figure out what's going on, I see Zander stand next to me and then he lifts the table off the ground, with one hand, as if it's just a piece of paper. I look at him in amazement, never having seen him use his gift except for at work while he's pulling weeds.

Zander turns his head and looks down at me, challenging me, "Okay, turn off my strength."

I look at my parents and sigh, complaining, "I don't know how."

My father places his hand on my shoulder and whispers, so no one else can hear, "Just look at him and think of how you feel about him, how you felt last night admitting it to him." Then suddenly without me even looking up, the table crashes to the floor and Zander steps back, taking in what just happened. I'm not even sure what just happened, but before I can even wrap my mind around it, Zander picks me up and twirls me around.

"Alexis! You're gifted!"

When Zander puts me down, I sit and look at the floor. *I'm gifted... I'm really gifted... I won't be separated from Zander... but... I will be from my parents.*

I look at my parents, "I'm so sorry..."

My mother looks at me surprised. "Alexis, why are you sorry?"

I get up, wrap my arms around her, and say, "Because now I will have to leave you like Tara did."

My mother returns my hug, touches the back my neck, and kisses the top of my head, trying to reassure me, "It's okay, we will still get to see you. You might not know who we are, but we will know you, and we are so proud. The gift you have is one your father and I have never heard of. You might be able to change things."

I look around to see my parents and Zander talking and laughing while I search my thoughts for answers. My mother's words float in my mind: *"You might be able to change things"—what is that supposed to mean? There are so many Elite and there is only one of me. There is no way I can change things. I am a fourteen-year-old girl who is apparently gifted, and will now lose my family.*

I look up at my loved ones enjoying themselves and yell out, "STOP! Just stop being happy about this! I can understand Zander's joy, because I share that." I turn to my parents and explain my outburst. "But I can't understand your joy, I don't see what is so great about Zander and I becoming Elite and never knowing you or his family again. We will have the haze, and we will be a part of the Core making sure you're all doing your jobs!" I finish my rant and run out of the house. The sun is up now so I head up to the fields and begin pulling weeds.

I'm so angry that the weeds pull out with one hard tug. I keep pulling and pulling, not stopping even at the site of blood on my hands. I am so angry I forgot to stop at the edge of the field and grab some work gloves. The events from earlier this morning are still playing in my head, making me angrier.

*How can my parents be happy about this? How can they be okay with losing both of their daughters?* As I continue to think of everything that happened, I begin to feel guilty about my outburst. *Wasn't I just thinking yesterday how I wish Zander and I were both gifted so we can be together? How can I be so stupid? My outburst probably made Zander think what I said last night wasn't true. This whole gifted and not gifted thing is getting annoying. I don't understand how I can be happy and sad about it at the same time. But what I really don't understand, is how my parents can be happy about this.*

I'm getting deeper and deeper in the field and blood pours onto the ground from my hands, when Zander's voice startles me.

"Alexis, your hands are bleeding, let me help you." I turn, look up at him, and hold out my hands. He takes a cloth out of his pocket and begins to soak up the blood. That's when we hear the Elite watching the field coming our way, so I turn to face them and to my surprise it is Tara. "Tara! What are you doing here?"

As she walks toward us I take her appearance in, knowing Zander and I will be Elite soon enough. There is no emotion on her face or in her eyes, she is walking stiffly almost like someone is moving her limbs for her. Her hair is flowing perfectly behind her showing off the Elite Core uniform. It's a sleek black jumper with dark grey detailing. On her chest is the Elite logo, it is a large circle with the letter E in the middle of it. Another circle surrounds it, with only a small space in between each one. The logo looks like our regions—the Inept Region is on the outside expanding around the Elite Region. Once I get past her uniform, I see that at least she looks healthy.

Tara looks at me with the haze in her eyes and responds, "Inept worker, I am here to heal your hands." My heart sinks at her words, her voice is steady but doesn't change in pitch. I desperately want to speak with *my* sister, not this imposter. I look up at Zander, he nods, and puts my hands into Tara's. She has a liquid that stops the bleeding, healing the cuts but the scars still remain. While she is working on my hands I can't help but stare at her in hopes that I can work my gift on her. A few minutes later my hands fall and she walks away.

"Zander, why couldn't I make her haze disappear?" I look up at him and realize this entire time it's the first thing I've said to him. He takes one of my hands and tells me his theory.

"I was wondering the same thing, I could see you concentrating, deep in thought. I assumed the emotions you felt seeing her would trigger it, like the feelings you use to

15

stop my gift. Maybe with everything that has happened today your mind was too full of different emotions to focus on the one."

I look down at our hands and lift them up, commenting, "But it's working on you right now, you're not breaking my hand."

Zander gives a small laugh, "No, I guess I'm not." Then he hands me a pair of gloves and the lunch my mother made me, and we get to work, not saying anything to each other.

When the work day is over, I'm more exhausted than I was yesterday. The rollercoaster of emotions that ran through me today, paired with pulling weeds, puts me on the verge of passing out. Once I reach the edge of the field I sit on the ground, pull my knees to my chest, and put my head down on them. Before I realize it I'm sobbing. I'm not normally one to cry out in the open; I don't like showing people my tears, I see it as a weakness, but my emotions are so raw today that I can no longer hold it together. I'm not sure how long I have been crying when I feel Zander's arms around me. He is sitting on the ground next to me, letting me get it out of my system. He hasn't said a word, he just holds me close and lets me cry.

When my tears finally stop he kisses my forehead, saying in a soothing voice, "It's better now that you let it all out, isn't it?" I shrug my shoulders and realize I owe him another explanation

"Zander, I'm sorry. I know it's better that we are both gifted, and I am truly happy that we will be able to stay together. That I won't lose you. I'm just confused with all this happening. I thought abilities get stronger, more out of control when you're fifteen?"

He chuckles a little, and sarcastically says, "Alexis, you're not fifteen yet, remember? That's next week." He places his hand under my chin again and looks me in the eyes. "Trust me when I say, controlling your gift is the hardest thing you will ever do. I wasn't surprised that you couldn't remove Tara's haze today. But I am surprised that you are able to stop mine whenever you please. When I first realized my strength I had a hard time not crushing my family. I barely have control now, but when I am with you it's like I'm normal. I don't have to concentrate not to hurt you, when I am around you with your ability I can let go. Last night when you asked me what I was thinking, I was dreading separating from you. I was thinking about becoming an Elite and never knowing you again. I can't bear that thought, but now that I know you are gifted, there is hope that I will get to know you for the rest of my life." Before he can say anything else I lean up and kiss him.

Zander walks me home, gives me a soft kiss on the cheek, and leaves. He knows I need the time to figure things out with my parents. As I slowly walk up the path to my home I start to notice its quirky beauty. In a lot of ways our home is just like me. It's not your typical symmetrical home—the windows on the second floor are a bit crooked, the paint is peeling, and the grass is long. I've never taken much notice to the outside of my home and I'm starting to wish I had. In a few months I will never walk up this path again, I will never get to look at this silly looking house, and I will no longer know the residents. I take a deep breath, open the door, and brace myself for the fight I'm walking in to.

When I close the door behind me, I notice my parents don't seem upset. They are doing their usual tasks at this time of day. My father is relaxing after his day in the factory and my mother is making us dinner. I'm starting to think this morning was a dream, that my tantrum never happened, and that I'm not really gifted. Just then my father asks me to sit down and he begins the lecture.

"Alexis Mea, I want you to know that your mother and I are not happy that you are leaving us." I start to protest but he raises his hand to shush me. "We are only happy because you will be happy. Once you have the cloud in your eyes you won't know the pain of losing us. All you will know is that the Elite Region is your home, that Zander is with you, and that life is good. You will get to have the privileges you would never get here. No more days working dawn till dusk, no more watching what you say, and no more walking around like the ground is made of glass. In some ways Alexis... you will be free."

I take my father's words in, hanging on the last one. *Free? How would being an Elite puppet make me free?* Instead of questioning that, I get up, walk over, and hug my father. Then I walk over and hug my mother tightly. When I let go of my mother I look at them both and say, "Thank you... for... everything, and I am sorry that I overreacted this morning."

Both my parents smile, then my dad takes one of my hands. His eyes are full of sadness. "Alexis, dear, what happened to your hands?" I had almost forgotten about the cuts because they don't hurt since Tara...

"Mom, Dad, I almost forgot to tell you!" I say excitedly. "I saw Tara today. At the fields! I forgot to grab my work gloves and I began pulling thorny weeds. My hands were bleeding and Tara came to heal them." My father then asks the question I knew was coming.

"Did you remove her haze? Were you able to get to her?" I shake my head slowly and begin to explain Zander's theory.

"Zander thinks that my emotions were too out of whack to focus properly, even though it was still working on him." My father looks at me deep in thought, but doesn't say anything. My family and I eat our dinner in silence and then I head to my room.

Instead of taking a shower, I run myself a warm bath hoping it will relax me. As the warmth of the water spreads through my body, I let my mind wander. I think about what it would be like growing up before the nuclear war. I try to imagine the walls not existing, not working every day for the Elite, and most of all, never having to lose the ones I love. My family would be whole, Zander would always be around, and life would be great.

Slowly I get out of the bath, empty the water, and throw on my pajamas. As I stare in the mirror I am taken out of my dream world, all I see staring back at me is a robot version of who I will become: my ordinary blue eyes cloudy, making them look almost grey. I shake my head for a few minutes trying to erase the image from my mind. I decide it would be best to try to get some sleep, to stop thinking of what could have been, or what might be.

I'm not sure why I thought sleep would be the answer to clearing my mind—all I do is have nightmare after nightmare, one so vivid I'm still trying to come out of it. *All I keep seeing is Zander with his wonderful blue and green eyes clouded by the haze. With all my might I try to remove the film in front of his eyes, to bring him back to me, with no success. I never give up and keep trying, until the Elite figure out what I am trying to do, and suddenly I am in the air unable to move, slowly my body begins to turn and I see Titen. Panic washes through my mind, but my body doesn't react. I try to turn Titen's gift off, but it's no use. Then I feel familiar arms around me holding me too tight.* I wake up filled with anxiety because in my dreams, Zander was killing me. I can't lay here anymore, so I get up, put my hair in a bun, and go downstairs.

"Alexis, sweetie, did you sleep at all?" my mother asks me from across the room. I shrug my shoulders, sit at the table, and begin to chew on some bread. My mother, being as kindhearted as she is, comes over to the table, and sighing, suggests, "There are still a couple more hours until you have to get to the fields, why don't you try to get some more rest?"

I give her a panicked look and in a tired, defeated voice say, "I can't. Well... I won't. There is no way I am ever sleeping again after the horrifying nightmare I had last night. And no, I don't want to tell you about it."

My mother nods her head and attempts to change the subject. "Today your group isn't in the cornfields, you will be in the berry fields. That should cheer you up, the weeds aren't so tough there!" I give my mother a weak smile and continue to chew on my bread.

Once I am finished picking at my bread, I go and change into my light pants and a deep red shirt, which indicates that I will be in the berry fields today. As I open the door to leave, I gasp and take a step back. Zander was just about to knock on the door as I opened it, and made me jump. I wasn't expecting to see his face, not yet, not before I could erase the terrifying images of him breaking every single one of my bones. As I catch my breath I can hear him laughing—apparently I scared him too.

"Look at the timing, I was just coming to get you so we could walk to the berry fields together." He gives me the brightest smile and all I can do is stare at him blankly. I try to pull myself together, remind myself the Zander in front of me is not the Zander from my nightmares. I say goodbye to my mother and head out the door. As soon as we are outside, he stops and says, "Okay, so what's the deal? Why do you look like you haven't slept for days?" I look up at him and make the rash decision to throw my arms around him and bury my face in his chest.

"Zander... I had the most awful nightmare last night. It took me a minute to snap out of it, but I'm okay, I promise." He hugs me, rubbing his hand back and forth across my shoulder blades. After a minute we start walking again and he asks the question I knew he would.

"Alexis, what was your dream about? Why did you look so terrified this morning?"

I look up at him and exhale. "I had a dream that you were an Elite and I wasn't. I was trying to lift the haze from your eyes and other Elites found out. Titen got a hold of me and I was suspended in the air, then your arms were around me. You were starting to crush me when I woke up." As soon as I finish explaining, Zander stops walking. I turn to face him and I'm about to apologize when he puts his hands on both of my arms and looks me dead in the eyes. "Alexis, I would never... will never hurt you, even if I am an Elite and you're not. I know in my heart I would never allow, even a vacant version of myself, to hurt you." Then he pulls me close and whispers, "I promise you, that even when my mind is clouded that my heart never will be." I smile up at him and we continue to walk to the berry fields. Telling Zander about my nightmare makes me feel as if a thousand pounds have been lifted off my shoulders. The rest of the day was peaceful as we pulled weeds in the berry field, enjoyed our lunch, and walked home together.

## CHAPTER TWO

I wake up to the sun shining in my face and a sweet smell filling the air. As I roll over onto my back, my mother comes into my room, greeting me with, "Good morning, dear, I laid out your dress for you today. Get showered, dressed, and come downstairs." I stay in my bed for a few more minutes trying to figure out what the special occasion is. Then dread pours over me as I realize that today I turn fifteen.

The day an Inept turns fifteen is one of the very few times we get an extra day off from work. Normally we only get one day a week off, mainly to regain our strength for the next week. Turning fifteen is a big deal to the leaders of the Elite—it means a possible gift may be discovered if it already hasn't been. On their fifteenth birthday, the child gets the day off with whomever he or she chooses. I of course had already picked my parents, Zander, and his family to spend the day with.

While I get into the shower I go over the last week in my head. I just found out I'm gifted, Zander and I are closer than ever, and now I get to spend the day with all the people I love. I quickly put on my one dress my mother laid out for me and let my hair fall to my back. It is nice not putting my hair up for once and seeing how different I look with it down. When I reach the top of the stairs the sweet smell gets stronger, so I inhale, taking the scent in as much as I can. Then I go to the kitchen and see my mother pulling a cake from the oven.

We never get treats like these except on our fifteenth birthdays. I take in a deep breath and say, "I cannot wait to taste that!"

My mother laughs at me and responds to my joy with, "Alexis, you have to wait until after dinner tonight." I give her a pouty face and go join my father in the family room. Shortly after there is a knock on the door and I know it's Zander and his family!

So I stand up and shout, "I'll get it!"

I open the door to see Zander with his father, mother, and little brother. Excitedly I greet them, "Hi, Mr. and Mrs. Rane, it's lovely to see you both!"

Mrs. Rane smiles and says, "Happy birthday, Alexis, thank you for choosing us to spend the day with you." Then Zander's parents go and join mine in our family room. I then turn my attention to Orion, Zander's little brother.

"Hey Orion, are you excited to have an extra day off?" He looks up at me, nods, and then joins his parents. Feeling a little hurt, I look at Zander, asking, "Does Orion not want to be here?" While I'm waiting for my answer, I notice the way Zander is looking at me and I begin to blush. He has never looked at me with such intensity, and before I can ask him what's wrong, he remembers how to speak.

"Orion is happy he isn't working today, but he's nervous. I told my family about your gift, and well, he's afraid you will turn his off."

I stare into the room where everyone is sitting and I gasp, "He's only twelve! How can he know he is gifted already? I mean I knew he would be, but he's so young. What can he do?"

After a minute, Zander sighs. "It's kind of awesome,

I'm a little jealous. Okay, so this is going to sound ridiculous, but he can sort of disappear."

"DISAPPEAR! How is that even possible?" Zander laughs at my amusement and explains.

"It's not like he's turning invisible, he has some awesome thing he can do to the mind to hide himself from people. When he first started seeing signs of his ability my parents would panic because they couldn't find him, but he was by my side the entire time and I could see him perfectly fine. It was kind of crazy for a couple days." I look over at Orion, who is pretending like he isn't listening, and I can't imagine him being gifted. Now not only my parents will be losing all of their children, so will Zander's.

Both my family and Zander's spend the morning chatting, laughing, and having a great time. Just after lunch, Mr. and Mrs. Rane are about to leave when Zander says, "Mom, Dad, wait, I want to try something." They both stop, then Zander takes me into the other room and tells me his idea. "Alexis, ever since I discovered my gift I haven't been able to hold my family. Our time here is getting shorter and shorter, and before I leave I want to hug them one last time without hurting them."

I look down at the ground. "I... I don't know if I can help you. So far it has only worked when you are dealing directly with me."

He pleads, "I know, but can you just try?" I give him a smile, walk into the next room, sit at the table, and focus my mind on Zander and his ability. My dad is about to say something, but stops when he sees Zander come into the room. Zander walks towards his family, wraps his arms around his mother, and lets out the breath he was holding in. I look up to see his mother holding back tears and hugging him back.

*It worked... I can't believe it.* For a few minutes I keep concentrating while Zander gently hugs his family one by one.

Then to my surprise I'm off my chair and in Zander's arms as he exclaims, "Thank you! Thank you so much, Alexis!"

I wrap my arms around him. "Anytime." Shortly after, Zander's family leaves, and my parents begin to cook dinner.

While holding his hand, I walk with Zander down the street, until we reach a small pond and sit next to it. We are sitting in silence just enjoying each other's presence when he says in the sweetest tone, "You look magnificent today." I try to hide my face in my hands as I blush, but he pulls them away, kisses me softly, and says, "Happy birthday, Alexis."

I lock my fingers in his and whisper, "Thank you. This has been the best birthday I've ever had."

After we watch the sun start to set, we head back to my home for dinner with my family. We walk into my house and join my parents at the table. My dad turns to Zander, asking, "How did you get her to stretch her ability today?" but before Zander can answer, I speak first.

"He told me how he just wanted to hold his family one last time. I didn't think I would be able to, but he asked me to try. So I tried and I don't know how, but I did it. Any other time I've tried I couldn't get my gift to work." Zander smiles in agreement, takes my hand, and holds it.

Then my father says, "Alexis, what were you thinking when you were doing it?"

"I was thinking of how it's wrong that the kids with abilities get taken away from their families," I say. "About how I will never know you two again, and how I wish the Elite and the Inept could be one region."

My father gives a little laugh and simply says, "Interesting." Just then my mother sets the food on the table, and we begin to eat and relive the afternoon. Once we finish dinner, my mother cuts the sweet smelling cake and gives us each a slice. With excitement I take my first bite and it's amazing—I never knew food could be this delicious. It is sweeter than any berry I have ever tasted but soft like bread. The cake is dark brown, rich with a flavor I've never had before. It's sweet but savory with a smooth cream on top with the same flavor only sweeter. I could get addicted to this flavor—I wish I knew what it was. I look around and notice everyone has the same look on their faces of pure joy. It was the first day in a long time we had spent outside of work all together, having a relaxing day, and eating something delicious.

Even though, I dread going to the Elite Region now that I've turned fifteen. Today is one of the best days of my life.

Zander went home a couple of hours ago, and my father went to bed. So I sit in the family room with my mother, too wound up from the day to sleep. I am laying with my head on her lap while she is running her fingers through my hair. Occasionally I'll glance up and she'll flash her brilliant smile at me. Then she whispers, "Alexis... can you promise me something?" I nod my head and she continues, "When you go to the Elite region, I want you to keep concentrating on the thoughts you had today. To never forget how you feel about the regions, your family, and Zander."

I sit up and protest, "But if I do that they will see my ability firsthand, and not just on their test results."

My mother nods. "Sweetie, I don't think you realize what you may be able to do. If you concentrate hard enough, you may be able to turn off the haze in the Elite's eyes and talk some sense into them."

My mind starts to race with panic trying to take in what my mother is saying. *Talk some sense into them? She's joking, right? I don't see how anyone would listen to a fifteen-year-old who hasn't got the slightest idea of how to control her ability.*

Once I get through my thoughts I ask her, "What do

you mean, talk to them?"

She looks at me with hope in her eyes, "I think if you can clear the haze you can get through to someone. Especially if it is an Elite not much older than you. With the control off their mind, they might remember their families. And maybe, just maybe, they can keep the Elite who is controlling their mind out of their head." I shake my head trying to understand.

"If it will give you peace of mind, I promise to keep my mind on the thoughts I had earlier. But I can't promise to change the world. I'm going to go to bed now. Mom... I love you."

She smiles. "I love you too, Alexis." I go up to my room, get ready for bed, and let the events of today play in my head as I drift to sleep.

I wake up and sit in my bed thinking of the dream I had last night. I dreamt again of the world with no walls. Only this time I saw myself doing everything in my power to break down the walls. I had gone to the Elite Region, and did what my mother asked of me. I somehow picked the right Elite, opened their mind, and convinced them to join me. One by one I cleared the haze from the Elites' eyes and opened their minds. Soon we had enough people with a range of gifts that we were able to overthrow the leader of the regions, the man who separates Inept families, our Commander.

I know it is wishful thinking, but maybe I *can* do something. Maybe enough of us can convince the Commander that what he's doing is wrong, that we can all live together peacefully with no walls, and no mind control. Maybe we can still have a Core to make sure crime doesn't happen, but they won't have the haze. If I can make this happen, if I can convince just one person, maybe things will be different.

I jump out of bed feeling determined to work on my

gift today, and get dressed in my berry field uniform. I rush downstairs to find Mr. and Mrs. Rane sitting in our kitchen. I stop in my tracks when I see the pain in their eyes. My father comes over to me and explains, "Alexis... Zander is missing." My heart stops, I sit on the bottom of the stairs and listen as my father continues. "Last night when he got home, Orion was so excited that he received a hug from his brother that he ran to him and... well, Orion didn't know you had turned off Zander's gift, he thought Zander gained control. Anyway, Orion came running down their stairs and when he was about half way down them he jumped to Zander. He couldn't just let Orion fall. He tried to catch his brother, and in the process he broke one of Orion's legs and one of his arms. Before anyone could do anything, he ran out the door and no one has seen him since."

I sit here looking down, the mood of determination for controlling my gift turns into determination to finding Zander. I push myself up from the stairs and run out the door. *How could he do this, he has to know it was an accident. This is all my fault, I should have never agreed to help him yesterday!*

Not sure where to look, I start in the fields, thinking maybe he put himself to work like I do when I'm upset. When I find he isn't there, I start to panic; *what if he ran into an Elite and hurt them? What if he was taken by Titen to the Elite Region to become a mindless robot already? I have to find him! He can't go without me, I need him.*

I run to the main clearing in the region, where the Coming of Age Ceremony is held each year, where Titen killed Benjamin. I can feel my lungs tighten and my fear growing with each step I take. Finally I reach the clearing and no one's here. *This is good, he's not being punished. But where in our enclosed prison can he be!* Then it hits me, I know exactly where he is!

*The pond...we were just there last night, it has to be where he is.* I run as fast as I can to the pond and reach it, gasping for air. "ZANDER!" I see him sitting at the edge of the water and gasp some more as I yell over to him, "ZANDER!" He turns and looks devastated. Still trying to get air into my lungs, I walk over and sit next to him.

I take his hand, and he pulls it away, saying, "Just don't."

I'm taken aback by how put off he is being and ask, "Don't what? Love you?" As the words come out, I wish I could take them back, I wish I had thought about what I said before I said it. *Why would I blurt that out! I'm so stupid, I'm going to scare him off.*

He looks at me and whispers, "No, never stop that. Don't try to make me feel better. I'm a monster who broke my brother's bones." Relieved that my words didn't scare him away, I take his hand again.

"Zander, I'm going to try and make you feel better, because it's not your fault. You're just learning how to control your ability, and Orion... well, he caught you off your guard."

"Orion's going to hate me, or worse, be afraid of me now."

I trace a small circle on the back of his hand with my finger and say, "No, he won't. Zander, despite being stronger than anyone, you are the gentlest person I know. You would never intentionally hurt anyone. Even if I can't make you feel better, we need to get back to my house. Your parents are there, worried as ever."

He looks over at me, his brow furrowed, asking, "Alexis, do you really... umm... do you love me?"

I can feel my face getting hot as I start to blush and all I say is, "Of course." Then I get up still holding his hand, and make him come with me to my house.

Neither of us say a word until we reach the path to my home. Zander stops and I tell him, "You need to see your parents. They need to know you're still alive." When he doesn't respond I look up at him and he pulls me close to him.

He takes a deep breath and lets it out slowly, "First, I need to say something to you that I've been meaning to say for a long time but couldn't get the courage." He laughs a little, continuing, "I guess being strong doesn't make someone a brave person... anyway, Alexis..." He takes his hands and places one on my back and the other on the side of my face along my jaw line, and looks deep into my eyes. "I love you, more than my lousy words can ever express to you." Then he leans over and kisses me more passionately than normal.

My mind becomes vacant and then I realize my own gift has shut off. His grip is too tight, his kiss too hard, so quickly before he can hate himself more, I pull my lips away, but I stay in his arms and simply say, "Zander, I love you." Then I can feel the control coming back I can feel his grip loosening. So I take his hand, we walk into my home, and join both our parents at the table.

His parents hug each other when we sit down, and his dad says, "Zander, we know what happened last night was hard for you, but do not blame yourself. Your brother is going to be fine, and he isn't worried about his bones... he's worried that he made his brother hate him."

Zander, looking disgusted, says, "Why would I hate him? Orion should hate *ME*, I'm the one who broke his bones."

"Zander, it's my fault, I gave him false hope," I say. "He didn't know I did anything to help you last night. Orion thought you learned how to control your strength. Please quit seeing yourself as a monster, because you are the furthest thing from it. You sacrifice being able to touch your family so you don't hurt them. You have done all you can to protect them, you will learn to control your gift, and you will be able to hold your family without my help."

He gives me a weak smile and then looking toward his parents, asks, "Should I go see him? I mean, does he want to see me?" They both nod their heads *yes*, and then Zander and his family walk out the door together. I lean back in the chair when the door closes and start to rub my neck where Zander's hand was holding me too tight. I should have known better than to start tending to my sore spots with my parents still in the room. My father quickly asks, "Did he hurt you? Was his anger too much for you to hold off his ability?"

I shake my head *no*. "Dad, I had kind of a lapse of judgment, it was my fault. I realized what happened and fixed it." Out of the corner of my eye I see my mother with the largest grin on her face, so I turn to her and ask, "What? Why are you grinning like that?"

She chuckles a little and teases me, "He kissed you, didn't he? Not just a peck, but a real passionate kiss." I nod and she continues, "That's what I figured, you rarely have a lapse of judgment in anything. Only a moment like that could turn off something locked in the 'on' position in *your* mind."

I look at her confused and ask her, "What do you mean I have something locked in the 'on' position?"

She gives me a look like I am losing my mind and says, "Alexis, how many years ago did Zander find out he was stronger than normal? And how many years have you been his best friend not being hurt by his strength?"

My mouth falls open and I respond, "Now I feel like an idiot, for at least two years now I've had this gift and I'm just now realizing it?"

This time my father laughs at me and says, "You have *always* had your gift. Remember our conversation the other day? When I told you that you used to tell me about how special all the other children were. You're probably the most special of them all. Your ability was always there, it's a powerful mind gift, and once you realize this you'll be able to tap into it more. You may even be able to keep it on while... umm... Zander kisses you." I just look at him in awe and giggle a little at how uncomfortable my relationship with Zander makes him feel.

Just then there is a knock at the door, so my mother goes to answer it. I hear her talking to someone but I'm not paying much attention. I'm regaining my determination to work on my gift, to strengthen it.

My mother comes into the kitchen followed by an... Elite. *This can't be good.* Then my mother says, "See, she is right here, she is running a bit late, but I wanted to make sure she got some food in her so she can work well in the fields today." I look around my mother to see the last Elite I ever want in my home... Titen.

I swallow hard, get up, and say, "I'm sorry, I will get to the fields at once." Apparently they do notice when someone is late, constantly. As I start walking to the door I stop and realize I can't move and my feet are leaving the floor.

At once my father slams his fist on the table. "You don't need to do that! She was on her way!"

Then Titen says the first thing since he's walked into our home. "This Inept worker is over two hours late, and now that she is fifteen the rules are stricter. If she has the Elite gene she needs to be watched more carefully. No fifteen-year-old Inept worker is allowed to be late."

Through a strained voice I manage to get out, "I... I didn't... kn... know. It... wo... won't... happen... a... again." Suddenly I drop to the ground and he escorts me out of my home. He's following me close behind when I decide that now is the time to try out my gift. So I stop dead in my tracks and turn to face him.

I concentrate on a free world, on the walls being torn down, and lastly on Titen's clouded eyes. I think of his dark green eyes with the slight tint of blue in them. I look straight into his eyes as he is lifting me off the ground and then I drop back down. He looks right at me, with clear eyes and says, "Alexis? What... what's going on?" In shock, I can't say anything, I just look at him in amazement.

*I did it! I actually did it!* I keep staring at him and his confused look, but as quick as the haze left, it is back. My face falls and I quickly turn and start walking again. When I reach the field, I notice Zander isn't here. Maybe they gave him a personal day to deal with his brother's injuries.

The day moves slower than normal, and I can't stop thinking about what happened. All I want to do is run and tell Zander and my parents. They will never believe what happened, but I can't wait to tell them that I did it! That there is hope, that maybe I *can* change things.

As I sit alone eating my lunch, looking around at all the other kids in the field, I try to focus on each individual one, to see if I can sense if they're gifted. From what I can feel, just under half of us have abilities. *I wonder how many people have gifts in the other workgroups.* After lunch I can't think of anything except controlling my gift, and making it grow.

Finally it's time to leave and by this time I am so full of excitement I run from the field to Zander's home. I quickly knock on the door, he answers it, and before he can say anything I blurt out, "Zander, can you come over to my place for dinner tonight? I need to tell you something important!" He smiles, yells goodbye to his parents, and walks home with me. I look at him, happy to see him in one piece, and ask, "Did you get a personal day to stay with Orion?"

He laughs a little. "You missed me that much that the first thing you do after work is sprint to my house and say you need to tell me something, just to ask that? Well, to answer your question, yes, I was given a day to attend to my brother. They originally were going to have one of my parents do it, but my mother thought it would be best for me to spend the time with Orion."

I give him a slight nudge. "Yes, I did miss you today,

but there really is something important I need to tell you and my parents. I will explain everything once we get to my house."

After what seems like forever, we reach my house and I ask my parents and Zander to sit in the family room. My parents sit quietly as I explain to Zander that Titen came looking for me today. He looks at me horrified and says, "I'm so sorry, I should have told you that they are stricter when you're fifteen."

"Anyway, Titen was escorting me to work, and I got the thought that it would be the perfect time to try out my ability, to see if I could remove the haze. So I stopped walking, focused on a world I would love to see, and it worked!"

All three of them look shocked. Then my father speaks up, "You risked your life hoping your gift would work at that moment?"

I'm appalled by his reaction. "He wouldn't have killed me for stopping for a minute! So now where was I? Oh yeah! When his haze lifted he looked at me, said my name, and asked what was going on. Only I was too amazed to say anything. The control that's over their mind doesn't erase anything! I think it just blocks their own minds and replaces it with whatever the Commander wants in there." I look around to see their horrified faces, and before I can realize what's happened, I am in Zander's arms. He is twirling me around like the night I first realized I'm gifted. When he finally puts me down, I can see the hope in my parent's eyes.

Once the excitement settles, we go to the kitchen and have dinner. No one says much after that; if they feel anything like I do, they're going to be deep in thought for a while. As soon as dinner is cleaned up, Zander leaves for the night to go and be with his brother. I head up to my room, lay on my bed, and think of the possibilities.

# CHAPTER THREE

Since I discovered my gift, the last few months have flown by. The Coming of Age Ceremony is only a week away, which means I only have one week left to be with my parents and work on my gift. Over the past few months my time has been split between four things—working for the Elite, spending time with Zander, being with my family as much as possible, and strengthening my ability.

I haven't been able to master controlling when my gift works, because my emotions play too big of a factor. Mostly I have been trying to focus on how I am able to continually, without trying, keep Zander's ability turned off. I've even tried to put my gift up against some Elites, with no luck. I keep trying to figure out what I did differently that day with Titen, but it was such a quick decision that I don't even know what I was thinking at the time. My parents and Zander keep telling me it will come with time, but time is running out.

Today Zander and I are working in the corn fields again. It's one of my favorite times of the year—harvest time. Picking the corn off its husks comes easily to me, it's definitely better than weeding. Plus harvest time means it's fall, my preferred season. The colors of fall have always brought me joy. The different shades of red, orange, and yellow are soothing. It makes being in the fields less stressful, and for a minute I feel like I live in a different world, like before the war. I must have stopped working because the sound of Zander's voice brings me back to reality.

"Alexis...is something wrong?"

I shake my head softly. "No, I was just daydreaming." He smiles at me and continues working. As we reach the end of our rows, we set down our baskets full of corn, and get ready to leave, when I look up and see Tara a few rows down making her rounds watching the Inept workers.

"Zander, should I try it on her?"

He takes hold of my hand and says, "Forgive me." I look at him confused and then feel a sharp pain on my palm as Zander cuts me with a small blade we use for the harvest.

"What did you do that for?" I pull my hand away from him and start to tend to my wound.

"We need a reason to speak to her without seeming suspicious... I'm sorry." Suddenly I'm elated, and we start to walk towards Tara.

I reach her and hold out my hand.

She looks at my cut, and says, "Inept worker, let me tend to your wounds." I look into her clouded eyes and try to focus while she works on my hand. I feel disappointed until Zander squeezes my other hand.

"You can do this, I know you can."

*He's right, this is MY gift, and I can do whatever I please with it.* So I look more intensely at my robot sister and relive my dreams of a world where we can be a whole family again. My still bleeding hand suddenly drops, when I notice her haze is gone. "Tara!" I shout and throw my arms around her. She must be in too much shock to say anything, and just returns my hug. Then, like Titen, as quick as the haze left, it's back.

She takes a step back, and with an even more confused look continues to heal my hand. I'm so filled with joy, I can't help but grin at her. Once she finishes fixing my palm, Zander and I start our daily walk home, only today I want to go to the pond first and relive that moment. "Zander, do you care if we make a detour before heading to my house?"

He chuckles, the soft chuckle I love, and says, "Of course we can."

Without asking he walks with me, almost as if he knows where I want to go. Then I realize it's the one place we both go when big things happen. As we reach the pond, we sit in the grass by the edge, and I take in the beauty. The slight breeze is making small waves in the water, the trees and their fall colors are reflected in it, and the smell of the fresh air coming off the water is breathtaking.

Zander puts his arms around me and says, "You haven't stopped smiling since you hugged Tara."

I rest my head on his shoulder. "I know… it was just so amazing, to see her eyes without the haze, to feel her hug me again, but it didn't last long, and I'm pretty sure it's only because you helped me."

"If I could help you with this I would love to, but I don't have a mental gift that can help you make yours stronger. All I did was tell you what you already know… that you can do it. You've already proven that with me… every day."

I lift my head up and kiss him on the cheek. "We better get to my house before my parents start to worry." I stand up just to be pulled back down into Zander's arms. I look at him and smile. "I take it you're not ready to leave yet?"

He shakes his head. "Alexis, you never stop amazing me. You don't have much faith in yourself, but I can see the impact you're going to make. I'm just grateful you want me by your side while you do great things."

I can feel my face blush. "I couldn't imagine being

able to do anything considered great without you by my side." Then he places his hand on the side of my neck and kisses me. I can never get enough of his lips against mine. For some reason, I always feel like it's going to be the last time we share a kiss. I return his kiss and get up. "Okay, we really need to get going now before I never want to go home again." Zander laughs and we head to my house.

When we get to my home, my father is attempting to cook while my mother pokes fun at him. He's not the greatest cook in our family. I walk into the kitchen and greet them. "Sorry we're late... we stopped at the pond. Something great happened today!"

My father looks at me apprehensively. "What exactly occurred?"

With a huge smile on my face I tell them about Tara. "Today we saw Tara, and I wanted to try and turn off her haze... and well... IT WORKED!" I'm too excited now to keep my tone down. "She hugged me! Even though she didn't say anything, she knew who I was!"

Both of my parents look surprised, then my mother says, "Alexis... that's wonderful! How long did it last? Will you be able to do it again?" I am feeling a little overwhelmed and can't answer my mother's questions. I look over at Zander, my smile gone, and he speaks for me.

"It didn't last long... just long enough for a quick hug and then she was back to her... umm... hazy self." Zander grabs my hand and squeezes it just like in the field. "I think she will be able to do it again... like I told her today, she just needs to believe in herself."

Normally I would have dinner with my family and Zander, but tonight I'm not feeling up to it.

*How could today go from one of the greatest days, to the worst? I haven't felt this horrible in a long time. I don't know why everyone thinks I will learn to control my gift in a week.*

"I'm sorry, but I think I want to go upstairs and be

alone." All three of them look at me like someone just died, which makes me want to escape even faster. I kiss Zander on the cheek and head for the safety of my room. As soon as I am behind my closed door I sit on the floor with my knees pulled up to my chest.

A knock at my door distracts me from my thoughts, but I don't answer. I don't deserve to see any of them. I'm too big of a disappointment. Still sitting on the floor I hear my door slowly open. "Can I join you?" Zander says in a soft voice. I don't even turn to look at him, and shrug my shoulders. He must have taken that as a yes, because now his arms are around me. He pulls me close to him, and I lay my head on his lap.

"Alexis... I know nothing I say can make you believe in yourself, but I'm going to try. Just look at us right now... if you didn't have a great ability I wouldn't be able to get anywhere near you. You know this, though, I have told you, your parents have told you, and you have even said so yourself. I wish you would see yourself the way I see you. You are a smart, brave, confident, and beautiful young woman. You can do anything your mind is set to, I have yet to see you fail at anything... and don't say you failed at using your gift, because as I said before, you're using it right now." He pauses, waiting for me to say something and then sighs.

"If you want me to leave, I understand because you have a lot to think about."

He starts to lift me off him to get up and all I can manage to get out is, "Please... don't leave me."

He stops moving and whispers, "Never."

I'm not sure how long we stay like this because I drift off to sleep. I wake up to the sun on my face trying to figure out how I got into my bed. I look around half expecting to see Zander, but he isn't here. I know he needs to be with his family too. Oddly I feel refreshed, like it was the best night's sleep I have had in a while.

I get up and start getting ready for work. I stare into my mirror looking back at myself while I fix my hair. I keep staring at myself while Zander's words swirl in my mind. *Smart... brave... confident... beautiful...* I repeat the words over and over again until I start to believe them. Finally I decide to go downstairs to face my parents and apologize once again. When I get downstairs I notice Zander is on the floor in our family room... sleeping. I go into the kitchen where both my parents are sitting. Concerned, I look at them, then over my shoulder toward the family room.

"Why is Zander sleeping in there?"

My father smiles and says, "He's keeping his word. You asked him not to leave and he said he wouldn't. I tried to get him to go home but he refused, he was worried about you. These past few months you have gone through a lot and I think he just wants to be one thing that doesn't make your emotions go crazy. So I finally agreed to let him stay on one condition."

My father glances over my shoulder and I know what the condition was without him telling me. There was no way my father would let his fifteen-year-old daughter's boyfriend sleep in her room. All I can do is smile. "Thanks, Dad, his family must be worried, though. Oh... and I'm sorry about yesterday. I'm feeling more confident today."

"I knew you would!" I nearly jump out of my skin when I hear Zander behind me, I wasn't expecting him to be awake yet. Everyone is laughing at my mini heart attack when Zander says, "Don't worry about my parents. Your father, very kindly, went to my home and let them know what was going on."

We all sit down and have some breakfast, the typical bland eggs and bread we have almost every day, before Zander and I head to work. On our way we stop at his house so he can switch from the shirt he wears in the cornfield to his berry field shirt. It's annoying only getting a select amount of clothes, with most of them being for work. I wonder what clothes the Elites get, I'm sure they have more than just their Core uniforms.

I follow him into his home, feeling a bit awkward that his family isn't here. I wait for him in his kitchen while he changes, looking around at how similar our homes are. They both have a similar layout, the stairs are the first thing we see when we enter our houses. There is a small hallway along the side of the stairs that branches off into the kitchen and family room. The second level has one bathroom and three rooms. If a family has more than two children a room has to be shared, but they are barely big enough for one.

As I make comparisons, Zander walks into the kitchen and I walk toward him. "I never got the chance to thank you for last night... I appreciate that you stayed with me, but you need to spend time with your family too."

He looks at the floor. "It's easier for me to be away. To get used to the fact that I won't know them anymore. I have talked to them about it, and they think it might be easier too. I still see them as much as I can, but when a situation like last night happens they understand."

"I'm sorry."

"Please don't be," he says with a smile. His smile is a bit uneven and looks more like a smirk, but it's the smile I've grown to love. There is something about it that's genuine, and I know he's truly happy when he smiles that way.

When we get to the edge of the field we pick up some baskets, and then begin harvesting the lush raspberries. They are deep red and plump with juice. We use the berries for everything, to try and make our food sweeter, but after a while I get sick of them.

A few rows down Zander is struggling not to squish them. It makes me sad to see him trying so hard and failing. He's the strong one, he's normally the one helping me out, but maybe I can help him out today. Normally I can only turn his gift off when he is close to me, but maybe I can turn it off now. It's a good way to practice my ability without having to deal with the Elite Core.

I try to focus my thoughts, emotions, and energy on Zander without drawing attention to myself. So as I pick berries, I concentrate on helping him. After a few minutes I look up to see him trying to harvest the berries without crushing them. For the most part he's accomplishing it, but I have to laugh to myself that he has to work so hard at picking berries when everything else comes so easily to him. Then I feel sorry for him, and I marvel at the range of emotions Zander brings out in me. Finally it's time for lunch, so I walk over and sit with him.

When I sit down he nudges me, and says, "Thank you!" I chuckle and try act like I don't know what he's talking about.

"Thank you for what?"

Then Zander puts one arm around me. "Maybe I should stay at your home more often. It seems to make your gift work better!"

I think about what he said, and respond, "I was able to do it because of what you told me... I kept repeating smart, brave, and confident in my head before work this morning." I purposely left out *beautiful* because that's the one I'm still trying to convince myself of. "If you wouldn't have told me that, I wouldn't have been able to help you today." He kisses me softly and then we go back to work.

This week before the ceremony is over before I can blink my eyes. My days with my parents are over. Tomorrow when the sun rises, the entire region will go witness the Coming of Age Ceremony, where the Inept children who have turned fifteen will be recognized and taken across the wall to the Elite Region.

Of course I can't sleep, so I keep tossing and turning, wishing I had asked Zander to stay with me tonight. Earlier today he asked if I wanted him to stay, but I told him no. As much as I may think I need him, his family needs a chance to say goodbye, which isn't something I look forward to in the morning. Saying goodbye to my parents, hugging them one last time, and never seeing them again, is not something I want to experience.

Soon I give up on sleeping, take a shower, and put on my one nice dress. I slip it over my head and straighten it out. My dress hangs down to my shins—it's a little big for me because it used to be Tara's. The entire dress is tan except for the dark brown ribbon of cloth that I carefully place around my waist and tie behind me. I put it in a bow and let the strands hang down my back. I look into my mirror while I get the knots out of my hair, and repeat the four words in my head that Zander told me: *I'm smart... I'm brave... I'm confident... and... I'm beautiful.*

I look out my window and see the sun start to rise, so I decide it's time to face my parents. I slowly walk down the stairs thinking about how much I am going to miss my home.

Once I reach the bottom I take in each room one by one, trying to make sure the images can never escape.

I'm about to turn into the kitchen when I hear my mother say, "Grant, I can't sit back and lose both of my daughters. This isn't right!" I stand by the door and listen to my parents talk.

"Evalyn, we need to be strong for Alexis. I don't think it's right either, but how is she supposed to have any confidence in herself if we are upset?" My father says.

"Just because the Elite are gifted, doesn't give them the *right* to take my babies from me! She is fifteen years old and they are going to take her from us, and *make* her marry someone. We can only hope it's Zander, but you and I both know there is no guarantee. Then when she is married we will *never* know if we have any grandchildren. For all we know Tara could be married and have two or three babies already. How do we just sit back and continue to let this happen? Our entire region just *lets* them take our kids for their own personal gain!" My mother manages to say.

My father softly speaks to her, "Tara and Alexis are strong, we raised them to stand up for what's right. Alexis is one of the most aware, and sometimes stubborn, kids that is going to cross into the Elite Region. If she wants something done, no one will get in her way." He pauses before he says, "We both know why our region lets this happen. People are scared, they know that rebelling against the Elite never ends well. Without any gifts we are no match for them. Remember a few years back when there was a small group that tried to rally against the Elite? Evalyn, they disappeared, no one has seen them since. If Alexis can strengthen her gift, we will have an even playing field. I know it's hard to lose our girls, but I truly believe someday we will have them back. Alexis is too passionate to fail at anything."

I can hear my mother sniffling, and I feel my own tears escape my eyes. *Come on, stop crying. They can't know I heard them.* I take a couple deep breaths, turn into the kitchen, and my father stops embracing my mother.

I notice breakfast is already on the table, so I assume my parents didn't sleep much either. There is something sitting in a basket that looks like a misshapen roll. "What's that?" I ask my parents while I point to the funny-looking roll.

My mother smiles and says, "It's a mixed berry muffin. I think there are blueberries and raspberries in it. The Elites delivered it as a gift for getting to be a part of the testing this year."

I frown at them both. "I don't know how to do this... I don't know how to say goodbye." Tears trickle down my face.

"Dear, you don't need to," my mother says. "I know

you will be able to convince them that we are equals, that things will change... if by some chance you can't, it's okay. We love you very much, and we always will no matter what happens. You will always be our little girl, clouded eyes won't change that." I can see her holding back tears in her already puffy eyes, and I can't say anything.

We eat our breakfast in silence while the sun rises. Once we are finished and the dishes are put away, we get ready to leave. Before we walk out the door, I grab both my parents together and hug them tightly. "I love... you both." I have a hard time telling them as I begin to weep, so quickly I turn and walk out the door with them following.

Before going to the ceremony we head to the Ranes' home to meet up with Zander and his family. Mr. and Mrs. Rane have never gone through losing one of their children before, since Zander is the oldest, so my parents want to meet up with them so they can support them through the day.

Zander is already sitting outside waiting for us. He looks so handsome in his nice clothes. He is wearing a long-sleeved, light blue button down shirt, with a pair of black slacks. His clothes are a thicker linen than our normal work clothes. I can't help but smile at him. He gets up and takes my hand. Then my parents go inside to get his family while we wait outside for them. "Zander, why aren't you saying goodbye to your family?"

"I've been waiting for you so I can wrap them all up in my arms," he confesses.

"So what are we waiting for?" I say. Just then his parents come out of their house and Zander embraces them. To my surprise, I don't even need to try—my gift is working without me even thinking... that's new.

I watch, getting a little tearful, while Zander hugs his family one by one. His mother's eyes have tears in them, which she is failing to hold back. My mother is by Mrs.

Rane's side with one arm around her waist, trying to hold her together.

As we walk to the ceremony, we see a large group has already gathered, waiting for it to begin. Zander and I give our parents another quick hug when our families get to the edge of the group. We stand in silence, holding hands, and look at the Elites that are taking their places around the Inept. They look intimidating in their matching Core uniforms, and their blank faces make me feel uncomfortable. Once all the Core members in our region are stationed, we all watch as one spot in the wall begins to open up.

Throughout the crowd there are gasps, some even start to applaud. Once the wall stops moving, a group of Elites walk through, moving to the stage that was built yesterday for the event. I look up at Zander, but he is just staring straight in front of him. We both know the Elites in front of us are probably more gifted than any of us combined, considering they protect Commander Avery.

The Commander makes my skin crawl. He's a tall, skinny man with dark hair. His face has some wrinkles, mostly around his eyes. His eyes are bland and dark, which makes me think that the haze would improve his looks. I can't imagine being one of his androids, it makes me feel sick.

I don't think anyone knows what the Commander's gift is, but I'm guessing it has to be amazing to have so much power. Once Commander Avery takes his place front and center, he begins his speech, which tends to make all the Inept people feel miserable. "Once a year, I grace you all with my presence, to look upon the Inept children who will be stepping into my region. Only a few are lucky enough to have the gifts to become part of the Core. I'm sure those few know who they are. We are not here to separate families, we are here to make better, stronger, Elite families. Because of me, those who are not chosen as an

Elite are spared. Before my time, the Commander would kill anyone who did not possess special abilities. I, on the other hand, believe and have proven, that the Elite gene sometimes skips a generation. Now let's start the Ceremony."

One by one they call the names of the children who are at the "glorious" age of fifteen. I don't recognize many names, but I know there aren't very many of us this year. I think there are maybe ten of us, if that. Then I hear it: "Alexis Gander." I try to swallow and walk toward the stage. The closer I get the more I can feel how gifted the Elite are. I have a feeling that the one who makes us into Elite puppets is here, maybe it's the Commander himself.

I shake hands with the Elite who called my name and I wait for what seems like forever until they say, "Zander Rane." I watch him as he walks up to the stage. When Zander gets to the man who called his name, he reaches out to shake his hand. I make sure I'm concentrating. It would be a bad situation, with all the Elites around, if Zander accidently hurt one.

Once his hand drops I realize I was holding my breath and let it out. I look up and down the line, and I only count eight of us. From what I can remember, it's the smallest group I've ever seen. Maybe people are trying not to have kids anymore, knowing they will get taken away in fifteen short years. Commander Avery starts speaking again, but I'm not listening, I'm coming up with my own ideas. What's weird is I feel like there is an Elite who isn't gifted, but it must be some of the kids standing around me. I'm positive an Inept would not be able to fool the tests.

I keep thinking of ways to turn off the haze, hoping my gift will grow and I will be able to do it to more than one person at a time. I'm also thinking about the possibility of keeping Zander's gift turned off—maybe if I can he can return to his family.

I wish calling up each of us was the end of the

ceremony, but unfortunately it's not. Now the Elites on the stage take turns one by one showing off their abilities. The first one up is Titen—we all already know his gift but he still shows off. He picks a random person in the crowd, without his consent, and starts to lift him into the air and flips and spins him around. His movements make him look like a fish out of water.

Finally Titen puts him down, and the man can barely stand. Then I hear Commander Avery laugh, saying, "Nicely done, Titen!" Before the next Elite goes, Titen picks a few more from the crowd and shows us that he can use his gift on more than one thing at a time. It's a bit frightening finding out his ability is stronger than we knew. Finally he steps back and a small girl, who I recognize from last year, steps forward.

As she stands there, she holds her hand out and all of a sudden a flame appears out of nowhere over her palm but doesn't burn her skin. I can't stop watching the fire dance in her hand. Then she shows us why we should all be afraid of her: she lifts her hand and blows on the flame, making it bigger. Before anyone has time to do anything, she throws it! Everyone gasps as it ignites a small tree near the stage.

Then the commander says, "That's enough, Brin." She looks up, smiles, and the fire is gone, almost as if we had all just imagined it. I hate to say it, but some of these gifts are amazing! I'm glad to know if I ever get on their bad side, I can shut them off. The next *performer* is coming from the crowd. It's one of the Elites assigned to watch the region.

As the Core member surfaces from the crowd, I can't help but cry out, "Tara!" I know as soon as it leaves my lips that it is a stupid thing to do. Almost instantaneously I am off my feet, Titen is working his "gift" on me. I start to gasp for air because he is starting to squeeze my airway shut, when Commander Avery comes and stands in front of me.

"Young lady, how dare you interrupt the ceremony?" Still gasping, all I can think of is my family watching one Elite daughter show off, while the other will be killed right in front of them. I can feel my eyes getting heavy, I know soon I will pass out and shortly after, be dead. Then I hear Zander try to talk some sense into the Commander.

"Sir, the girl Titen is suffocating is Tara's sister. If you like Tara's gift, can you really chance losing whatever ability Alexis may have?" First Commander Avery looks disgusted that Zander spoke to him, then he looks back and forth from me to Tara. I must have passed out before he decided, because the next thing I know my body hits the stage like dead weight. I feel Zander's arms around me as I come to. He pulls me to my feet and holds me up, only his grip is too tight, and it is starting to hurt. The lack of oxygen must have weakened my ability, and I'm unable to turn off his strength.

Once I feel my lungs filling back up with air, I'm able to think straight and look up to see my sister still showing off. She can leap from the stage to the end of the crowd and then back again. One thing I notice about her growing gift is how she can suspend herself in the air now. Before she could only jump as high as our roof, but now she can jump so high I almost can't see her anymore. She's so elegant while she does it that it's hard not to wish I had a physical gift. While we all watch Tara jump around beautifully, I can feel Zander's grip getting looser. It's nice to know my lack of oxygen didn't permanently damage my gift.

One by one the Elites show off. Some can manipulate different elements, like fire and wind. Others have extraordinary mental gifts. An Elite named Len made us all believe there were insects crawling all over us. The Commander of course was left out of the fun, so he could watch us all squirm. By the time the Commander is done showing off his favorite Elites, the sun has set. Then he leaves through the wall with the group of Elites that escorted him in.

When the wall closes in front of us. We look at each other confused and Titen comes up behind us. "Preparations are being made for your arrival. Tonight you will stay here and await our orders to cross into the Elite Region." Once the Elites clear the crowd and take down the stage, they form a barrier around us. I don't remember the Inept children being forced to stay outside the night after the ceremony.

Instead of worrying about why we have to stay here tonight, I enjoy spending a little more time with Zander. He's sitting with his back against a tree and one of his arms around me. Ever since I was almost suffocated to death, Zander hasn't left my side. No one is saying anything, and I'm pretty sure it has to do with the Elites surrounding us. Finally I can't take the silence anymore, and I ask, "Zander, why are we out here? Why didn't we follow Commander Avery into the Elite Region?"

Zander chuckles. "I'm thinking he didn't want us to be anywhere near him when we disgrace his land with our presence." I want to protest, but I know he's right. I lean over and lay my head on his lap, while he slowly runs his fingers through my hair. "How are you feeling?" Zander asks.

I shrug. "I'm fine... I should have known better, but it just slipped out." He stops running his fingers through my hair, puts his hand under my chin, and makes me look at him.

"I'm not fine," he confesses. "I thought you were going to die right in front of me, and all I could do was watch. Even with all my strength, watching you take your final breaths made me the weakest I've ever been." Then I see a tear escape one of his eyes. I've never seen Zander cry before.

I brush the tear off his cheek and reassure him, "It's okay, I'm right here and I'm not going anywhere."

He smiles and repeats the words I spoke to him the first night he stayed at my house: "Please... don't leave me."

I whisper, "Never."

The events from today had been hard on me, so shortly after our conversation I drift off to sleep. It feels like I haven't been asleep for long when Zander shakes me. I look up at him dazed, and see that the Elites have brought us some food. Until now, I had forgotten how hungry I am. None of us have eaten since breakfast, so all of us start to eat without second guessing anything.

The food is amazing, it's a lot better than what we're used to. We are eating a creamy soup, I'm not sure of the flavor but it's nothing plain like the tomato soup we're used to. They also brought us the freshest bread I've ever had, it's so soft it almost melts in my mouth. Once we are all finished eating, everyone goes back to their own space. A little while after, I start to feel weird. I look up at Zander and his forehead is creased and I know he is feeling off too. I start to feel light-headed, and have a hard time focusing. I grab Zander's hand in desperation and say, "There's something wrong! I don't... feel... right." Then my eyes close and I pass out.

I'm not out for long, but my body still feels like lead. I try to look around but my head won't move. I can hear the Elite talking about us, one of them saying, "The drug took effect quickly this time, they must have upped the dosage."

*The drug? They drugged us?* I start to feel a little lighter and I can now slightly move my head. I look slowly side to side until I see Zander, whose eyes aren't open but I can see his chest moving so he's still breathing. I wonder why the drug is wearing off me so fast. I ate just as much as everyone else.

Then another Elite says, "It's hard to believe that a drug can take out potential Elites."

The first Elite responds, "It's not just *any* drug, they

were able to infuse some of Thyn's blood in it. Since the Elite gene is unique in everyone, it's a signature in our DNA. So basically they drugged them with his gift."

I almost can't believe what I'm hearing! The more I think about it, the more it makes sense that its effects aren't as strong with me. My mind must be protecting itself, and without me even having to think about it, I turned off whatever Thyn's gift is. I've never heard of this guy before, I wonder what he can do.

The lead feeling must be from the drug itself because I can't seem to get rid of that. My mind is clear, though, and as I think about what's happening, it hits me! *Thyn must cause the haze!* There's no other explanation for how our minds just shut off! His blood is in the drugs, so we are paralyzed both physically and mentally. Now I know who I need to find—if I can turn off his gift I can remove the haze from everyone!

I notice that we are no longer outside, Titen must have moved us when we all passed out. I think we are in an Elite vehicle, because I can tell that we are moving. I keep opening my eyes just enough to see Zander, hoping I can wake his mind back up, but it's no use, so I try to move my arm to reach out to him. Maybe if I can touch him I can open his mind back up, but I can't move no matter how much I try. I decide to close my eyes to hide my consciousness from the Elite.

It seems like we have been traveling forever. I wish I would have gotten to see the outside of whatever it is we were traveling in. I have only heard rumors about the technology the Elites have. Hopefully once we reach our destination I'll get to see if any of the rumors are true. I feel the vehicle come to a stop, and start to hear the Elites talking.

"Titen, make sure you're gentle with them, we don't want them to think we're monsters!" I hear a female Elite say. I hear someone huff, who I assume is Titen in response to the female's remarks. Then I feel my body lifting into the air, so I make sure to keep my eyes shut tight so they don't know I am awake.

Once I am set down I can hear the Elites debating about how to position us. The female Elite says, "That girl over there should be placed with this boy. I think that they will be less upset if they are together." I hate to say it, but I'm starting to like whoever that female Elite is. I feel myself being moved again and set back down.

It's a crazy feeling having full control of your mind but not being able to make your body respond. I didn't like getting moved around against my will. Shortly after, I hear the door close and assume the Elites have left. Pressing my luck, I open my eyes searching for Zander. I find him next to me right away, which is nice—the Elite is right, I am less upset with Zander near me.

Once I know he is by my side, I look around the room we're in. It's absolutely breathtaking. The walls are a bright white with different paintings of what I can only guess to be parts of the Elite Region. Delicate lights hang from the ceiling, with silver fixtures holding them up. Around the lights is a lace work of diamonds that make the light dance off them onto the walls. The only thing that looks odd to me is the floor, which looks like there is fur on it. This room alone is so different from the Inept Region. We don't have fancy lights, just plain ones that are very dim. Our walls are peeling, and our floors are stained. It makes me angry that this one room is more luxurious than my entire region.

Finally I'm starting to get some feeling back in my body. First I can slightly move my head, then my fingers loosen up, and finally my entire arm. I look over at Zander and touch his face hoping he can open his eyes, but he doesn't respond. My voice has returned to me so I whisper, "Zander, wake up! Open your eyes."

He doesn't respond, and I get frustrated, so I think to

myself, *Zander Jae Rane, wake up this instant!* Then I concentrate on removing the drug from his mind and opening it up. Finally his eyes flutter open and I exclaim, "Welcome back! I've missed you!" He looks at me confused, and starts to panic. I lay my hand on his chest and explain, "Zander, it's okay, they drugged us to move us here. I know that sounds bad, but the drug didn't fully work on me. My body was paralyzed but my mind wasn't! I heard them talking about this guy named Thyn whose blood was infused with the drug—it shut our minds off. I'm pretty sure he is the one who creates the haze! I think if I can shut off his gift, that everyone's haze will disappear." Zander is still looking at me shocked, and I just want to comfort him. I test my body to see what has unthawed and I can move everything but my legs. So I twist toward him and give him a soft kiss on his frozen lips.

Finally after what seems like hours, the drug wears off. Everyone is able to move around and talk about what has happened. The only people not talking about the events that just took place are Zander and me. Since I already explained everything to him while he was still paralyzed, we start talking about the room we are in. I take his hand in mine and say, "Isn't it beautiful? I wish they would share some of this stuff with us, it's wonderful."

Zander complains, "I don't think it's that great! It's just another way to make us feel inadequate to the Elite. They deprive us so when we come here we drool over what they have and we don't." I'm hurt by what he said. I wish I had some of the things in this room.

"Zander, just because they have nicer things doesn't make us inadequate. The Inept Region has an important thing that this place will never have."

He looks at me frustrated. "What's that?"

"The people in the Inept Region have *love*. The Elite have their spouses chosen for them to create the best Elites possible. I would rather be deprived and get to love whoever I please, than have all this and never be with you again."

Then Zander pulls me close and kisses my forehead. "You're right."

"I know!" I tease, playfully nudging him.

Shortly after our conversation an Elite comes into the room and says, "You will all be staying here for the rest of the day and tonight. Tomorrow you will get a tour of the region and then go to the Testing Facilities." Then the Elite turns and leaves the room.

I take Zander's hand. "I don't know if I'm ready for this. What if they ask me to prove my ability? I can't always do it on demand."

He sighs. "You'll do great, plus I'm sure they have technology to detect a gift somehow."

I'm sure he's right, but I'm still nervous. We spend the rest of the day just enjoying each other's company. Things get a bit awkward when everyone starts going to sleep. We are in one big room with small cots that we unfold to sleep on, and the only room connected to ours is a bathroom. Zander sets up our cots next to each other and I lay on mine.

He leans over and gives me a passionate kiss, "Alexis, I love you." Then he tries to get comfortable on his cot.

"I love you too." Soon we both drift off to sleep not knowing what tomorrow has in store.

# CHAPTER FOUR

I wake up to the sound of an Elite coming in the door. Sitting up slowly, I stretch out, stiff from sleeping on the cot, and look toward the door. Unfortunately the Elite they sent to us is Titen. He's not my favorite Elite, considering each time I've ran into him it involves me getting abused by his ability.

Titen waits for everyone to wake up, then says, "You all need to be ready in ten minutes, that is when your tour will begin." Then he turns and walks out the door.

Once I stand up I see that there is a pile of clothes with our names on them. I walk over to where they are laying and see Zander's first. "Hey, Zander, I think these ones are yours." He comes over and grabs them, while I look for mine.

Finally I see a label that says 'Alexis' and I grab the clothes to examine them. There is a pair of black pants with a logo on the hip, like the one the Elites have on the chest of their Core uniforms. There is also a long-sleeved white shirt with the same logo on one of the sleeves. As I look around, I notice everyone has the same outfit.

We all glance around realizing it will take too long for us to go one at a time into the bathroom to change, when one of the girls has an idea. "What if the boys turn and face the wall while the girls change, and then we will do the same for you guys?" Everyone agrees, and we all get changed within a matter of minutes.

A few minutes later, Titen returns and instructs us, "Okay, everyone, come this way." When I walk past Titen, I almost go into shock. His haze isn't there! All I can do is think, *Am I doing this?* But I'm pretty sure that I'm not, considering he's not having the same response as that day in the Inept Region.

Outside our room is a narrow hallway that leads to one other door. When we enter through that door, everyone gasps in awe. For the first time, we lay our eyes on an Elite transportation vehicle. I can't get over how big it is—it is large enough to fit all eight of us and four Elites with room to spare. It is white, pretty much like everything else in this building, and it is hovering about a foot off the ground.

I look over at Zander and ask, "How is this possible? Why do we have to walk everywhere when they get these?" He doesn't say anything but shakes his head and looks at the vehicle with anger in his eyes.

Once we are all in the vehicle, an Elite slides large sections of the side of the vehicle open, exposing large windows, which leaves us all in awe again. When she turns to sit, I notice she doesn't have the haze either. I touch Zander's hand softly and point at my eyes, then to the Elite. He looks up and makes eye contact with the Elite sitting on the other end of the vehicle. Zander's forehead creases, and he looks just as confused as I feel.

When the vehicle begins to move, I suddenly become nervous, so I reach over and take Zander's hand. As the vehicle pulls away from the building, Zander and I begin to stare out the same window. The building we were staying in is small, and located directly inside the wall. As we get farther from the building I notice that the Elite Region is bright—most of the homes are white with silver or black trim. There are also larger buildings that are black; even their windows are tinted. *I wonder what those buildings are used for.* I also notice that their roads aren't dirt like ours, they are solid black and look smooth. I can't help but stare out the window with my mouth hanging open, trying to take in how different it is just on the other side of the wall.

As we are taken past some more homes, I notice they aren't crooked, the paint isn't peeling, and they are big, unlike ours. The more things we pass by, the angrier I get. So I stop looking out the window and start focusing on the four Elites that are in the back of the vehicle with us. I clear my throat and ask, "Are we allowed to speak, and ask questions?"

One of the female Elites answers, "Of course, we want to make your journey as comfortable as possible." A little shocked by her answer, I stare at her until finally I come up with something.

"Well, it seems that you all know our names, can we know yours? Could we also know what your gifts are so we aren't caught off guard?"

The four Elites look at each other and must have silently agreed, because the female Elite that first responded to me begins. "My name is Acey, I am able to sprint quickly. When I was young, I started out beating all my friends in races but as I grew I became faster and faster. Now I can reach speeds up to fifty miles an hour without getting winded."

I can't believe these Elites are opening up, and I'm stunned by Acey's gift.

One of the male Elites continues before anyone can say anything. "I'm Kian, I have the ability to influence water. I can make it appear wherever I choose, and can manipulate it to move any way I please."

I look over at him and ask, "Can you make it rain?"

He simply nods and the next Elite says, "I'm Sacri, and I can heal."

Zander asks, "Heal? What do you mean?"

She smiles, then runs her fingernail down her arm, drawing blood. When only a few seconds have passed, the scratch on her arm begins to fade. The sight of that makes us all speechless.

Finally the last Elite, who we all already know, says, "My name is Titen, I can move objects with my mind." Since Titen scares most of us, no one asks him any questions. We all sit in silence until we reach our first destination.

The vehicle comes to a stop, so we all step out and face a giant statue. Once everyone is outside, Acey explains, "This statue is an exact replica of our founder, Ean. He created the two regions in hopes of creating a better life for the gifted. He was able to move objects with his mind, like Titen. The stories say that when he discovered his gift it was frowned upon, and he became an outcast with the other gifted children. But once his gift began to grow, he was able to make the regions and gain power over the ungifted."

No one says anything, we all just look up at the statue to see the person who started the horrible tradition of tearing families apart. I'm annoyed that this man was selfish enough to build the regions. I'm also angry that people who did not possess any gifts are part of the reason this all started. I can see why Ean would separate himself and other gifted children, but I can also see why having a gift used to be a bad thing. I wonder if he meant for it to come this far, for the Inept to be treated poorly. After a couple minutes we are ushered back into the vehicle, when I can't take it anymore.

"Why don't you guys have the haze?" I blurt out. The four Elites look at me suspiciously but don't say anything. Getting more agitated, I'm almost yelling by now. "We aren't stupid, we know when you are in the Inept Region that there is a cloud over your eyes, and there obviously isn't right now!"

To my surprise, Titen is the one who answers me. "The Commander thinks it's best for us to have our minds controlled so we can focus on our responsibilities without being distracted by our Inept families. I guess I've been here long enough now I forgot it places a... haze?—in our eyes."

It takes me a minute, but I finally manage to ask another question, "So you guys aren't forced to be robots every day of your lives?" They all shake their heads, and then I have one more question, "Is it true... that marriages are arranged here?" This seems to hit a sore spot in Kian because it suddenly begins to rain in the vehicle.

"KIAN!" shouts Titen, snapping Kian out of his sadness.

"Oh sorry!" is all Kian says, the drizzle stopping.

Zander says, "So I take that as a *yes*." When all the Elites nod in agreement, Zander squeezes my hand and frowns at me, which Acey notices.

"If you don't mind me asking... Zander... Alexis... what are your gifts?"

Clearing his throat, Zander says, "I'm not sure I want to say exactly what they are since we haven't done any tests yet. But I have a physical gift, and she has a mental gift."

Acey smiles and says, "Maybe since you two are fond of each other, and are both probably going to be Elites, they might pair you two together. We have a lot of couples with one having a mental ability and one having a physical ability." I give her a weak smile, and hold on to Zander's hand tighter.

For the rest of the tour I don't look out any windows, all I can do is stare at the Elites. Acey is petite with long, straight, blonde hair. Her eyes are a light blue that sparkle when she looks out into the sun. She looks up at me and gives me a slight smile, so I look away. I draw my attention to Sacri—she is kind of like me, not a typical beauty. She has reddish brown hair that only reaches to her jaw. The cut of her hair makes her jaw line stand out, and the color of it brings out her golden brown eyes. I try not to stare at her too long so I move my attention to Kian. He looks taller than Zander, with tan skin and dark hair. He has it so short that it's almost gone. His eyes are dark, darker than I've seen before. For some reason I can't quit staring at him—I feel for him, knowing he must have loved an Inept.

"Kian... you were separated from someone you loved, weren't you?"

He looks up at me with sadness in his eyes, saying unconvincingly, "I don't know what you're talking about... I love my wife and only her."

"I'm not saying you don't love your wife... it's just when we mentioned the arranged marriages you made it drizzle in here. So it must have upset you."

He turns his head and looks out a window. "Yes, I was much like you two," he says, gesturing at Zander and me. "I came here with her four years ago. I knew we would be separated, but I couldn't make myself let her go... until I had no choice."

I look at Zander then back to Kian. "I'm sorry... I—"

"That's enough questions," Titen interrupts. "We are almost to the Testing Facilities. I'm sure I don't need to remind all of you to be on your best behavior."

A little shocked, we all shake our heads, and then Acey says, "Titen, that was uncalled for, I'm sure none of them are going to get out of line."

I can feel Zander's breaths getting shorter. He's getting angry. He must not have been able to hold it back anymore, because he yells, pointing at Titen, "Of course we wouldn't get out of line, especially with *him* here. We all know what he is capable of, or you did you forget you tried to kill one of us already!"

"What are you talking about?" Titen asks.

I look at Zander, whose anger has faded into confusion. "Zander, I don't think he knows… I think the haze… well, the mind control shuts them completely off… they don't even know what's happening when they are in the Inept Region."

Titen nods in agreement then says something I never expected from him: "I'm so sorry, whichever one of you I… uhh… tried to kill."

I reach over the Inept sitting next to me and touch Titen's arm. "It's okay, I understand now that I know it wasn't really you." He looks at me and tries to smile.

No one says anything else while we pull up to the Testing Facilities, we are all too busy trying to catch a glimpse of it. It's a large black and silver building, and on the front there's a sign that reads "Inept Testing Facilities." None of us can take our eyes off it. The Testing Facilities seem to be made up of four smaller buildings connected by something. Unsure of what's connecting it, I ask, "So what's that between the buildings? I've never seen anything like it."

Without taking my eyes off it, Acey answers, "They are suspended walkways, basically it's a hallway enclosed by walls. That way people can get from one building to another without having to leave the facilities." This annoys me—my home is barely standing and they have buildings for their hallways!

Our vehicle enters the gates of the facilities into a tunnel. I tap Zander, point to my eyes, and then to the Elites. Their haze is back, and it upsets me because I was starting to grow fond of them, especially Acey.

My emotions must have empowered my gift, because suddenly Acey's eyes are sparkling blue again. Zander stiffens, and I try not to look guilty. Acey looks around as the vehicle comes to a stop, and for the first time, as an Elite, she sees the haze in her comrades' eyes. She's shocked, maybe even scared.

Zander looks down at me and whispers, "Alexis, you need to stop using your gift on her."

"I don't know how," I tell him. "I didn't even mean to turn it off!" Then quickly Acey gets up and closes all the openings in the vehicle, trying to figure out what has happened to her.

Titen stands, commanding, "Everyone file out." The fear I feel from Titen must be affecting my ability, because Acey's panic fades and her haze is back. Before I can think about what happened, Zander pulls me up and we get out of the vehicle. Once everyone has gotten out, someone says, "This way everyone."

Zander takes my hand and we follow them around the vehicle, when Tara comes toward us. She is still in her Core uniform, her eyes are clouded, and she's moving stiffly again. My breath is gone, and my heart begins to race. I can't handle this, I can't follow my zombie of a sister around the Testing Facilities.

Just then she says, "My name is Tara, and I will be guiding you to the first building where you will see your living quarters for the duration of your stay here." I can feel tears filling my eyes, but I don't let them fall. I can't let the Elite affect me this way. So I focus all my energy on Zander and try not to get myself into trouble.

Tara turns and begins to walk toward a door and we and the other Elites follow her. I wonder why they think they need five Elites to escort us. Maybe they think we are going to try and leave. Once inside the door, we go up some stairs. At the top is a walkway with a solid floor and ceiling but walls made of glass.

Walking suspended in the air is a terrifying experience, but I make myself look out the window. I am hoping to see the wall, to maybe be able to see over it, but it's no use, the Testing Facilities must be in the center of the Elite Region because all I can see are their beautiful homes, gardens, and ponds. I wish I could have gotten one last look at my home.

Finally we reach the other side of the walkway and enter a large room with a kitchen and family room. Tara turns to face us, and says, "This will be your living quarters, and everyone will share the kitchen and family room. As you can see, on either side of the family room there is a door. On your left is the room the young men will be sharing, and on your right the young women." I look around and notice there are only two other girls, so it won't be too overwhelming with only three of us in there.

I walk over to the kitchen and examine the differences from my home. They have different equipment and I'm not sure what it's used for. I keep staring, hoping I will somehow be able to figure out how to use it. I think we cook with it, but I'm not sure considering there isn't a fire pit underneath it like we use in the Inept Region. I look around to see all the other Inepts' eyes on me. So I turn to Acey, whose eyes are still clouded, and ask, "Can you show me how to use this? We don't have things like this in our homes." Acey nods, comes over to the equipment, and pushes a button on the side of it. A transparent picture appears in front of my face, suspended in the air. I lift my hand and put it right through the middle of the picture. My fellow Inepts are looking at it with me in confusion. Acey pushes another button and letters appear on the picture.

She looks at me and says, "Pick any food you want to test it out on."

I think for a minute, smile, and say, "Cake." Acey spells out 'cake' by touching each letter. Confused I look at the picture, and say, "But I just put my hand through it, how are you picking the letters?"

When she finishes spelling, she says, "It can sense which letters you choose when you touch them, the cake will be ready shortly." All I can do is smile—at least we will be getting one good thing out of this!

Then the boys enter their room, and I join the girls in ours. There are three beds that take up most of the room, and a dresser at the other end. It's almost set up like my room at home, but everything is twenty times nicer. The dresser has three drawers, one with each of our names. I open mine up and see three different outfits. They are all black pants and white shirts like the ones we are wearing, but each outfit has one difference. On the opposite arm of the Elite logo it says medical, physical, and mental. I'm assuming those are the tests we will be taking, and we will have to wear the specific clothing for each one. I close my drawer and head back to the family room.

Once we all return to the family room, Sacri announces, "Later today I will come back to lead you all to a gathering in the yard. You will then be addressed by the Commander, and hear more about the Elite Core." The Elites start to leave, showing us a button by the door we can press if we need anything. I can smell the sweetness of the cake I requested earlier but have no appetite right now to even think about enjoying it. The day is only half over. If we were still in the Inept Region, we would be having lunch in the fields.

I start thinking about having another visit with Commander Avery. It makes me start to feel overwhelmed. So I walk over to the kitchen, sit at the table, and lay my head on it. Apparently everyone thinks this is a good idea and they join me at the table. One of the boys grabs the cake, some plates, and some silverware. As he hands it out, I lift my head up and start to take a good look at everyone. I never realized how young we all look compared to most of the Elites we've just met.

The boy who brought over the cake starts to talk. "So now that we all actually have a moment, we met all those Elite, know all their names and abilities, but we don't even know each other." He's right—considering how spread out the Inept Region is, I have only seen maybe one or two of these other kids when I was there.

He continues, "My name is Aron, and I can… read

minds. I try not to listen, though, so don't be mad!" I'm a bit shocked by this, but I'm not mad. His gift is so interesting, it brings me back to reality and I start paying attention. Aron is a tall, skinny boy with brown hair that reaches his chin. His eyes are a gray color that will probably look white with the haze.

A boy to his right says, "My name is Crayton, I'm not gifted." I look over to him and notice he is shorter with dark skin and hair, but his eyes are almost purple in color. I am glad he will get to go home and be with his family again.

On his right is a girl who looks just like him, only her hair is long and curly, and her eyes are brown. She looks over at Crayton, then back to everyone else and says, "My name is Fatima, unlike my twin brother I'm gifted, my dreams show me what's to come."

In awe I ask, "So you can dream the future?"

She smiles, saying, "Kind of, right now it's still weak, I can only dream about what might happen the next day, and only with people I have met. But the future is never set in stone. If someone changes their mind, my dreams are incorrect."

On her right is another boy, he is short but bigger than the other boys. His hair is a sandy color and his eyes are a lovely blue. "My name is Reece, I don't have any special abilities." He frowns.

I'm next. "I'm Alexis... I can... umm... turn off other people's gifts. I've also been able to... I guess... feel if people around me have abilities." All of them look at me like I am crazy, like I knew they would.

Then Zander says, "Here, I'll prove it since you all seem to doubt her." He stands up right next to me and lifts the table over his head. Then he looks down at me and since I'm feeling a bit embarrassed, I make sure to touch him just to be safe. Suddenly the table comes crashing down and he tries to lift it again, but can barely nudge it.

THE GIFTED

People still look skeptical when Aron blurts out, "It has to be true! When I stand close to her I can't read anyone's mind, when right before everyone's thoughts are screaming in my head."

I smile and say, "Thank you."

Zander introduces himself with, "I'm Zander, and you all obviously already know my ability." I smile at him and he takes my hand.

Then the girl next to him introduced herself. "My name is Mya, and I am ungifted." She is about my height, with gorgeous red hair that flows to her waist, and her eyes are a soft light green.

The boy next to Mya has dark hair so long that he has it pulled back into a ponytail, and it hangs straight down his back. He's more muscular than Zander, but not so much that it's intimidating. His eyes remind me of my sisters, they are a caramel brown, but have darker spots in them. Then he says, "My name is Noah, I'm gifted. I can enhance other people's abilities."

A little confused, I ask, "What do you mean *enhance?*"

Sighing, he says, "It's not much of a gift for myself, it's more for other people with abilities. I can help make someone's gift stronger, more controlled. Right now I don't have much control over it, though. Sometimes I have to touch people, while other times I do it without even trying. I'm concerned that they will make me use my ability with some of the more intimidating Elites, like Titen." After he finishes, no one says much, and Aron starts dishing out the cake. I barely touch mine, but I watch as everyone else takes a bite.

While everyone eats, Mya breaks the silence with, "So you two are pretty lucky that you're both gifted and won't end up like Kian."

Zander and I look at each other and he responds, "Not necessarily, they might not think our abilities together will amount to much. I'm hoping for the best, but at the same time preparing for the worst. At least for Kian, the woman he loved was Inept. If we get separated, I have to spend the rest of my life watching her have a family with someone else." I sigh, but have nothing to add, because he is absolutely right, we can still be separated even though we are both gifted.

Everyone continues to eat until Sacri comes in and says, "Everyone, please follow me." We move toward the door that we first came in and go back down the stairs. We follow her around the transportation vehicle and out another entrance. All of us stand motionless at the sight in front of us. At least thirty Elites are standing at the other end of the yard.

# CHAPTER FIVE

Cautiously we walk toward the Elites. When we get about ten feet in front of them, Sacri says, "That's close enough."

We all stand side by side facing the Elites when Commander Avery walks out from behind them and says, "Welcome to the Inept Testing Facilities. I'll try not to keep you too long so you can all get your rest. You have a lot in store over these next few days. Behind me is the Elite Core, they are the ones with the best gifts that contribute to our society, although people of the Elite Region can be called upon at any time to help the Core. For example, some of our less gifted Elites are occasionally placed in the Inept Region. We try to keep the faces different as much as possible—we don't want the Inept getting too comfortable, do we?"

My hate for the Commander grows the more he speaks. He has no respect for the Inept Region, even though it's where most of his Elite come from. My line of thought is interrupted by the change in voices, and when I look up, I see a small man with dark hair that has streaks of gray in it. His face has some wrinkles and he looks to be middle aged like my father. One big difference between him and the other Elites are his haze-free eyes. He introduces himself,

"My name is Thyn, you could say I'm the second in command here." He explains, "When you are chosen as an Elite, your first few weeks will be about patrolling the Inept Region. Many of your gifts are still a bit out of control, but I have full control of mine. When I enter your mind, I will be able to use your gifts properly. Another reason the Commander and I have decided to use my ability on the Elite is so you will not be prone to rejoining your families. Until you show that your loyalty is to the Elite Region, this method will be used for our region's safety."

*So it is him… he's the one who controls the Elites.*

I stare at Thyn trying to turn his gift off, to remove the haze from the thirty-plus Elites standing inches behind him. Unfortunately, I'm unable to get even one Elite's eyes back to normal.

Then Commander Avery takes the spotlight again and says, "All of you should feel honored to be standing here today. If you are chosen, your lives will improve beyond your wildest dreams. You will no longer have to work day in and day out, and you will get to enjoy all of the privileges of being a part of the Elite Region."

If it wasn't for all the Elites standing behind him under Thyn's control, I would have given the Commander a piece of my mind. The way he speaks to us makes me feel inadequate and angry. The only thing I think is worthless is him and his beliefs that the gifted are better than the ungifted. I ball my hands up into fists and grind my teeth, trying to keep calm.

I'm not the only one on edge at the Commander's words, because Reece begins screaming at him, "The Inepts' lives don't need to be improved! We are some of the kindest people you will ever meet! If the roles were reversed and you were outsiders for being gifted, we wouldn't think twice about it! We would let you live in harmony with us, and we wouldn't run stupid tests on you!" I know he shouldn't have said anything, because I'm familiar with the wrath of Titen under Thyn's control. Suddenly Reece is a foot off the ground moving toward the Commander.

Once he is right in front of Commander Avery's face, the Commander says to Titen, "You can set him down, but don't let him move."

The Commander grabs Reece's jaw and spits, "You don't have the slightest idea what would happen if the roles were reversed. You see us as monsters, but the regions exist to protect us! Not that any of you could do anything to stop an Elite!" He lets go of Reece, who begins to get moved back toward the line when the Commander says, "Wait. Titen, can you show our guests here that they can't do anything to stop us?"

Just then both of Reece's forearms bend in half, shattering his bones. All of us look away in horror and I cover my ears. The sound of Reece's screams are going to haunt me forever. Then Sacri walks toward Reece, who is still in Titen's control, and pulls out a bottle of clear liquid. Titen snaps back both of Reece's arms, and Reece screams again. Sacri pours the liquid on his arms, healing them almost instantly. Then Reece is back in line, no longer under Titen's control. Tears are running down his face and his whole body is shaking.

Thyn clears his throat to get our attention. "Now that you all know your place, I am positive there will be no more outbursts! Commander Avery and I are going to leave you with the Core now, so you can ask them anything you would like to know." Then Thyn and the Commander walk into the building and the haze is removed from all of the Elites.

Reece collapses to his knees, heaving like he might get sick. I walk over and kneel on the ground next to him, running my fingers through his hair like my mother does to me when I'm not feeling well. Soon his heaving stops along with his tears and he looks up at me with fearful eyes, saying, "Why didn't you turn off the haze?"

I tell him, "I tried. I don't have control over my gift yet. Reece, I'm so sorry." Then he pushes up off the ground and walks away.

Acey comes up to us and asks, "Is there anything you would like to speak to us about?"

I huff, "Yes, there is, but you probably wouldn't agree." I push myself up off the ground and cross my arms in front of my chest. *How can they not see what happens here? How can they just sit back and let this happen!*

I go and sit on the ground where I can watch everything that is happening in the yard. The Elites are talking and laughing like normal people, and it makes me sick. I'm frustrated that they don't care about what happened to Reece. I'm mad that they have never thought to stand up against the Commander. I keep watching as the Elites take turns speaking to the other Inept kids one by one. I see Titen a few feet away from me so I get up and start walking toward him. I say to him, "Hey Titen, can I speak to you... privately?"

He nods and the Elites around him walk away. When the other Elites are no longer in hearing distance I ask him, "Do you remember anything that just happened?"

He looks at me and says, "No. When Thyn uses his gift on us, we lose time. Chunks of our days are missing from our memories. Why do you ask?"

Frustrated I say, "Don't you wonder what happens when he is in control?"

He shrugs and says, "Not really, we are told that when he is controlling us that our gifts won't be used, that our presence alone makes the Inept obey."

This makes me angrier and I say, "Titen, we told you already about how you nearly killed me. Do you want to know what he made you do today?"

His forehead creases and he says, "Yes."

Trying to calm down, I explain what he did to Reece.

Looking horrified, Titen says, "I would never... I could never hurt someone like that. How many other people has he made me hurt?"

I shake my head. "I have no idea. I know once he made you snap someone's neck, and then he made you use your ability on me twice. Other than that I haven't heard about you hurting anyone else." I'm not sure if Titen is in shock or what, but he walks away and heads over to Reece. I watch as Reece starts to back away from Titen, but Titen moves towards him slowly with his hands up trying to signal he won't hurt him. Once Reece calms down, Titen takes him aside, but Reece still looks terrified.

I sit back down and watch Zander with the Elites—he is showing off. *Ugh, I really wish he wouldn't do that, pretty soon they won't even have to test him.*

I am snapped out of my thoughts by Noah sitting down next to me, who says, "So that was pretty crazy, huh? I can't believe Titen had the nerve to go and talk to Reece after breaking his arms!"

I give Noah a disgusted look and say, "When the Elites have the haze, they don't know what they're doing. I even talked to Titen about it, and he said when Thyn is in control they lose time. They have holes in their memories. He had no idea he hurt Reece, and he feels horrible." Noah sits here for a moment taking in what I said.

Then he looks at me and says, "I bet if we told enough of them, we could get them to stand against the Commander. With your ability, you could shut off Thyn's gift."

I shake my head. "I don't have control over my gift yet. I tried today, but it was no use."

"Maybe someday," he says with a shrug.

Despite my anger, I enjoy watching the Elites act human. Acey is sprinting around the yard so fast she is hard to see. Kian is pouring rain on some Elites and laughing as they get soaked. Maybe the Elite aren't that different from the Inept. The only thing making them different is being controlled by Thyn and the Commander.

The sun starts to set so the Elites gather together, and Titen says, "Please follow me back to your living quarters." As Titen walks toward the entrance we all walk behind him, with Reece in the back. He must not be comfortable with Titen even after their talk.

Once we are back in our living quarters, I realize I am starving. I walk over to the kitchen and hit the buttons we were shown before. I think for a minute, then touch the letters to spell out tomato soup and bread. Then I walk over to the table, remove the leftover cake, and begin cleaning the dishes we used. According to the picture on one of the machines in the kitchen, it looks like it cleans dishes for us. I debate for a moment whether or not I want to use it, but I decide against it. Doing something somewhat close to my normal routine calms me down.

When the dishes are clean, I reset the table and wait for the food to be finished. When the soup is done I turn to set it on the table and see that everyone has already taken a seat. I fill a bowl for Reece and say, "This should help relax you." Once everyone has soup and some bread, we begin to eat.

The soup warms me up and makes me feel at home for the first time since we arrived here. I begin to think about my parents, wondering if they are with Zander's family. I have only been gone for a day and a half but I miss them. I don't think any amount time away will make me forget them.

I look over at Aron and ask, "Can you tell what Thyn's ability is all about? Since you can read minds, I was wondering if maybe he was thinking about it."

Aron stops eating and nods, "It was actually a bit weird for me. The only minds I could hear when he was controlling the Elites were his and the Commanders. Thyn's ability controls a person completely. It was weird when he went from controlling Titen to Sacri. I could tell he was still using his ability on both of them, but it was like his point of view changed. When he was using Titen's gift it was like he was looking through Titen's eyes. Then when Sacri came up the thoughts changed, and it was like he was looking through hers. I was near Titen when he was speaking with Reece, and I believe him that they have no idea what's going on."

I sigh. "Can Thyn read minds?"

Aron laughs a little. "No, if he could, half of us would probably have been hurt like Reece."

After that, I was too lost in my thoughts to notice if anyone had spoken while we ate. When everyone is finished, I get up and begin to clear off the table. Mya starts to help me and says, "Thank you for doing all of this for us."

"No problem," I say with a smile. "I just wanted this place to feel like home before we begin testing tomorrow."

When the kitchen is cleaned up, I join Zander in the family room. He puts his arm around me and asks, "Are you okay?"

I lean my head on his shoulder and confess, "I don't know, I have a weird feeling about all of this. What if we go through all this testing, get picked as Elites, and still get separated? I can barely deal with losing my family, I don't think I would survive if I lost you too."

He holds me tighter. "They can make me live with someone else, but they can never make me love anyone but you." I can't help but smile at him.

Then I sit up and give Zander a kiss. "I think I'm going to go sit in the girls' room. I just want to try and clear my mind. I'll see you in the morning."

Zander hugs me. "Okay, that sounds like a good idea."

I get up and head for the room designated for myself, Mya, and Fatima. I walk over to the bed with my name on it and sit down, my legs hanging over the edge. I let my body fall back onto the bed and cover my face with my hands. I try to repeat the four words that Zander said to me... *I'm smart... I'm brave... I'm confident... I'm beautiful. I can do this, I can show them I'm gifted. I can become an Elite, learn to control my ability, and turn off the haze.*

My thoughts are interrupted with the sound of the bedroom door shutting. I move my hands off my face and prop myself up on my arms. "Oh sorry, were you sleeping?" asks Mya.

I smile and shake my head, "No I was just trying to calm my nerves for tomorrow." I sit up farther, move to the middle of my bed, and cross my legs.

Sitting on her bed, Mya asks, "Do you have any siblings?"

I'm a little surprised someone is actually asking about my life, so it takes me a minute to answer. "I have an older sister, you actually met her today... Tara."

Looking a little shocked, she says, "Wow. I have two siblings. My sister is older and ungifted like me. My brother is younger, we aren't sure if he's gifted or not."

"It might be better for all of you to be ungifted—your family won't be torn apart then."

Shrugging, she says, "I guess, but none of us are unique. We're just Elite slaves."

I get up and sit on Mya's bed next to her. "Maybe someday it will change. Did you notice how the Elites are just like us, when they aren't controlled by Thyn? Maybe I can strengthen my gift and make the two regions one. My family and Zander seem to think I can, but I'm not sure. When I see people get abused by the Elites I start to think I can do it, that I can help everyone."

Mya smiles. "That would be a wonderful world to live in."

I nod. "It would be, but can we talk about something else?" I think for a moment and ask, "Where do you like to work best? I enjoy the fields. The only bad part of them is weeding, that's how I got these." I hold out my hands and show her the scars on them.

She touches my hands and says, "How did you get these? I thought everyone gets work gloves."

"I was overwhelmed the day I found out I was gifted. I was happy because I would get to stay with Zander, but my parents seemed to be happy too, which upset me, so I ran to the fields and began pulling weeds... anyway you still haven't answered my question."

Looking down, she says, "I'm not sure, I don't really like any of it. If I had to choose... I would pick working in the clothing factory. My mother makes clothes for us when we have extra money for cloth. She taught me, and I love it."

I nudge her and say, "I thought you said you weren't unique? I think being able to make your own clothes is an unique ability. I probably couldn't even if you taught me. I dread the clothing factory. They make me wash everything because I tend to poke my fingers with the needles more than the cloth!" Mya laughs at me, and I realize it is the first time I've heard her laugh. It's so soft it's almost hard to tell she's laughing. I only know because she's holding her stomach and has a huge grin on her face.

I look at the door. "I wonder how late it is... do you want to try something with me?" She nods, so we get up and she follows me to the kitchen.

As we walk through the family room I notice Fatima sitting on the couch next to her brother, but I don't see anyone else; they must have gone to bed. Mya and I enter the kitchen and I press the two buttons on the food processor. I say, "Think of anything you want and I will push the letters for it."

She thinks for a moment. "I think I would like some pudding."

I smile and spell out 'pudding,' and then I add my

own. "I think some cookies would go nice with that pudding."

As we wait at the table for our food, the kitchen fills with an amazing smell. It is better than the smell of the cake I had on my birthday.

Inhaling deeply, Mya says, "I wish we could get food like this in the Inept Region. We might be more willing to work for them if they treated us a little better. I don't understand why they have to treat us so badly. I get that the Commander thinks that the Elite should have better lives, but we don't deserve the lives they force us into." Tears build up in her eyes, but she holds them back. "Alexis, please believe in yourself. I saw Acey's eyes become clear in the transportation vehicle. I know you did that, and I know you can do it to Thyn."

I try to smile and say, "I can only tell you what I've told my family—I will do my best."

Our food is ready, so I get up and place the bowl of pudding in front of Mya. Then I grab the plate of cookies. They must have it set to make enough for all eight of us, because the amount of pudding Mya has in front of her would last my family a month.

Mya and I stuff our faces with cookies and pudding until we can't eat anymore. I like Mya, and I wish she was gifted so we could stay friends. We don't have the energy to put away the dishes once we are done eating, so we head to our room, where we find Fatima already asleep.

As quietly as we can, we get into our beds, and Mya whispers, "I'm glad I met you, Alexis, and I'm glad you will be around for a few more days."

Tiredly I said, "Me too."

I drift off to sleep until I wake up to Mya shaking me, and Fatima looking worried on her bed. I realize I am sweating and Mya says, "Alexis, it was just a dream! It's okay."

Suddenly my dream comes back to me: *I was watching*

*a hazy-eyed Titen kill everyone I love. He started with my parents, snapping their necks like he did with Benjamin. Then he moved on to Mya, breaking her bones one by one. Finally he had reached Zander, taking his time to make him suffer. All of this happened because he found out my plan. Thyn found out I was after him.* Without warning I start to cry, and Mya wraps me in her arms, then I panic and yell, "Zander! I need to go see if he's okay."

Mya stops hugging me and says, "I'll go get him." Before I can say anything she is out the door, and back before I can even blink. Then I see Zander walk through the door and I start to cry even more.

He sits down next to me and pulls me into his arms. "Alexis, what's wrong?"

I sniff. "I had a horrible nightmare that my family, Mya, and you were all being killed because of me."

Hugging me tighter, he says, "That will never happen, when you get upset your gift works better, they can never hurt anyone you care about." I try to take in what Zander has said, because I know it's true—I've accidently removed the haze from Elites before I even knew I was gifted. When my emotions are running high I seem to be able to do it better, still out of control, but it can be done.

I give up on sleeping, but I convince Zander to go back to bed. He only agrees after Mya offers to stay up with me. I am guessing there's only an hour or so until we will be off to the first day of testing, so Mya and I try to figure what to make everyone for breakfast. We decide to keep it simple with eggs and bread. While it's cooking we clean up the mess we made last night and set the table for everyone.

# CHAPTER SIX

A knock on the door startles us. We turn to look as a female Elite we haven't met comes in. "Today all of you will begin with Medical Testing. Please make sure everyone is ready, with the proper attire, in one hour." She turns to leave, shutting the door behind her. Mya and I look at each other, and without saying anything we go and start waking everyone up, then change into our Medical Testing uniforms.

I finish changing before everyone else and go to the kitchen to serve our breakfast. I barely touch my food because the closer the test gets the more nervous I become. Zander must have noticed, and he puts one of his arms around me. This brings me some comfort, especially after the nightmare I had last night.

*What if wanting a world with no walls gets the people I love killed?* I don't think I can live with myself if they are gone because of me. The hour seems to be creeping by, only making me more anxious. *I wish they would hurry up, I just want to get this over with!*

Giving up on eating. I get up, clear my plate, and go and sit on my bed. I position myself with my knees pulled up to my chest, and the door slowly opens. "Do you want some company?" Zander asks softly.

"I always want your company." I try to smile at him, but I can't do it. "I'm sorry I'm such a wreck lately."

He sits next to me and sighs. "It's understandable, if anyone in our situation wasn't they would have to be crazy."

I look at him trying to figure out what he's talking about. "But you're not falling apart."

Apparently what I said is funny, because now Zander is laughing at me. "Trust me, I am freaking out, I just hide it better. It doesn't help that you put a ton of pressure on yourself. Alexis, I know everyone has been stressing the importance of your gift, and what you're capable of... including myself... but if it's affecting your happiness, you shouldn't do it. I don't need the walls torn down to be happy, I just need you."

I look straight ahead, I can't say anything. All I can do is argue with myself. *He's right, I don't have to do this. But it doesn't mean I shouldn't... ugh!*

Zander sits with me in silence until Mya comes in, announcing, "The Elite is here to take us to the Medical Center." I nod and start to head out the door, then suddenly stop.

Zander doesn't notice I've stopped and nearly knocks me over, asking, "What's wrong?"

I turn around, wrap my arms around his neck, and kiss him. "Zander, I love you."

He smiles. "I love you too." Then we both enter the family room where everyone is waiting.

The Elite waits while we join the others then introduces herself, "My name is Giana, I will lead you to the Medical Center." I stare at her as she speaks to us, she is short with tan skin and long curly black hair. I wish I could see what color her eyes are, but they are clouded.

Giana doesn't say anything as she leads us down the walkway, which gives me an eerie feeling. We are all deep in our own thoughts. Of course mine are terrifying, as normal. I'm thinking about them shoving different needles into my skin, making my blood pour out, dissecting me on the spot to retrieve my gift for their own use somehow. My heart starts to race, and I can feel my lungs trying to get air. I'm hyperventilating, when I feel someone's hands on me, which makes me panic more because I can't figure out what's happening. Eventually my heart slows down, and my breathing becomes fuller. When I can finally focus I see a hazy-eyed Giana touching me. *How can someone who has a panic attack at the thought of needles change things?*

Slowly my heart finally returns to normal, so Giana drops her hands and starts to lead us again. I pick up my pace and join Giana asking, "What's your gift?"

"I am a healer," she says in a monotone voice.

I think for a moment. "Is it like Sacri's? Can you heal if you get cut?"

Without looking at me this time she answers, "No, Sacri can only heal physical injuries on herself. I can heal internal illnesses, on myself and others."

Finally we reach the Medical Center and we follow Giana in. All of us look around at the machines next to each bed. I'm not sure what they're used for but I'm not concerned about them. I'm more concerned about the tools that are laying out. Some of them look sharp, some have needles, and some have tubes attached. I can't figure out what they would need all these things for. Wouldn't taking some of our blood be sufficient? I'm starting to feel less and less human. It seems like we are only objects for them to poke and prod for their little experiments. These thoughts make me angry, and I want to leave the Medical Center.

Giana orders us to take our seats at our assigned beds, then turns and leaves the room. One by one we sit down on the beds with our names on them. Fatima is in the first one, followed by her twin Crayton. I'm in the third bed with Aron next, followed by Noah. Mya and Reece are in the next two beds. Zander, unfortunately is in the last bed. It makes me uneasy that Zander and I are separated, especially since I'm sure I won't be able to see him when we are lying down.

Suddenly several people in white trench coats enter the room. They have their faces covered so we can't see who they are. This frightens me because I can't tell if their eyes have the haze or not.

Apparently they can see through whatever is over their heads since they walk around the room without tripping or running into anything. My heart stops as I watch one of them approach each of our stations.

As one of the trench coats gets closer to me I start to get more nervous. My heart starts to race, and I can feel myself getting pale. *I can't do this, I'm going to be sick!* I drop off my bed onto my hands and knees and start to heave, but there isn't anything in my stomach. Now I'm glad I didn't eat anything before we came here.

By the time I'm able to get ahold of myself the Elite in the trench coat is staring at me. So I slowly get up and say, "I'm sorry, I'm just nervous."

She whispers, "It's quite normal to be nervous. Could you please get into your medical bed and lie on your back?" I quickly nod, and do as the trench coat asks. I can feel my body shaking, when the examiner grabs my right arm. Without thinking about it, I try to pull my arm away, which is a very stupid thing to do, because now the examiner is putting restraints around my wrists and ankles. I try to keep calm, but let out a slight scream—I try to compose myself, but I can't. I can feel something stabbing into my arm, slowly pushing something through my veins.

I don't want to be drugged, I want to know what they are doing to me. I can feel the drug moving up my veins in my arm. It takes effect quickly because my arm already feels dead—I wouldn't be able to move it even if they removed the restraints. I wish it would spread faster, because now I can feel the examiner stabbing my body with other wires. Then she takes a small clear tube and wraps it around my head right above my mouth. The tube is blowing something into my nose, and I hope it's just air but as it fills my lungs I can feel myself starting to lose consciousness. Shortly after that I lose the battle with my eyes and they shut heavily.

To my surprise I can hear everything going on around me. It's a weird feeling being completely aware, but not having control over any part of my body. I can't even get my eyes to open. I start to wonder if it's just my ability protecting my mind again, or if everyone can hear what's going on. I hope Zander and Mya can't. I'm not even sure if I want to hear what they are doing or saying. I can hear the examiners walking around, checking on each of us to make sure the drug has taken effect properly.

I hear one of the examiners say, "Let's start with the first station. We need to extract some blood so we can check her DNA." I'm glad when they get to me that I won't be able to feel the needles going in... I hope. Then I hear them speak again, "The drugs seems to be working well, she didn't even flinch when the needle went in. Now that we have her blood, let's start on the brain examination"

*Brain examination...* that can't be right. How can they examine our brains without killing us? My question is answered with a sound so alarming that if I wasn't paralyzed I would have jumped out of my skin. They're going to drill into our skulls to get the information they want!

Maybe the other two tests are a ruse so we don't know that we just walked into our final resting place. I'm not ready to die... there are so many things I still want to do with my life.

As panic races through my mind I hear the drill grind

on something hard. Immediately when the drill starts to grind Fatima gives a bloodcurdling scream! I can feel myself trying to fight against the drug, but nothing I do or think makes me move. I just want to get to Fatima, to stop them from killing her! Fatima's scream fades when the drill turns off.

Then an examiner says, "I will place the tip of the sensor in her brain tissue and it should show us any brain activity she may be having. If she does not have a mental gift there won't be anything on the tests since the drug we gave them will make them comatose. But if she possesses an ability of the mind, the drug won't suppress it and the activity will show up on the analysis. The way their brain acts while on the drug will show us what type of mental ability they have. So far the results on this one is interesting. Her brain is reacting like she is asleep and having a vivid dream. That's fascinating."

I am trying to figure out everything the examiner just said but it's hard to focus when I still have Fatima's scream replaying in my mind. To me it sounds like the examiner is saying that our gifts are the only thing functioning, which explains what they said about Fatima's examination, because she's dreaming. So that means half of us will have something show up on the test results. I wonder what mine and Noah's will look like, considering we need other gifted individuals around to make ours work—unless that's why I'm completely aware, maybe I'm turning off whatever is in the drug. I wish someone would just tell me what they are drugging us with. I'm pretty sure the Inept would cooperate more if they told us what is going on.

I'm so focused on my thoughts that I don't notice them moving closer to my station. The sound of the drill turning on startles me again. When it starts to grind on Crayton's skull he doesn't scream like Fatima. I wonder if his pain tolerance is higher, but then I erase that thought. No one could have a higher pain tolerance to someone digging in their brain. So the ungifted and physically gifted must react differently to the drug.

Only four of us here will know the pain of our skulls being opened and our brains examined. The examiners aren't talking as they work on Crayton, which leaves me alone to my own thoughts. I'm getting more terrified with each passing second—soon they will be done with Crayton and move on to me. I wish I could get up and run away, I wish I was an Inept, and I wish I didn't live in this world! I can hear the examiner's moving around, their steps coming closer to me.

Then I feel something stab my arm, they must be taking my blood. I keep trying to brace myself for the sound of the drill, but it never comes. Apparently there is a lot more they do before the drilling that I didn't hear with the others. They don't speak as they work on me, they must be hooking up different equipment. I want them to forget about my brain, to walk away without opening my skull, but of course they don't. I can feel them tugging on my hair, moving it out of the way. Then the drill starts up, and I feel it touch my skull as it tears through my skin.

I open my eyes, confused. I'm lying on my back, not in the Medical Center but in the bedroom of our living quarters. I sit up and my head begins to pound. I reach up to rub it and feel a slight bump, which I'm assuming is the scar from the drill. I'm thankful that they have medicine here that can heal anything, I don't think I would enjoy walking around with a head wound. I can remember everything up to my head vibrating from the drill coming into contact with my skull, but nothing after. I'm not even sure if I screamed.

I look to my right and see Mya. She looks peaceful like nothing happened to her. Then I look over to Fatima—she is awake but looks traumatized. She is lying on her side with her knees curled up to her chest and her hands over her ears. I want to comfort her, but I don't want to upset her more. Instead I get up, and almost fall back over. The drugs must not have fully worn off. I regain my balance and head toward the family room. I want to find Zander, to make sure he's okay.

When I enter the family room, Zander isn't here. He's probably still sleeping, he was the last one worked on so he will probably be out the longest. I see Aron sitting in the family room staring straight ahead.

I join him and he gushes, "I heard *everything*—Fatima's scream, my own, and Noah's... the thoughts of the examiners... I heard your thoughts until they began drilling on you. But I couldn't hear Crayton, Mya, Reece, or Zander's thoughts. I think the drug they gave us numbed them completely, mind and body. But like the one examiner said, the drug didn't suppress our gifts. So the few of us with a *wonderful* mental gift got to be tortured. I don't understand how you couldn't scream, how suddenly your thoughts vanished. I... I thought he drilled too far and killed you. The examiner who ran the drill is a horrible human being. The entire time he was thinking about torturing each and every one of us until we died a slow painful death. He was hoping we were all Inept so he could 'punish' us without the others blinking an eye. Alexis... he *enjoyed* when we screamed. It makes me sick!"

I'm taken aback. I shake my head trying to sort it out. "What kind of person would want to kill another? I heard Fatima scream too... I wanted to get up and help her, but I'm sure you already know that."

Nodding, he says, "I did too. Alexis, do you remember anything that happened to you during or after your examination?"

I sigh. "No, the last thing I remember is the drill ripping through my skin like it was paper, and then I woke up here. I think I must have blacked out from the pain or something."

"Really? You think you blacked out when the rest of us didn't? Think about it, we were already out. Our bodies were in a coma like state, the only reason our minds worked is because we have a mental gift. Have you ever turned your own gift off? I know you can turn others off, but does it happen to you too?"

All I can do is nod. This upsets Aron and he takes a deep breath trying to keep calm. "You turned your gift off, you didn't have to feel the pain of them picking in your brain. You could have done the rest of us a favor and helped us out too."

My eyes start to water. "I wanted to, I wanted to do anything I could to help you guys. My *gift* is uncontrollable right now, I didn't even know I shut mine off. I didn't try to, my thoughts have been on staying with Zander. In order to do that I have to become an Elite, so if I had control of it I wouldn't have turned it off." Then I lose control and my tears run down my face.

Aron reaches over and brushes one away. "I'm sorry, I didn't mean to upset you."

I bury my face in my hands. "No, Aron, I'm sorry." I lean over and give him a hug, wishing I had control over my ability so I could have saved them from the pain and the memories.

Then I get up and tap on the boys' bedroom door. When no one answers I slowly open the door up and walk in. Crayton and Reece are out cold, just like Mya, but I'm focused on Noah. He's sitting on the floor facing the corner of the room, rubbing the spot on his head where they drilled. As he rocks on the floor he mumbles to himself, but I can't make out what he's saying.

Quickly I scan the room for Zander, and he's on his bed peacefully sleeping. So I walk over to Noah and touch his shoulder. "Noah... are you okay?" He turns and looks at me like I am the enemy.

Before I can react, he tackles me, screaming, "I

WONT LET YOU DO IT AGAIN! STAY OUT OF MY BRAIN!" He knocks the wind out of me, and I hit my head when we land on the floor. I try to fight him off but he is bigger than me.

"Noah, please, I'm not an examiner... it's me, Alexis." He won't listen to me. Instead he grabs my shoulders and starts slamming me repeatedly into the ground. I do the only thing I can think of—scream: "STOP! SOMEONE HELP ME!"

Noah stops slamming me against the floor and slaps me across the face. My skin burns where he hit me and tears roll from my eyes. His weight is making it hard for me to breathe, and when I start to gasp I try to call for help again: "Zander! Please wake up... Plea... se..." Noah wraps his hands around my throat, cutting off my oxygen. I try with all of my strength to pull his hands away, but can't. I can feel my lungs start to seize when someone tackles Noah.

I take a deep breath and rub my neck. I sit up to see Zander holding a blue-faced Noah up against the wall with his feet off the ground. I quickly get up and slide myself between Zander and Noah, yelling, "Zander, stop! You're going to kill him!"

Noah suddenly drops to the floor gasping for air and Zander wraps me up in his arms. "What happened?"

"It's a long story, but I think Noah is traumatized. He was sitting in the corner, and I touched his shoulder. He thought I was an examiner."

Noah looks around confused and says, "What's going on?"

"You kind of beat me up, but it's not your fault. You were in shock," I explain.

Zander shakes his head. "What do you mean he was in shock? We were knocked out for the entire examination."

Rubbing my neck, I explain, "No... you, Crayton, Reece, and Mya were... the four of us with mental abilities heard and felt everything... Zander they drilled a hole in our skulls and put some kind of sensor in our brain to see if any of us have a mental gift." I turn my head and show him the lump where the hole was. Then he reaches up and touches his head.

He looks at me and then takes Noah's hand, helping him up. "Noah, I'm sorry, but you were going to kill her, I had to stop you." Before Noah responds, Zander pulls both of us close to him and hugs us.

I go to the kitchen to make some stew and wait for it to cook. Zander and Noah sit down at the table together and Aron is still in the family room. Everyone who is awake is out of bed, except for Fatima. She won't come out of the bedroom no matter how many times I ask, so I'm hoping the food will get her to come out.

I sit down next to Zander and take his hand. Squeezing mine, he says, "Do you feel like telling me what happened?"

I look down at the table. "I guess I can, but I don't know everything. Maybe Noah can fill in what I missed?" He nods and I continue, "When they started to work on us... I got nervous... I tried to fight it, but my examiner put me in restraints. Anyway, once the drug had taken effect, my body was paralyzed but because I have a mental gift my mind wasn't affected by it."

Zander sighs. "Of course you would try to fight it."

I shrug. "Anyway, when everyone was out they started on Fatima. I could hear everything they were doing to her. Then I heard the drill, and as it dug into her head she screamed. I still can't get it out of my head. Crayton didn't react like Fatima because he doesn't have a mental ability. When it was my turn, I could feel them stabbing me with different tools, and then the drill was back on and ripping through my skin. I think I turned my gift off, so I was out for the rest of it like you. I don't remember anything after that." Zander just stares at me, his forehead creased.

Noah clears his throat, saying, "Alexis, you pretty much know everything, you only missed out on Aron and I being tortured." I can't say anything to him, I know like Aron, he wishes I would have helped them. I hate that I couldn't. I hate that I was selfish and saved myself.

When the food is almost done I get up and head to the girls' bedroom. Fatima is still in the same position as earlier, so I go and kneel next to her bed. Slowly I brush her hair away from her face, saying, "Fatima... please get up... there's stew in the kitchen. You need to try to eat something... Fatima... I'm... I'm so sorry I couldn't help you. I tried, I wanted so badly to get up and stop them, but the drug was too strong."

Without saying anything she gets up and walks out the door. Then I cross the room to Mya, sit on the edge of her bed, and softly shake her awake. "Mya, wake up, it's time to eat." She opens her eyes and smiles. We walk to the kitchen together and join everyone else who is waiting for us. It's easy to tell who was aware during the examination and who wasn't.

The ones who weren't look well-rested and happy. The rest of us who know what happened look like we haven't slept for weeks. Aron looks the worst, his hair is messy, his eyes are vacant, and he blankly stares across the room. I would give anything to have been able to help them, no one should have to be tortured the way we were. I'm more determined than ever to tear the dreaded walls down so no one else ever again has to live through what we did.

After dinner Zander and I go to the family room. He sits down and I lie with my head on his lap. He brushes his fingers through my hair and I drift off to sleep. However, I'm not asleep for long. *I am in an empty building with Fatima's screams echoing in every direction. I search and search, but can't find her. When I finally do find her, the screaming has stopped and she is on the floor in a pool of blood. Aron's voice rings over and over again, "Why didn't you save her?"*

*I put my hands over my ears, crying, "I tried! I swear I tried!" I keep my eyes tightly closed and my hands push harder and harder against my head.*

Zander wakes me with, "Alexis… it's okay, it was just another bad dream." I slowly open my eyes and see Zander with a worried look on his face. I am getting sick of these dreams.

I lift my hand and stroke his face. "Zander, can we stay out here tonight? I don't think I can be in that room."

"Of course we can. Anything for you." Then he leans over and gently kisses my forehead. "You can go to sleep, I'll be right here." I close my eyes and dreamlessly sleep in Zander's arms.

# CHAPTER SEVEN

I wake up to Zander and Mya talking. Sounding concerned, she says, "She's been asleep for a long time... is she sick?" Zander lightly snickers and says, "Nah... she's just had a rough few months. When she learned about her gift it was hard, because now her parents are alone. Now it's hard for her because she couldn't help anyone yesterday. I think she really needs some sleep." I keep my eyes closed while Zander runs his fingers through my hair. I'm not ready to be awake yet, I don't want last night to end. I haven't slept this well in who knows how long.

Then I hear Aron say, "You know, she's not asleep anymore... she's eavesdropping."

Keeping my eyes closed, I smile and say, "I'm not eavesdropping... I just don't want this to end." I finally open my eyes and look up at Zander. He is intensely looking at me, but he looks worried. "Zander... what's wrong?" I ask him.

"Nothing. I'm just thinking about the testing today. An Elite came in a little while ago to tell us to be ready soon. We are heading to the Physical Center today."

Without saying anything I get up to get ready for the

day. I go into the bedroom to grab my clothes, and then head for the bathroom. I take a long, warm shower and get dressed. I'm tired of wearing the Elite logo. I hope once we are Elites that we get normal clothing to wear when we aren't serving the Core. I stare at myself in the mirror, and pull back my hair to see the scar on my temple. I touch it, wishing they would have hidden the scar in my hair. I already look awkward enough without a pink scar on the side of my face. Because of the scar, I decide to leave my hair down, but it still peaks through.

Finally I give up on hiding it and go out to the family room to join the others. When I walk in, my sister is standing by the entrance to the walkways, and it looks like everyone is waiting for me. I glance over at Zander and then to Tara. She's looking down at the floor, moving her foot in tiny circles. She always did that when she was impatient. Then it hits me! Thyn wouldn't know that! I run over to her and throw my arms around her. She hugs me back and says, "Hey Ale."

I had almost forgotten she called me Ale when we were younger. Everyone picked up on it, but when she became an Elite I started to hate the nickname. It doesn't feel right without her around. "Tara! I... I can't believe you're here and not umm... under *his* control like you were a couple days ago." I take a step back to look at her eyes, tears are filling them. Then she brushes my hair back and looks at the scar on my temple. I push her hand away and say, "It's fine, I'm fine."

She lets out her breath, like she's been holding it. "Oh good, so you don't have a mental gift. When I came here the ones with mental gifts told us horrifyingly gruesome stories of the examinations. I was worried it might happen to you."

I can't look her in the eyes. "Tara... I know what happened... a few of us do." Before I can say anything else, her arms are around me. Then I realized something.

"Tara, why don't you have the haze?"

She smiles at me. "Because I asked them if I could speak with you. I know some of the examiners and they said you put up quite a fight when they were hooking you up. So I went through the long process of communicating with Thyn and Commander Avery. They agreed I could come and take you to the next test without the haze. Considering they think since I'm Elite that you're probably going to be one too, they didn't see the harm in it... oh, that reminds me! We better get going and get you guys to the Physical Center."

Tara holds the door open for everyone, and we file into the walkway one by one. When Zander is through the door I take his hand in mine and we follow my sister. She turns to look at me, glancing at our hands, and laughs. "Does Dad know about this?"

I can feel myself starting to blush, explaining, "Yes, he knows, and Mom embarrasses me about it." I look over at Zander and he's smiling. Then another thought occurs to me. "Tara, are you... married?" She doesn't look back at me, or even stop walking. When she doesn't answer I assume it's because we have reached the Physical Center. She holds the door open for us again and shuts it behind her.

She takes my other hand and leads me away from the group. "Alexis, one thing you need to understand before you're an Elite is that you may not be arranged to marry Zander, even if you grew up together, they probably won't care. I didn't want to get married at all, but the second you're chosen as an Elite they start to decide what gifts will combine well to make the next generation stronger. I wasn't paired off right away, so I got to live alone for a year. The next year, when the new group came here, there was someone chosen for me. You know him pretty well, and he's told me a lot, which is another reason I wanted to come and talk to you."

I can't help but look at her confused. "But that means you were only sixteen when they chose your partner. Why do they make you get married so young here? Wait... what do you mean I know him?"

"They explained that they want us to get married soon to get past the awkwardness of living with a complete stranger, so we can learn to love each other and create an Elite family."

I start to get angry. "Tara, what do you mean that I know him?"

She looks down and starts twirling her foot again. "I'm married to Titen... please listen for a minute. I know he hurt you, but he's not a bad guy. I believe him and you, when he told me about what Thyn made him do. Just please remember that it's not really Titen."

I'm so shocked I can't say anything, but then I have to ask, "Do you love him?" All my sister does is nod. Then she places her hand on her stomach. I gasp, unable to hold it back, and I blurt, "You're *pregnant*—?!" All she does is nod and no matter what my feelings are toward Titen, I love my sister. I wrap my arms around her again and say, "I'm happy for you, and I love you."

Smiling, she says, "Thanks. I love you too." Then she turns and leaves, so I rejoin the group.

As soon as she leaves, a male Elite comes in. He's a tall man with blonde hair, and he looks thick with muscle. He greets us with, "My name is Hunter... the physical test is different than the medical one. Instead of being at stations, you are all free to roam. A physical gift isn't only strength. It can be many things, maybe you can influence water, or some other element. Anything you have to *physically* do or touch to produce it will be tested here. The examiners from the medical test will be in shortly to observe you."

Panic shoots through my veins, I don't want to see the trench coats. I don't want to see the man who gave me the scar on my temple. I look over and see that Aron has a look of horror on his face, and Noah has turned pale and looks like he might pass out. Fatima can't hold on and is lying on the floor sobbing while her brother tries to comfort her. I hope they still have their masks on so we don't have to look at their faces. None of us can handle that right now.

Instead of waiting to figure out his gift, Zander asks, "Hunter, what's your ability?"

With the same monotone voice all the Elites have under Thyn's control, he replies, "I can influence plants. That's why all the plants here in the Elite Region are exquisite." Zander chuckles a little and Hunter scowls at him, saying, "Is something funny, Inept?"

Zander shakes his head. "I figured with how you're built that your gift would be physical, not mental."

Hunter glares at him. "My gift is physical, I have to touch the plant. I can't think about it and have it appear." Zander shrugs as a door opens.

Then the examiners come into the room wearing the same trench coats. Luckily they are all still wearing something over their faces like yesterday. They take places around the room, and Hunter says, "You may begin showing them your abilities."

For a moment all of us stand motionless. I walk over to Aron and ask, "Can you tell by their thoughts which one did this to us?" I touch my scar and he nods. I look around and ask, "Which one is he?" Aron nods across the room. I swallow hard. He's standing near the heavy objects where Zander will be, which means I'll be there too. Since I don't have a physical gift, my plan for today is to watch Zander enjoy showing off his.

Zander comes over to me and says, "Alexis, I know how much you don't want me to use my strength, but don't stop it. I need to show them what I can do." I nod, take his hand, and we head over to the station he will be using. I stand out of the way while Zander begins piling heavy objects on top of a platform. The examiner steps closer to watch him when Zander effortlessly lifts the platform over his head.

The man in the trench coat gives a deep laugh, exclaiming, "Well, would you look at that? I was wondering which one of you Inept would actually have a gift." I feel disgusted that he is speaking about Zander. Turning to me, the man says, "Do you have anything to show me?"

I keep staring at Zander and say, "No... I don't think so. I'm sure you got everything you needed yesterday. I don't have a physical gift."

He steps into my view and says, "Hmm. Why would an Inept like you be following this boy around then?" He glances suspiciously at me and Zander and laughs. "Oh my, you think that boy *likes* you... HA! A potential Elite is too good to be with someone like you!" He's leaning toward me in a way that makes me feel uncomfortable. Then he leans in even closer to me and whispers, "You are a worthless Inept! You will never be good enough for an Elite. Have you taken a look in the mirror? No one will ever want to be with you unless they are blind!" He steps back laughing in my face, while tears fill my eyes.

I stare at him with hate and scream, "You don't know anything. What makes you so special?" I hear the platform Zander is using crash to the ground and I realize my anger has triggered my ability.

The trench coat looks to be shaking, when finally he tears off his mask. He has black, shaggy hair, and he's glaring at me with his haze-free, grey eyes, like he wants me dead. "How DARE you! I am the offspring of two powerful Elites! I am worth more than your insufficient life ever will be!" I look around and everyone is watching us, even the other examiners have come closer. He must have noticed this too, because he says, "This one needs to be taught a lesson! She needs to learn when to keep her mouth shut! First she fights us during the medical test, and now this!" One of the other examiners nods, then he grabs my arm and starts to pull me towards the door.

*Why does this keep happening to me? They must know something. I wonder if they have heard me talking about my gift!* I keep eye contact with Zander while I am being dragged out of the room. He looks torn. I know he wants to help me, but if he does, it will just make things worse. So before I can be pulled through the door, I grab onto the frame and yell out, "I'm sorry... I'll be fine!" Then I can't hold on any more and I am in the walkway with the examiner.

He slams me against the wall and gives me an appalling smile. "You shouldn't have told them you'll be fine..." Then he hits a button in the walkway and orders, "I need Titen up here immediately!" Turning back to me he says, "You're going to regret being a sarcastic brat!"

I try to get loose from his grip, but he is stronger than me. I would give anything to have a physical gift right now. I keep trying to look away from him, but he grabs my face and makes me look into his eyes. *This guy is crazy! I didn't do anything that I should be punished for!* I hear footsteps echoing along the walkway and know Titen is on his way. So I shut my eyes trying to concentrate on my gift. Maybe I can get him back to normal and he can help me.

Then I hear Titen say, "What can I do for you today, Axel?"

*Axel.* At least now I know who will be punishing me. I feel his grip loosen so I open my eyes and look at Titen. I try not to say anything when I notice he doesn't have the haze.

Axel says, "I need you to take my *patient* to the medical center. I will meet you there once I finish observing the physical tests." He lets go of me and quickly walks back into the room. I glance up at Titen and he sighs.

"Are you going to make me use my gift on you, or will

you just walk with me?"

I can barely think straight, but I manage to say, "I can walk, if that's okay." He nods and I follow him to the Medical Center.

We don't say anything to each other until we are in the room. When he opens the door, he gestures toward the bed with my name on it. "If you could take a seat at your station, I would appreciate it." I deliberate for a moment, then go to the medical bed.

I swing my feet off the edge and ask, "Titen, what is he going to do to me?"

"That depends on how upset you made him." Then he sits down next to me. "What did you do?"

I fidget with my hands. "I asked him what makes him so special... but it was only after he said horrible things to me." I turn to look at him. "Why don't you have the haze?"

"Because Thyn isn't here today. He trusts us to do our job. He only uses it on us when we are with him or in the Inept Region."

I get up and start to pace. "I know it's your job to keep us *in line*, but could you do me a favor?" He nods. "If he kills me, will you tell my sister I love her?"

"He won't kill you. That's not what he's about. He's not even Elite..."

I walk over to Titen and look him dead in the eyes, "What do you mean he's not Elite?"

"I shouldn't have said anything, but since I already did... we are similar to the Inept. Two Inept can have an Elite child, and two Elites can have an Inept child. The only difference is the Inept children here get to stay since both of their parents are Elite... I heard when he found out he wasn't gifted he dedicated himself to learning about medicine so he could administer the tests. We all think he's lost it, and enjoys torturing the people going through testing. I think it's because he's jealous that some of you might have an ability. It's worse to him because we come from Inept families."

I can't say anything I'm in such shock, so Titen fills the silence. "Alexis, I'm sorry in advance for what he will make me do. If I don't *do my job* he could hurt my family... your sister."

I nod my head. "It's okay, do whatever you have to. Keep her and your baby safe. My parents expect me to become an Elite anyway, so if he kills me they won't know I'm dead. They will just assume my gift is needed in the Elite Region."

Waiting for Axel is more torture than anything. My mind keeps filling with endless possibilities of how he can hurt me. I wish he would just get here and do whatever it is he's planning.

Then Titen startles me. "Alexis, what exactly is your gift? I've only heard that it's a mental one."

"I can turn gifts off, I guess. I did it to you once. I'm not sure if you remember it but I removed the clouds in your eyes. You even recognized me."

He rubs his eyes. "I remember. I really wasn't sure what happened. Are you in control of it yet?"

"I wish. I only have control with one person, Zander. My mother thinks it's permanently on when I am dealing directly with him. I didn't even know I was gifted until a few months before we came here. I assumed he had control of his."

His eyes widen. "That's incredible! Just wait until you can control it."

"Everyone says that, they think I can *change* things. That I can make it so we can all live together in peace, but I'm not sure if I can."

Titen laughs. "Well, if you ever decide to attempt it, let me know. I know your sister is with me when I say we will help you."

This makes me smile, but I quickly wipe it off my face when the door opens and Axel walks through. "Ah nicely done, Titen. Will you do the honors of assisting me?" I glance at Titen, who gives a slight nod, which elates Axel. "Wonderful! I need you to hold her down while I do further examinations on her."

I can feel my body move, and now I am lying down. Then I feel my limbs go rigid and I can't move. I look up at Titen and he has an apologetic look in his eyes. "Axel, would you like me to hook up the drug for you?"

Axel lets out a laugh. "No, no. We won't be needing that today. She needs to be able to feel this. Someone needs to teach her some respect." He pauses and adds, "Oh, and feel free to let her speak, no need to hold her mouth shut." Then he looks toward me with that horrid smile again.

As I lie here motionless I can hear Axel digging through the tools, looking for something specific. When he finds what he is looking for, he holds it in front of my face. It's a long metal tool that has a blade on the end of it. He slowly runs the dull side of it along my face, down my chest, and over my stomach.

I try not to panic as he begins making incisions down my arms and legs. I try not to make any noise—I don't want to give him the satisfaction, but when he pours something onto my skin it burns and I can't help it, and I scream, "STOP, please stop!" I can see Titen trying not to watch and placing his hands over his ears.

Axel continues, "I thought you said you would be fine? A little of our *enhanced* gel shouldn't bother you." He stops just to start digging through his supplies again. I can feel the blood dripping down my arms, when I hear the last noise I ever want to hear again—the sound of the drill. I scream as he drills into my feet and legs. I can barely see through the tears rolling down my face. I try to look at Titen, but he's only a blur. I plead with Axel, "Please, I'm sorry. Just please, stop." He laughs at me as he drills into my forearms.

I'm starting to feel weak from the blood loss when

Titen finally says, "If you don't stop the bleeding, you're going to kill her. If she's possibly gifted, Thyn won't be happy."

Axel yells, "She's not gifted! She's a worthless Inept. Nothing showed up on her medical results, and she doesn't have a physical gift!"

Titen protests, "If you don't let Thyn do his test on her, it won't be good for you. Do you think you'll get away with it?"

"Fine!" Then I can feel him pouring something on my wounds and my strength starts to come back. "It gives me more time to experiment on her. Now where was I?"

*I wish they would let me die! From now on I'm done trying to defend everyone. All it does is get me abused. First by Titen, then by Noah, and now by Axel! How am I supposed to change anything when I end up constantly near death?* My thoughts are interrupted as I feel him lift my shirt. Slowly he runs his fingers across my body and I cry out, "Don't touch me!"

He laughs a little then I feel more pain. He is opening up my stomach—I can feel the cool gel pouring onto the incision he made down my torso. I begin to throw up from the pain and choke, then I feel someone lift me to my side and hit my back. I am finally able to breathe again, and see Titen gently laying me back down. This is the first time I've ever seen him touch someone to move them.

Axel isn't happy about this and says, "Titen. What are you doing? Get back over there and do as you're told!"

Titen steps back, looking more upset than before. "Why are you doing this to her?"

"She deserves it! She's trying to seduce an Elite! When I'm done with her, no one will fall for it!" Then he lets out another laugh.

Appalled, Titen says, "She's fifteen years old. How can you think that way?" Axel responds by running his hand along my pant line. I take a deep breath and he begins to unbutton them.

*"Please don't!"* I beg him, I would rather be dead then have him touch me that way.

When Axel doesn't stop and is about to remove my pants, Titen says, "Violating her that way won't stop someone from wanting to be with her. There is no need for that!"

He stops and thinks for a moment, "You're right, but I know what will." Then he comes into my view and I feel a blade run down my face. I keep my mouth shut, because screaming only makes it worse. I wish I could control my tears, because they burn the cuts on my face. Finally the constant pain is too much and I pass out.

I can feel my body moving, but I'm not walking. I open my eyes and see that Titen is carrying me. "What's going on?"

He sighs in relief. "Oh good, you woke up. Once you passed out it wasn't *fun* for him anymore. So he healed you and left. I let you lie there for a while to see if you would come to. When you didn't, I decided it would be best to take you back to the living quarters. I'm sure everyone is worried about you. Although they won't be relieved when they see what he did to you. Alexis, I'm so sorry."

Confused, I start to look at my arms and gasp, "How bad is my face?"

He shakes his head. "It's not as bad as the rest of you. You have three scars on your face. One is from your temple to your chin, and the others are smaller. One on either side of the long one." I touch both sides of my face, and feel the scars on the same side as the one on my temple.

"Can you put me down so I can walk?"

"Sure, but if you feel too weak let me know and I will pick you back up." He sets me down, and I wobble a little but don't fall. We aren't far from the living quarters when I stop and put my hands against the glass wall.

"I can't go in there. I can't let them see me like this. Mya will be terrified, and Zander... I don't even know what he will think." I start to hit the glass when I can't move my arm anymore. "Titen, stop doing that!"

"No, I'm not going to let you hurt yourself because of Axel. If Zander loves you he won't care about the scars! He will only be concerned about how you are holding up. With the way it looks right now you're not doing well!"

I turn and glare at him. "I'm fine! Axel only made me want to succeed even more!"

"Good! Like I said before, I'll do what I can to help you. I'm tired of living in a world like this. I'm tired of my ability hurting and killing people."

I sigh. "Titen... did he do anything to me when I passed out? Like he was about to before you stopped him, before he cut my face."

He hesitates. "No, he didn't... I think he knew I wasn't going to let him, it's one thing to make me participate and watch him torture you. But it's a different story if he would try and make me help him... *violate* someone."

I can feel my eyes fill with tears, but I ignore them and pick up our conversation we were having before Titen answered my question. "We probably shouldn't talk about going against the Commander and Thyn, not until I'm officially an Elite." He nods and walks me to the entrance to the living quarters. I give him a hug and say, "Thank you for trying to stop him today." He returns my hug and walks away.

Slowly I open the door, hoping everyone will be asleep considering how late it is. When I get inside I don't see anyone, so I head straight for the bathroom. I take a deep breath and look into the mirror. Apparently he didn't feel the need to clean up all the blood like they did during the actual testing. I look at all the dry blood, trying to figure out how I didn't bleed to death. Then I jump in the shower. I can't let Zander see me like this, he will be horrified.

Once I'm done I have no choice but to put the same clothes back on, since all my other clothes are in the bedroom. Axel must not have moved my clothes out of the way when he cut into me because they are covered in holes and blood. Now that my skin is cleaned up, I look at my wounds. My arms are covered, along with my legs and stomach. Slowly I look up into the mirror then quickly away. I can't hold it in anymore. I pick up anything I can and throw it at the mirror—I can't stand looking at myself. The mirror shatters, and I hear a panicked knocking on the door. It's Mya. "Alexis, open the door!"

I drop to the floor. "Go away!"

She tries to get in but the door is locked. "I'm not going anywhere, neither is Zander!"

"Alexis, please open the door," Zander pleads.

"Just leave me *alone!*" I scream.

I can hear them talking to each other. "Come on, Mya, she will come out when she's ready." Then I hear their steps going away.

*I can't go out there. I know they will want to know what happened, but I can't relive it... not yet.* I try to compose myself, and clean up the mess I made. I stand against the door, trying to get the courage to face them, when a soft knock surprises me. "What?" I ask wearily.

"Please, Alexis. I need to see you... I need to know you're okay."

"Zander... I... I can't come out."

"Why not?"

"I just can't, okay?" I start to lose my composure again.

"Do you remember a few nights ago when I asked you not to leave me?" When I don't respond, he continues, "You told me *never*. You swore you would never leave me. I am here for you, we can get through whatever happened if you will just open this door." I'm not sure if I'm crazy or if I like to be disappointed, but I unlock the door.

"It's unlocked, but I'm not coming out." Defeated, I face the opposite wall and place my hands on it, leaning my forehead over to touch it. I still don't want him to see me. The door slowly opens, then quickly shuts. I feel his hand on my shoulder, and he turns me around to face him. I put my hands over my face before he can look at me.

Zander gasps, "What did he do to you? Your arms!"

Still hiding my face, I cry, "It's just not my arms... it's... all of me." I can feel his arms wrap around me but I pull away. "Don't pity me. I'm horrifying." I let my arms drop and Zander looks at my face. As I expected, he's shocked! "I shouldn't have let you in."

He softly touches the scars on my face. "Alexis, I'm sorry this happened to you..."

"But..." I let the word linger.

"What?" he says, looking at me confused.

I turn away. "You're sorry this happened, but you can't stand to look at me."

"You're the one who keeps turning away. You are beautiful, you always have been, and you always will be. A few scars won't change the way I feel about you!" He says defensively.

"That's why he did this... he thinks I'm Inept, and that I'm trying to get an Elite to fall for me. He scarred me so no one would want me," I explain. When Zander doesn't say anything I tell him almost everything that happened, including my conversations with Titen. When I finish, he still hasn't said anything. I turn to look at him, and see that tears are running down his face. Zander is a strong person, he never breaks.

After a moment, he takes my face in his hands and kisses me. "I love you... and no one, not even someone as insane as Axel, will change that." I give in and press my face against his chest. "You need to go out there. Everyone has been worried. We were all in the kitchen when you came in. But you were too quick and we got to the family room as you shut the bathroom door. We wanted to give you some privacy. But when I heard you breaking down I couldn't sit back and wait anymore."

I squeeze him a little tighter. "I'm sorry."

"You have *nothing* to be sorry for."

I take a step back and take his hand into mine. "Will you walk in front of me so I don't shock anyone right away?"

He leans over and gently kisses me on the forehead. "Of course."

We walk out. Then I hear Mya say, "Oh, Alexis, are you okay? Why are you hiding behind Zander?" I tighten my grip on his hand.

Zander clears his throat. "She doesn't want to upset you guys." I wish I could stop thinking about it. I know Aron is probably watching it replay in my mind. I slowly let go of Zander's hand and walk out from behind him. Everyone stares at me, but Aron has a painful look in his eyes.

"Aron, I'm sorry… I'm trying not to think about it, but it keeps replaying in my head. I can't get it out." Still no one says anything, then Aron comes over to me and wipes the tears from my face like the day of the medical test.

He looks at my arm. "Don't be sorry… you didn't do this."

I look up at Zander. "I'm going to go change… I'll be right back." I go to the girls' bedroom and change into the first outfit we were given. I sit on the floor with my back against my bed. I am about to break down again when Mya walks in.

She gives me a weak smile. "I'm glad you're still alive. Aron said when the examiner came back to the physical test, that he was thinking about the different ways to punish you. They all led up to you dying."

I nod. "I probably would have died if it wasn't for Titen. Luckily he didn't have the haze and was trying to get

Axel to stop." I get up, walk past her, and she follows me out of the bedroom, but no one is in the family room. "Mya, where is everyone?"

"They are probably in the kitchen."

We head toward the kitchen, and sure enough everyone is sitting around the table. I take a seat next to Zander and I can feel everyone's eyes on me. I'm assuming Aron filled them in, because even Zander has a different look to him. I purposely left out some details so he wouldn't worry too much, but I'm guessing he knows everything now. Then Noah stands up.

"Alexis, the way we get treated was tolerable until today. They crossed a line, and we want to help tear the walls down... we have all talked about it, and think we can get enough help to make this work. Of course it may take a while considering a lot of us don't have much control over our gifts yet. In the meantime, I think we can start planning what to do. Mya, Reece, and Crayton have all agreed to gather as much help from the Inept Region as possible. Once I gain more control over my gift, I will be able to help make yours stronger."

"You guys don't have to do this. Your families could get hurt because of this... But if we do this I don't think we should talk about it here. I don't want anyone we can't win over to hear about it. I already have Titen and my sister on board. Mya, I need you to find my parents when you get back... they decided on this before I even had a chance to think about it. I appreciate all of you for this. It's not going to be easy, but it's better than sitting back and taking it. Just remember not to speak of it anymore here. I don't want Axel catching wind and killing any of you."

When I am done telling them my plans, Mya gets up and serves everyone some leftover stew. I don't want to eat anything, so I get up and sit in the family room. Being alone might not have been the best idea, but I can't be in the kitchen with all of them staring at me anymore. I sit with my legs pulled up to my chest, like usual, trying not to close my eyes. Every time they get heavy, Axel's sadistic smile enters my mind and I can almost feel him touching my waist.

# CHAPTER EIGHT

After dinner everyone gathers in the family room. I think they feel obligated to keep me company, but I can see how tired they all are. We sit in silence, which is worse than sitting by myself. Occasionally they glance at me, making me feel uncomfortable. I can't stand it anymore and say, "You guys can go to bed... I'm fine... I swear." Apparently that did the trick because slowly one by one the room empties, leaving Zander and me alone. Then Zander starts to get up. "Where are you going?"

He stops. "I thought you might want to be alone." I shake my head *no* and he sits back down. "I feel like there's something you're not telling me... Aron already filled in some missing pieces, but there is something else, isn't there?"

I sigh, defeated. I can't keep it from him anymore. "I'm sorry I haven't been completely honest. I didn't want to worry you more than you need to be but... when Axel was *examining* me he mentioned that my medical tests didn't show that I'm gifted. When he said I was Inept before, I thought the results from the test weren't ready yet. That wasn't that case at all... Zander, my gift turned off during the test. If I can't convince them in the last test that I'm Elite, I'll be sent back to the Inept Region... if that happens, can you promise me something?"

"Anything."

I take a deep breath, trying to hold myself together. "If I get sent back, promise me that you won't forget about me... about us."

"Don't be silly. Nothing will make me forget you. We have known each other our whole lives... I have loved you for as long as I can remember." Putting his hand behind my head, he places his forehead against mine. "I plan to spend forever with you... if we get separated I will fight to get you back. We know your ability works on me. So if you get sent back, I believe you can remove the haze from me. Somehow we will be together."

I pull away from him, and say, "After all of this, I can't lose you... I won't let it happen."

He smiles. "I know you won't." Then he kisses me so passionately that for a moment I forget about all the terrible things that took place today. I want it to last forever until he runs the back of his fingers across my face into my hair. Immediately I pull away and place my hand over the scars on my cheek.

Zander gives me an apologetic look and then moves my hand. "Alexis, it's okay... I don't think or feel any differently about you because of these." He gently touches the scars on my face, then pulls me into his arms.

I sigh and he asks, "What's wrong?"

"There's something else I didn't tell you, and I'm not sure if Aron did."

"You can tell me."

I take a deep breath and explain, "Zander, he put some kind of gel on my skin. It burned, and he said it was enhanced. I don't know what it was, but it was so painful!" I burst into tears, unable to keep my composure.

Zander tightens his arms around me, and I sob into his

chest. Softly he says, "Alexis, it's okay. He can't hurt you now. I should have helped you when he was taking you away, I should have stopped him!"

I continue to cry while Zander holds me, and that's where I stay for the night, avoiding sleep.

Occasionally through the night I would fall asleep and my dreams would wake me up. Each time, my heart would race and I would feel sick. I'm not sure if it's because Zander is next to me, but no matter how bad the dreams are, I never scream. He is still asleep when I go to the kitchen. I'm a little surprised when I see Aron sitting at the table. "When did you get up?"

He shrugs. "I'm not sure... I really never slept. Any time you fell asleep I could see your dreams like I was having them myself... I think my ability is strengthening, because it used to only be voices. But the past couple of days it's been more vivid, and sometimes it's a picture playing in my mind."

I sit down across the table from him. "I'm sorry... I'm trying my hardest not to think about it, but it's difficult. Every time I close my eyes I see his face, and I can feel the pain all over again... honestly I'm trying to figure out how I'm not dead from the blood loss. I'm just happy Titen stopped him from..." I let my sentence trail off, I don't even want to think about it.

"Stopped him from what?" Aron looks at me confused.

"Don't you already know?"

Shaking his head, he says, "No... I can only hear or see thoughts when someone is thinking about them. From what you've been thinking, I only saw him cutting you and putting some gel onto your skin."

I rub my hand down one of my arms looking at the different scars. "He was touching my stomach... Aron, he was about to take my pants off, but Titen stopped him. If Titen hadn't been there..." I shudder at the thought.

Suddenly there is a loud crash in the other room. Aron

and I both jump up and run to the family room. As we reach the entrance there is another loud noise. I slowly round the corner to see Zander angrily throwing the contents of the room around. I've never seen him act like this. "Zander! What are you doing?"

He picks up a large chair and throws it against the door leading to the walkways. Then he looks at me and falls to his knees. "I overheard you two talking!" He bends over and pounds the floor, leaving a dent where his fist hit it. "I will never allow him to hurt you again! What kind of monster wants to violate someone like that? How can they let him work on us? If the Elite gene is so important to them, this shouldn't happen. If any of them had an ounce of humanity in them that man wouldn't be anywhere near us."

I start to cross the room to him. He stands back up and is about to throw some more furniture around.

"Zander, stop! If you don't, they will punish you too!" The chair he is holding drops to the floor. I can see the anger in his eyes and I raise my voice. "I won't let you do it... I won't let them have a reason to hurt you." Everyone has gathered at the edge of the room. The noise must have woken them all up.

Annoyed, Zander storms off. "I need to be alone for a minute." He walks into the boys' bedroom and slams the door. Moments later the door that connects to the walkways opens. We all look over to see Tara walk in the door, followed by Titen.

Slowly she scans the room. "What's going on here?" I need to hide, I can't let her see me. I'm sure Titen told her, but I don't want her to worry. Quickly, before she sees me, I duck back into the kitchen.

I can hear Aron saying, "Zander got a bit upset... but don't take him... he didn't hurt anyone. I think he did it to release some of the emotions he's been going through."

Of course he would know exactly how Zander feels... I would give anything to read his mind, to know how he really feels about everything.

I hear Titen's muffled voice. "Where is she?"

*She...* why are they looking for a girl? They know Zander destroyed the family room. Just as I finish my thought I can hear someone enter the kitchen. There is nowhere for me to run to, so I step out to face whoever is coming. I look at the floor as Titen says, "Alexis... are you... doing okay?"

"I'm not sure... I haven't slept... he's not going to get in trouble, is he?"

He shakes his head. "No, Zander will be fine... with the results of his first two tests he's definitely going to be an Elite... we don't get *punished* the way you did. Plus Tara is with him right now, making sure he's okay." I can't think of anything to say. Then he clears his throat and says, "I told your sister about yesterday... she was going to speak with you today, but then we heard the commotion up here and came earlier."

"Why are you already here?"

"We stay here for the duration of the testing... all the Elites that you have interacted with are still here. Like Acey said on the tour, we want to make your stay comfortable. So we try to keep the same faces around so all of you don't get stressed out."

I can't help but roll my eyes. "Oh yes, my stay here has been *wonderful!*"

He catches on to my sarcasm but doesn't respond to it. "Let's go in the other room." I nod and follow him out. When we enter the family room, everyone is sitting along one wall. Titen points toward them, so I walk over and sit next to Mya. Then he joins Tara and Zander in the boys' room. Waiting here is killing me. I just want to get to Zander and comfort him.

I look over to Aron. "Can you hear any of their thoughts even though they're in the other room?"

He nods. "Kind of, it's hard to make out, though. It's

like static in my head." Noah is sitting right next to Aron. He reaches over and touches Aron's arm. "Wow, this is amazing... I can hear all of you at once, but I can somehow separate it and pick out distinct thoughts."

I get impatient and start to shake. "Aron, focus... what's going on in there?"

He straightens up and says, "They are talking to him about why he destroyed this room... Titen is thinking about what happened yesterday... I'm guessing that's what he thinks is behind Zander's anger... Zander isn't saying much, but I can feel the intensity of his thoughts. He is thinking about what Axel did... Alexis..."

He pauses too long for me. "Aron what?! What's going on?"

His eyes are closed and he begins to smile. "I can almost feel how he does, his thoughts are so intense... he truly loves you... it's incredible, his mind is filled with you..." Then Aron opens his eyes and says, "I lost it... everyone's thoughts are buzzing around again." Noah removes his hand from Aron and looks exhausted from enhancing Aron's ability.

"Noah, did you sleep at all last night?" I scoot away from the wall to look at him better.

"Yeah, I slept pretty well actually... I've noticed I get drained after intentionally using my gift. I think it's because it's still weak." I lean back against the wall and wait. Finally the door opens, and Tara walks out.

"Alexis... could you come here for a second?" She holds her hand out waiting for me to take it. So I get up and put my hand in hers. She keeps glancing at me, but never holds her eyes on me. When we enter the room she shuts the door behind me. Immediately I run over to Zander and throw my arms around him.

He embraces me back. "Hey there... I'm sorry about what I did in there." I tighten my hold on him when I hear someone clear their throat. Blushing, I step back.

Looking down at the floor, Tara says, "Could you take a seat next to Zander, please?"

"Why are you acting so weird?" She looks down at me with aching eyes. Titen puts his arms around her and she begins to weep. "Tara, you are freaking me out! What's going on?"

After a minute or two she pulls herself together. "It's my fault that happened to you." She gestures to the scars on my face.

Almost like instinct, I cover them with my hand, pleading, "No... don't ever say that. Axel is crazy! Aron read his mind... he's been looking for an excuse to do this to someone. It's no one's fault but my own. I'm the one who ticked him off." I get up and take my sister's hand. "Please don't blame yourself." She simply nods and then I get suspicious. "Wait... this isn't why you brought me in here, is it?" No one will look me in the eyes... not even Zander. "Well, what is it? You guys are making me worry!"

Before I know it, Zander is standing behind me, and he turns me to face him. "Alexis... Tara thinks we shouldn't be so obvious about our relationship when we go for mental testing today. If Axel happens to be there... I just don't want you to get hurt." He pulls me close to him and reassures me, "I won't be too far from you, though... they said when we go we'll be in a line and will take the test one by one. So I figured we could put a couple people between us." He looks deep into my eyes, insisting, "I don't want to do this." Then he looks up at Tara and Titen. "For each test we walked into it hand in hand... I'm not sure I can do it without her..."

Tara looks angry and raises her voice. "Do you want her to DIE? Axel thinks she's Inept, if he sees you two together again she'll be tortured! Worse than before! If he doesn't think she learned from last time she'll... she'll be begging for death!"

"I'll do it…" I lay my head against Zander's chest. "I don't want to do this, but I don't want him to turn on you too… it's only for the test." He nods in agreement and I leave the room to change into the clothing for the mental test. After I change I lie on my stomach across my bed, which is a bad idea, because the scars are more sensitive there. I roll over, cross my arms, and grip my sides, waiting for the pain to stop. After a couple minutes the pain only gets worse. Then Mya walks in.

"Alexis… are you okay?" The pain is too bad, I can't say anything, so I shake my head. Quickly Mya yells out the door, "HELP! Someone come quickly."

The pain is starting to overwhelm me when I see someone standing above me. In a moment of panic I scream, and start to push whomever it is away. When my body goes rigid I know it is Titen. I calm down and say, "I need my arms." Right as I ask, I can feel that my body is back in my control. Quickly I roll to my side and wrap my arms around my torso. "Titen… why does it hurt?"

He doesn't answer me, but apparently Tara is in the room too. "Tara," Titen tells her, "I need you to go to the walkway and page Giana." Tara pauses and he says, "Tara… go! She will be fine once we get Giana!"

I feel someone touch me, and start to move my hair out of my face. "Zander… Zander?"

"I'm right here." He brushes my cheek with his hand. "Giana will be here soon… you'll be okay."

I try to sit up but there are multiple pairs of hands pushing me back down. "It hurts so much! I need to move."

"Alexis, it would be best if you stayed lying down until Giana gets here… I would appreciate if you do it yourself so I don't have to force you to." Titen sounds serious, so I lie still.

I start to shake from the pain when I hear Giana ask, "What happened?"

I reach out and tell her, "Giana… it's… my…

stomach..." I can barely get the sentence out before I begin convulsing out of control.

"Titen, she's having a seizure, hold her still so I can help her." I have no control over my body, but I can feel it trying to shake even with Titen using his gift on me. Then I feel Giana pressing down on my forehead and stomach. "I don't know if I can heal this... it's not from an illness. I will do what I can but we need to get some medication into her... over there in my bag is a bottle of clear medication... it might help." I can feel my body relaxing... the seizure must be over with.

Then Tara says something for the first time since this all started. "I need the rest of you to get changed into your mental test uniforms. We need to leave in less than an hour."

I try to move, but Titen is still controlling me. "Zander... don't go."

"I won't." I can feel him take my hand in his. Giana is still working on me, when I feel her lift my shirt. She gasps when she sees my skin, and Zander's grip tightens.

"Alexis, I'm going to rub a numbing cream on you... then I'm afraid I will have to reopen your wound so I can pour some medication in it."

"NO! You're lying! I swear I'm not Inept! Zander, don't let her torture me."

"Alexis, she's trying to help you... trust me." I look up at Zander and close my eyes.

"Okay... get it over with." I keep my eyes closed, waiting for my skin to tear, but I never feel it. After a moment the pain starts to go away. "Is it over yet?"

I feel Zander run his fingers through my hair. "Almost. Just a couple more minutes."

I can feel Titen has stopped using his ability on me, so I know it's over. I start to sit up, and Zander helps me. I sit next to him with my head on his shoulder. "Giana, what's wrong with me?"

She looks devastated. "I'm not sure... but I didn't need to use the medication... I think I'm losing my mind." She holds up a small silver oval. "This was in you. I've never seen anything like it before, but if it's like the other things they are creating..." She pauses. "I, um, I don't know what this is, but I think it was the cause of your pain. You should be okay now."

"Thank you." I look up at Titen then back to Giana. The look on his face tells me he agrees with me—Giana needs to know what happened. She is such a good soul that there is no way she wouldn't join us.

The door opens slowly and my sister walks in and says, "I need you two to come with us, we will be going to the Mental Testing Center shortly." Zander and I both get up and walk to the family room followed by Giana and Titen.

Once we are all together, Titen addresses us, "I'm going to go page Thyn and let him know we're ready. The other Elites will join us and we will be under his control. So if you don't mind, can you line up so we can get started without... without anyone getting hurt?" As Titen leaves the room, we all file into line. Out of habit I stand behind Zander, holding his hand.

Tara clears her throat, and I remember our conversation from earlier. Slowly I let go of his hand and go to the back of the line. After a few minutes, we watch as Tara and Giana become mindless puppets. Slowly the haze fills their eyes and they begin to look like different people. The door opens and we file out one by one. Everyone is here—Acey, Kian, Sacri, Hunter, Titen, Giana, and Tara. We walk in silence, the Elites surrounding us.

The Mental Testing Center is the farthest from our living quarters. As we walk through the different walkways I gaze out of the glass walls. I start to admire the new world where Zander and I will be living. In the distance I can see their large, beautiful homes. I imagine living my life with

Zander. When I start to visualize it, I don't see us in one of the large, beautiful homes, I see us in a small house, but not run-down like houses in the Inept Region. I see us in an equal world, where privileges are shared.

Suddenly Aron stops in front of me and I collide with him. He whips around and says, "You shut the voices off... I almost forgot what my own thoughts sound like." All I can do is smile, then he turns around and keeps walking. I find it odd that I only shut Aron's gift off and not a single one of the cloudy-eyed Elites came back to life.

Finally we reach the door to the Mental Testing Center. Titen steps in front of the door and says, "One at a time, each of you will enter the room behind me. Walk straight in and sit down in the designated chair. Thyn will administer the test. The examiners will be watching carefully and will take note of any gifts you have."

I start getting dizzy... *examiners*... that means Axel will be in there. My mind starts replaying my second *medical test* in my head. I can hear Aron let out a sigh, so I whisper to him, "I'm sorry, it just popped into my mind." All he does is shrug and keeps his eyes ahead of him.

I'm so deep in thought that Titen startles me when he speaks, "Crayton, please enter through the door and into the examination." Crayton turns, gives his sister a small smile, and disappears through the door. "I want the rest of you to sit against the wall. You will wait here until it's your turn." Then Titen enters the examination room.

I sit with my back to the glass wall watching the Elites. Hunter and Acey are standing in the middle of the walkway, blocking our path if we decide to make a run for it. The rest of them stand along the other wall facing us. I can't help continually glancing at Tara. I miss her caramel eyes; the haze in them blocks their true beauty. Looking at her makes me miss home. She looks so much like our mother, and I'm sure she will be a wonderful mother too. I'm sure her baby is going to be gorgeous, with my sister's gracefulness and Titen's bone structure. My heart starts to ache knowing that their child will grow up around some horrible people, especially if it's Inept.

Aron nudges me and whispers, "How did you clear my mind earlier?"

"I was hoping you could tell me... maybe I was thinking of something specific to make my gift work. If I want to stay with..." I cut my sentence off, remembering I'm supposed to pretend that I'm not with Zander. "I mean... if I want to be an Elite I need to show them my gift... they haven't seen it yet."

He gives me a weird look. "Since when do you *want* to be an Elite?"

I don't have an answer for him, he obviously knows I don't. *But wait—he can read my mind!* Without speaking, I tell him in my head, *Aron... I don't want to be an Elite. I was going to say something about Zander but I'm not supposed to. That's what we talked about earlier... we're trying to get Axel off my case. The reason he hurt me is because he thinks I'm Inept, and is disgusted that I was hanging around Zander.* He looks at me a bit surprised then nods his head once, acknowledging that he heard me.

Just then Crayton comes back through the door followed by Titen. He sits down next to Fatima and Titen gestures for her to get up. Then he escorts her into the room and quickly shuts the door behind them. *Aron... what is Crayton thinking?*

He smiles and says, "It's nice to use this as communication... normally I just feel like I'm snooping around in someone's mind. He's not thinking anything... mostly he's confused, he doesn't remember anything."

"At least it doesn't seem to last long," I say, trying to sound positive. "And he doesn't look traumatized! Maybe this will be the easiest test of them all." *I'm not sure how you feel but the physical test was easy for me. I just had to lie there!* I give Aron a little smirk.

He can't hold back a laugh as he says, "At least you have a sense of humor about it!" It is nice to laugh about it. It makes me feel like Axel has less power over me. He can damage my appearance but he can never damage my soul. I'm a good person—scars can't change that. Aron lets out another chuckle and whispers, "Someone's jealous."

*Who's jealous of what?*

"Do you really have to ask? You know who... he's jealous that I get to spend time with you and he can't... but he's glad that you're smiling and happy." I look around for a moment and notice that none of the Elites' eyes are on me, so I lean forward and am able to make eye contact with Zander. I mouth *I love you* to him, which puts a huge grin on his face.

Aron nudges me and says, "He loves you too..."

"I know... I'm not sure if I deserve him, he's so kind. It's sort of crazy because he never worries about anything, or at least doesn't show it. I would give anything to hold my composure the way he does."

Aron's smile fades. "Considering everything you've dealt with since you've been here, I'd say your composure is astonishing... and he worries, mostly about you." Then he says, "I don't think he needs to worry about you. You're a strong person, I think you can handle pretty much anything."

Before I can answer him, Fatima emerges into the walkway and takes her place in line. Then Noah stands and enters the room with Titen. My nerves start to act up when I realize it's almost Zander's turn. I look over at him again, not caring who sees. He gives me a weak smile but I know he's scared.

Trying to relax my mind, I focus on Aron. "So tell me about yourself, we've been here for a few days and I only know Mya."

"There's not much to tell." He shrugs. "I'm an only child, I went from home, to work, and back home. When I started hearing thoughts I would shut myself away in my room. It was extremely overwhelming, my head would fill with so many different voices. It's starting to get better, I'm able to focus on individual thoughts now. What about you?"

I laugh. "Really?"

"Just because I can read your thoughts doesn't mean I don't want to have a normal conversation."

"I'm sorry. Well, obviously everyone knows I have a sister." I gesture toward Tara. "According to my father my gift didn't develop, it was always there. Part of my gift is sensing other people's abilities. When I was really young I used to tell my father about all the special kids. I knew Titen and Tara had gifts before they even discovered them, before I thought it was just a feeling. Like intuition... until I realized that... umm... *he* doesn't have control over his yet, but I was able to interact with him like no one else could."

Aron looks down the line at Zander. "How did you guys meet?"

I can't hold back my smile. "I've known him my whole life... our families don't live too far from each other. He's my best friend... I have always had a *thing* for him, but I didn't know he felt the same until a few months ago."

He looks over his shoulder out the glass wall. "You're lucky... you have an amazing ability, and multiple people love you. Ever since I discovered my ability I grew distant from my parents. Don't get me wrong, I'm sure they still love me, but it will never be the same again."

I look out into the Elite Region with Aron. "It might be... but I'm hoping someday it will be different."

We all look up when we see Noah come back in. Like the two before him, he looks confused. Titen stands in the door waiting while Reece gets up and follows him in. *What's Noah thinking?*

I watch Aron as he closes his eyes and concentrates.

"He had a conversation with Thyn after the test... Thyn likes his ability."

Suddenly I feel angry. "Of course he does! He'll use Noah to enhance his own ability! That could ruin everything!" When I look up I see Aron smiling again. "What are you so happy about?"

"I like when your emotions are running high... I get wonderful moments of peace and quiet."

"For a moment I thought you were smiling for a different reason. Sorry."

"It's understandable, it was bad timing on my part. I just couldn't help it."

I'm surprised Reece comes back so soon. *That was quick.* Aron nods his head once in agreement. When Reece sits down I see Zander get up. He looks back at me, but all I can do is stare blankly at him. It takes everything I have in me to stay sitting here. Then he disappears with Titen through the door.

Without warning, Giana is next to me and she places her hands on me before I completely panic. After a few minutes she goes back to her place, and the battle in my mind starts up again. *I'm never going to accomplish anything if I freak out at the smallest thing... someone else should have my ability, so they can use it properly.*

"No... your ability is unique to you, you have it for a reason. You wouldn't panic so much if we weren't here—if we weren't seen as dispensable objects. Alexis... you're the perfect person for this ability, you have too much to lose," Aron says softly.

Then Mya says, "I agree with Aron. I'm not sure what he heard you think, but I know you can do it." She leans forward to look at me and smiles.

"Thanks." I'm still not feeling very confident in myself, so I try to clear my mind. I don't want to share my thoughts right now.

"Then turn my ability off," Aron says, laughing a little.

"Just concentrate... you could even try closing your eyes like I do."

I roll my eyes. "It's not as easy for me... I've noticed it works best when I'm directly dealing with someone." I think about it for a minute, then place my hand on his arm. I'm assuming it's working, because he leans his head against the wall and looks peaceful. It's nice to practice my ability without all the pressure.

I sit here with my hand on Aron for a while, then decide I want to try without having to touch him. As I lift my hand, his peaceful look disappears. "Why did you stop?"

"I want to try something. If it doesn't work I'll do it the normal way." I try to focus on my gift, concentrating on turning off Aron's ability. I think about his ability and how I want to clear his mind.

"Nicely done," Aron says, returning to the peaceful look he had before.

"Hang on, I'm going to try one more thing." I stop concentrating but his expression never changes. It's nice to get some control over my gift, it should only get better from here!

Then we hear familiar loud crashes in the other room. Everyone looks toward the door. I hope Zander isn't doing that. Maybe Thyn is controlling him... seeing what his ability can do. I wish I was able to turn his ability off through the wall, but I can barely do it with someone next to me. Finally the chaos in the other room dies down, and we all sit here, stunned.

Soon Zander comes out of the room, his eyes down, not acknowledging any of us. Once he is seated Mya joins Titen and leaves. I nudge Aron. "What's going through his mind?"

Aron shakes his head and says, "You're still blocking my ability, I can't read it." I refocus on opening Aron's mind back up. It must have worked, because I watch him close his eyes in concentration.

"He's confused and a little scared... all he remembers is going in there and sitting down... then a while later he saw that the room was destroyed like our living quarters. He's scared that he has no memory of what happened, and doesn't want to know what Thyn will use his ability for." He opens his eyes, looking concerned.

I can't think of anything to say, so I lean over trying to see Zander. He is sitting with his arms crossed on top of his knees with his head down. I've never seen him look so defeated. What little hope I had is starting to diminish. With Noah's ability combined with Thyn's, I'll never be able to stop any of this.

Then Aron laughs loudly, "This is *unbelievable*. The two of you are quite a pair!"

"What are you talking about?"

Aron raises his voice so everyone can hear him, "Both of you are concerned for the other, and believe that the other can do amazing things... but both of you have absolutely no faith in yourselves. How will things ever be different if no one has hope?"

He's completely right. I can't even think of a valid argument. Zander lifts his head and finally looks at me. Somehow the look in his eyes makes me feel more hopeful. If he can believe in himself like I do, I can believe in myself like he does.

Satisfied with himself, Aron smirks and peers out the glass wall again. Then Mya comes back through the door, and his smile fades. He's next.

Once Mya sits down, he slowly stands and heads into the Mental Testing Center. I move over to sit closer to Mya. "How are you holding up?"

"It wasn't painful, so I guess that's a plus."

"I would say that's a huge plus! I'm sorry I've been distant lately."

"It's okay. I understand... how are *you* holding up?"

"I'm fine... now that the pain is gone I'm feeling good. The only thing I can't shake are the images that replay in my mind... but let's not talk about that. Are you excited to go back home soon?"

Mya nods. "Yeah, I'm tired of being here... I miss my family." I take her hand in mine and gently squeeze it. We sit here in silence for a while as I try not to look at Zander on the other side of her.

Then I ask her, "Is it frightening in there?" Mya nods and I begin to get more nervous knowing I'm next, knowing that Axel is in there waiting to see how he affected me. "Do the trench coats have their masks on?"

Mya simply says, "Yes." I let out a sigh of relief as Aron returns to our group. Like everyone else he looks confused. Quickly I move back to my spot in line and he sits down next to Mya. I take in a deep breath to calm my nerves, stand up, and walk over to the door where Titen is waiting. He holds it open for me and I enter the room.

The Mental Testing Center is the smallest one yet. It's a tiny room with one chair in the middle of it. On one end in front of the chair, Thyn is waiting patiently, and on the other end behind the chair are the examiners. I try not to look at any of them as I sit down.

Thyn approaches me and asks, "Oh dear... what happened to your face?"

"Oh nothing... it was a misunderstanding on my part."

Looking skeptically behind me, he says, "Alright then... before we get started I want to give you a chance to tell me about any gift you may have. Also that this won't be at all painful, you'll only lose a few minutes of the day."

I look at the floor. "I'm not sure what my gift is... I only know it's a mental one. It's a gift my parents have never heard of before, so I don't know what it is."

He chuckles. "No worries, dear, I will figure it out for you."

I lift my head and glare at him. "My name is Alexis...

I would appreciate if you would use it and not call me dear or anything like it."

His smile fades, and I begin to wonder if I will be punished again. I hear shifting behind me when Thyn glares at the examiners and says, "There will be no need to restrain her. I'm going to start the test now, just unwind and examine it like you're supposed to!" I can feel my palms getting sweaty. I know exactly who he is talking to without even seeing him. "Okay, Alexis, sit back and relax. The test will be over before you know it."

I stare up at him, wondering what it's going to feel like losing complete control of myself. Suddenly I feel a weird pressure in my head, almost like my mind is trying to escape. I can see the haze filling my eyes, but I'm still aware. Then I hear my voice—it sounds weird, and I'm not trying to talk. *Thyn must be controlling me.*

"I thought you said this one was Inept," Thyn says, through me.

"Sir, all her other tests are negative, her blood doesn't even show it!" Axel's voice rings out, sounding a little fearful. Before I can hear any more of the conversation, everything is gone.

The next thing I remember is an empty room. Only Titen and I are inside it. I'm a little disappointed; I assumed I wouldn't be able to be controlled by him. Maybe since I wasn't in control of my own mind it didn't work against him. I notice Titen no longer has the haze covering his eyes. "So I take it he's gone since your eyes are back to normal?" He nods and we leave the room. Everyone in the hall is standing around enjoying conversations together. It's weird seeing the difference in how we act around the Elites when they have the haze and when they don't.

Immediately I find Zander and take his hand in mine. He smiles and says, "I missed you."

I feel my face get hot as I start to blush. "I missed you too... it was so hard sitting two people away and not being able to interact with you." After a moment the Elites lead us back to our living quarters.

I am starving, so I go to the kitchen and make some chicken and potatoes for everyone. I set the table and call everyone in when it is ready. No one talks about any of the testing as we eat. It's nice to see the innocence of everyone in this moment. It reminds me of the first night here when we hadn't been experimented on yet.

After dinner we all go into the family room, which has been repaired, and enjoy each other's company, laughing like normal fifteen-year-old kids. Eventually everyone goes their separate ways into the bedrooms except for Zander and me. I relax into my favorite spot in his arms, with my head on his lap, and drift into a dreamless slumber.

# CHAPTER NINE

After everyone wakes up and we have breakfast, we are joined by the eight Elites that have been with us every step of the way. Zander and I are in the kitchen with Titen, Tara, and Acey. Everyone else is in the family room having a worry-free day. I'm glad they're having a good time, but I can't help thinking about my worries. After today we find out if we are chosen to be Elites or deemed Inept. I'm afraid that my ability didn't show up on any tests and that I'll be separated from Zander.

Titen is busy telling Acey everything that has led up to our decision to fight how we are being treated. As he reaches the end of his story, he asks her, "So will you join us? Tara, Giana, and I are all on board along with all the kids who entered testing. Even the ones without abilities are willing to help us."

She is quite for a moment sorting out her thoughts. "Will I get to see my family again? Are you positive this will work?"

Titen says, "If we succeed, you will be reunited with your family. I can't tell you if it will work or not. I can tell you I believe it will. I believe if we get enough people to go against Commander Avery and Thyn, we can do it. It's not something that will end quickly, but I'm tired of being forced to be a monster."

"I'm in!" Acey decides.

Our numbers are growing, but I'm concerned that we don't really have a plan yet. I guess that's something that will come with time. Then Mya comes into the kitchen, announcing, "They want everyone to gather in the family room."

We go into the family room and I notice the Elites there already have the haze. I turn to see Titen's, Tara's, and Acey's eyes slowly cloud over. I'll never get use to how that looks, how the haze overcomes them—honestly it's a little creepy. The Elites direct us out the door toward the transportation vehicle, which we pass through to the place where we met the Elite Core a few days ago. Like before, there are at least thirty Elites standing at the other end of the yard.

A few minutes pass when Commander Avery and Thyn come out from behind the Core. Then the Commander addresses us, "Congratulations on finishing your testing. Some of you have shown great potential and will be accepted into the Elite Core. Immediately after our gathering you will start your life in our captivating region. Unfortunately, those of you who are Inept will leave the facilities and make your journey back to the Inept Region. You will return to your work groups and live the rest of your lives working for us." He gives us a shining smile that none of us return.

Then Thyn clears his throat to get our attention. "When I call your name, please step forward and join our ranks. Aron, you're ability to read minds is fascinating." Aron hesitates, then joins the Core. As soon as he turns to face us, his eyes are clouded. "Fatima, I have never seen dreams as vivid as yours." She quickly hugs her brother, takes her place next to Aron, and then her eyes change.

I start feeling more and more nervous. I know

eventually he will call Zander's name and he will be a Core member. I hope they call my name before his, so I don't have to watch his wonderful eyes become dull. Just then my thoughts are interrupted by Thyn, "Noah, I am truly excited for you to gain control of your gift. It will come in handy." He joins the others with the same hazy look. "Zander, the strength you have is truly unique."

I look up into his eyes, trying to take them in as much as I can. Then he wraps his arms around me and whispers, "I love you."

"I love you too."

Thyn must have thought he was taking too long to join them. Before he even turns to walk over to the Elites, the haze clouds the beauty of his eyes. Under Thyn's control he turns and joins the Core. I'm the last one left... my nerves are starting to make my knees shake when Thyn says, "I'm sorry but the rest of you are Inept. All of the test results you four received are negative. You will be sent back across the wall, never to return to our region again.

*What? But... I'm not Inept! He's wrong... the tests are wrong!* Without even thinking about it I scream out, "NO! I'm an Elite... *please* retest me!"

The Commander laughs at me. "You're not the first one to try that. Our tests cannot be fooled! Unless you think your DNA can lie to us?"

I can feel my heart breaking... I'm being separated from Zander, and my sister is being ripped out of my grasp again. I take a few steps forward, ready to plead with them, when Thyn cuts me off before I can. "If you know what's good for you, you'll stop right there. Not everyone gets to live a life of privilege, and it makes you more pathetic that you are begging us!"

He's right, if I don't pull myself together I'll just be put through more pain. Defeated, I fall to my knees and watch as the Commander and Thyn leave. Everyone in the Core turns to follow them except for the ones who will be taking us home. I watch Zander as he walks away from me, not turning to acknowledge my existence. I can feel my anger building up, but I still can't remove the haze from Zander. If I had, he would have noticed, but he keeps walking until he is out of my view.

Slowly I get up, still in shock, and turn to see Mya looking at me in disbelief. "Alexis... how is this possible?" I shake my head because I have no idea.

Moments later the haze lifts from the four Elites who originally brought us here. Titen is the first to notice I wasn't chosen. "Alexis? What are you doing here?"

"My test results were negative... I tried to convince them that I'm Elite but they laughed at me."

Acey interrupts us, "We need to get to the transportation vehicle before Thyn realizes we're taking too long."

Everyone starts to follow her toward the building, but I can't make my legs work. My mind is going through everything that has happened since I've been here. *How am I not an Elite?*

Before I can figure out the answer, Mya starts pulling me with her, commanding me, "Come on, we have to leave!"

Once we reach the transportation vehicle, Acey, Kian, and Sacri get in with Crayton, Reece, and Mya. Titen is waiting by the door for me to get in, but I can't. If I get in I'll never be back. Everything I've been planning has been destroyed. "Titen, do you think they know? Is that why I didn't get chosen?"

He shakes his head. "No... if they knew what we are planning they would never let you out of their sight. I don't know why you didn't get chosen."

Slowly I get into the vehicle followed by Titen. I take a seat next to Mya, who says, "It's okay... we'll figure something out." I nod once, but I don't believe her.

As the vehicle starts to leave, Sacri opens up the

windows and I start to gaze out one. As we leave the Inept Testing Facilities, I see Tara standing in front of the building with Fatima, Aron, Noah, and... Zander. Losing it, I scream out the window, "ZANDER!" He looks up and I can see the pain on his face. All I want to do is get to him. Before thinking about if it's a good idea, I start to climb out the window. I can feel my feet being pulled back and I yell, "No! Leave me alone!"

Titen orders, "Stop the vehicle!"

*What? Titen is helping me?*

Slowly the vehicle comes to a stop. Looking nervously at me, Titen says, "I will give you a chance to properly say goodbye, but I need you to keep it short. If I think you're taking too long I will *make* you come back."

I can't be more thankful, so I throw my arms around Titen. "Thank you!" He smiles and I rush out the door. As soon as Zander sees me get out, he starts running toward me. After what feels like forever I reach him and I am in his arms. "Zander, they didn't pick me! They think I'm Inept!"

He looks at me like he is trying to memorize my face. "I know... Tara told me there was nothing on your test results." He pauses for a moment, running his fingers through my hair. "Alexis, I love you. We can still do this, we can still be together... please don't forget about me."

Laying my head against his chest, I tell him, "I could never forget about you, I love you too much. I will try to figure something out." I take a step back so I can look into his glorious eyes, hoping this isn't the last time I will see them. "I'm going to miss you."

"Me too." Then he kisses me. "You better get back, Titen just stepped out of the vehicle."

I hug him tightly one more time, then slowly walk back to the vehicle. Once I reach the door I look back at Zander, then get in. I take my place next to Mya again, and we start moving. I stare out the window until I can't see him anymore.

When he is out of sight, I lean back and close my eyes, I want to remember everything about him—his kindness, the sound of his voice, his touch, and the way he makes me feel. I try to ignore everything going on around me but it's difficult. Everyone else is so happy that they're going home. I'm glad I will get to see my parents again, but at what cost? I get my sister torn away from me again, along with Zander, and now I will never get to know my niece or nephew. I'm also going to miss some of the great people I've met in the Elite Region, and it's almost more painful to be going home instead of staying here.

I can hear them talk about the wall in the distance, and I'm trying to prepare myself for all of the questions that will surround me shortly. Finally I open my eyes and the site almost makes me sick. Everyone is smiling and laughing like these past few days never happened! Even though they were comatose for the medical exam doesn't mean they don't have the scar. They know someone was digging in their brain, but it looks like they don't care. I'm starting to get angry, mostly at myself. If my gift didn't show up on the tests, it must be my fault. The only reason I can think of for this to happen is that I turned my ability off. I would give anything to redo the tests with Zander next to me so I can show them what I can do.

Suddenly the sun isn't shining into the windows anymore. We're pulling into the same building we were kept in when we first arrived. Once the vehicle stops, Titen says, "You will be staying here for the rest of the day. First thing in the morning I will escort you to the wall."

I bend over and place my face in my hands. I want to have my own room where I can shut the door and lose it. I have cried, screamed, and lost my composure way too many times in front of everyone. After a moment, someone taps me so I sit up and notice only Titen and I are in the vehicle. "Sorry, I'll get out." The last thing I need is more trouble.

He shakes his head. "Take your time... if you want to talk, I'm a pretty good listener, at least that's what your sister says. We both know she's a talker."

I try to smile but I can't. "At least I'm not the only one who thinks that!" Then a more depressing thought hits me and I ask, "How long until he gets paired with someone else?"

He looks away. "I don't think that is something you need to worry about."

I glare at him. "You just said I could talk to you, and now you won't answer me?"

"It depends... your sister was placed in a home and spent a year alone. I was placed with your sister immediately after I was chosen. That's what Tara was doing with them when we left. They were being told about being placed, or paired as you say it. When she's done explaining everything she'll take them to their new homes. Each year they send an Elite to kind of break the ice, and make sure there aren't any problems before they leave."

"I wish there was some way you could find out for me, but I know you can't. Tomorrow you'll be in Thyn's control, so even if you found out you wouldn't be able to tell me," I say as I exit the transportation vehicle.

I reach the door and just stand here. "Titen... how soon will he be in the Inept Region?"

"Again it depends, it could be immediately and it could be weeks. I'm assuming since he has a physical gift it will be sooner than later. That's how it seems to work."

I nod and walk into the room to join everyone else. Once I have joined them, the Elites leave us for the night. I take a moment to look around, and I see that all the clothes we came here in are still where we left them. I pick up my dress and go to the bathroom to change. I look in the mirror at my scars and I'm starting to feel like I went through all of this for nothing. When I'm done changing, I head back into the room with the cots, and walk over to the other clothes. I pick up Zander's black slacks and blue button-down shirt. I stand here for a moment trying to motivate myself to move.

Finally I walk over to the wall where we sat together before. Slowly I sink to the ground, gripping his clothes tightly. When Mya joins me, she says, "I bet if you put on his shirt it would feel like he's here. It's worth a try, right?" I glance at her then the shirt. I put my arms through it and button it up. "It's nice to see you smile again," she tells me. I didn't even know I had smiled until she mentioned it.

I put the shirt up to my face, taking in a deep breath. "I think I smiled because it smells like him. Thank you, Mya, you're a good friend even when I haven't been one."

"You're a great friend!" she insists. "I understand you've had a rough few days, I'm not going to condemn you for it... as long as you promise me that we will hang out when we are back home."

"I promise," I say, trying to smile again.

I don't talk to anyone else, I continue to sit in the same place and stare across the room at nothing. I'm trying to figure out where to go from here. Zander has always been my confidence builder—he's the one with all the great ideas for how to use my ability against Thyn. Now I'm left to do it on my own.

Eventually everyone falls asleep except for me. The past few nights I've been sleeping with Zander's arms around me. It's just not the same without him and I'm not sure if I'll ever sleep again.

# CHAPTER TEN

While everyone sleeps my mind is having one of its typical arguments. *Everything is ruined, I will never see Zander or Tara again... the dream I had of a world with no walls will never come true... but I could still do something... I could get help in the Inept Region. If I can remove the haze from one Elite it's still possible.* My thoughts keep spinning, one moment positive, the next negative, as I struggle with having any confidence in myself at all.

Exhaustion finally catches up to me and I fall asleep, but it couldn't have been more than ten minutes when a familiar voice wakes us up with, "I need all of you to get up and come with me." I open my eyes to see Titen, his eyes clouded over, standing near the door. Slowly I stand up, making sure I have all of Zander's clothes. I am still wearing his shirt that's too large for me. I fold up his pants, tuck them under my arm, and head for the door.

Soon Mya is by my side, and the boys are behind us. Titen leads us out the door, but we walk past the transportation vehicle. The sun is too bright and my eyes are having a tough time adjusting. When I can finally see normally I notice how close we are to the wall. Then Mya gets my attention, asking, "How many people do you think will be waiting for us?"

I had almost forgotten that the family members and friends of those who get tested always wait on the other side of the wall as an unofficial welcome home party. "I'm sure your whole family will be."

"They already told me they would be, do you think yours will be?

"No... I'm pretty sure Zander's won't be either. They don't expect us to come back. If you don't mind, I would like to meet your family."

"I would love that!" Mya says.

Moments later we reach the wall and Titen walks up to it. We watch as he opens a tiny door that has a series of numbers on it. Quickly he presses a few in a special order and the wall begins to open. He shuts the tiny door, then turning to us, says without feeling, "Please enter the Inept Region." It takes us all a moment, but we walk through the opening and it shuts immediately when we are completely on the other side.

I look behind me to see that Titen didn't follow us. It confuses me a little, I guess I never knew how the wall shut behind the Elite before. The Core must come in groups and designate one person to stay behind to close the wall. By the time I look forward again, Mya, Crayton, and Reece have found their families. I'm not sad that mine didn't come... just disappointed that I'm standing here alone instead of in the Elite Region. I look around and do a double take. I could have sworn I saw Orion standing by a tree, but when I look back, no one is there.

I head to the tree to see if he ducked behind it when Mya cuts me off with, "Hey Alexis, did you still want to meet my family?" I nod as she drags me over to them. "Alexis, these are my parents." I look at her mother and she is a beautiful woman with the same brilliant green eyes and red hair as Mya. Her father has a more common look, with brown hair and eyes. Then she ushers me past them to her sister Maria and introduces me to her. I notice that Maria looks like her father, only her brown hair has a hint of red in it. I'm a little embarrassed because I can't think of anything to say to Mya's family.

When I don't say anything Mya turns to a boy standing near her and says, "Last but not least, this is my little brother Myles." He has lovely mix of both of his parents' looks, with the same green eyes as Mya, but his father's dark hair.

I give a small laugh, and say, "Maria... Mya... Myles."

Mya turns a little red. "Yeah... my mom has a thing for the letter *m*. I'm glad you're laughing, though! Did you want to come over?"

I think about it for a minute and say, "I better not, I should go home and see my parents. I will see you around." Before I can walk away she embraces me for so long that I almost lose my composure. She finally lets me go and starts to walk away with her family.

I feel a little bad that I lied to her, but I want to be alone. I'm not sure when I'll go home, I'm not ready yet. Automatically my feet take me across the region and I end up at the pond Zander and I spent a couple evenings at. I sit at the edge of the water looking across it, letting the cool breeze hit my face. Then I hear a noise behind me and my heart almost comes out of my chest. The events from the past few days have made me even more jumpy than I used to be.

I turn to see who's there, but it's no one. *Great! Now I'm going crazy!* I lie back against the ground when I hear the noise again. I quickly sit up and turn around to see Orion walking towards me. "Orion... what are you doing here?"

He shrugs and says, "I followed you."

I look at him confused. "So I did see you there, how did you run off so quickly?"

He has a satisfied smile on his face. "I didn't... I've been working on my gift, I'm getting pretty good at it."

I can't help but laugh. "How do your parents feel about that?"

"Ever since you guys left, they've been different... wait... why are you here?"

My heart sinks. "Apparently my gift is stronger than I thought... it didn't show up on the tests, so they think I'm Inept. Right now my gift is too influenced by how I feel, and I had a rough time there."

Orion sits down next to me and stares at my scars. "What happened? Did they do that to Zander too?"

I shake my head. "No... he's fine. It was during the second test... the physical one... I was watching Zander and one of the examiners thought... thinks... I'm Inept and was trying to *get with* an Elite, so he disciplined me." I notice this upsets him so I try to cheer him back up and say, "So how good is your gift now?"

His smile returns. "It's great! I can hide all day if I want. I've gotten out of work a lot. Plus I like to mess with people—I'll walk by then hide myself. Then I'll walk to the other side and show myself again. It's pretty entertaining, I'll have to show you sometime."

When Orion is done talking, an idea hits me. "Have you ever hidden anyone besides yourself?"

"No. I don't know if that's part of my gift or not."

I smile at him. "Let's try... let's go mess with an Elite!"

He doesn't respond, he just gets up with me and we run until we find an Elite. Luckily it's someone I don't know, so my emotions won't stop Orion's gift. "Okay, let's try it, first do it by yourself."

He nods, walks past the Elite, and stops. The Elites' eyes follow Orion as he walks away. I watch as Orion vanishes then pops back into view in front of the Elite, who stops in shock. Confused, the Elite turns to look where

Orion had stood before, but when he looks forward again Orion is gone! The look on the Elite's face is priceless. He has no idea what's going on, and probably thinks he's losing his mind.

After a moment Orion appears next to me. "Okay, how do I do it with you now?"

"I'm not sure, but I know when I'm trying to shut off other people's gifts I think about it working on them. Maybe try that... try and imagine me hidden with you."

He nods and we begin to walk by the Elite. I'm assuming, by the look on the Elite's face, that Orion did it! He hid both of us! I tap him and whisper, "I think you did it—look at his face!"

Orion is overcome with laughter, which only makes the Elite look even funnier! I can't imagine what I would be thinking if I saw two people disappear and then heard laughter coming from nowhere. Quickly, before Orion's gift gives out, we run back to the pond.

We sit on the ground trying to catch our breath when I look over to him. "Orion... do you feel like helping me with something?"

"Sure."

I fill him in on everything Zander and I discussed about going against Commander Avery and Thyn. When I am done he sighs and asks, "How is my gift going to help you?"

I look out over the water. "I haven't thought about that yet, but we need everyone we can get. We hadn't really gone over any plans. We assumed we wouldn't need any right now because we thought I would be an Elite."

"Okay, let me know what you need," Orion says. "I just want my brother back."

That reminds me, I am still carrying around Zander's pants and wearing his shirt. I hold out the pants toward Orion. "Here, these are Zander's, you should take them home."

I start to unbutton Zander's shirt when Orion says, "You should keep that. He means as much to you as he does to me. Plus I have a ton of his belongings at home. Speaking of home, I should probably get back before my parents worry." I watch him as he gets up and walks away. I never noticed how much he looks like Zander before. It makes me miss him. Then I slowly get up and start to walk toward my house.

I drag my feet, taking my time, feeling more and more nervous the closer I get to my home. I'm worried that my parents will be disappointed in me. I stop at the end of our little path and stare at our crooked little house. I'm getting overwhelmed, I want to see my parents but at the same time I know they will have questions. Slowly I walk up our path and stop at the door. I don't know if I should just walk in or if I should knock. I debate for a moment and decide to act normal. I open the door, walk in, and try to quietly shut it behind me.

I am facing the door when I hear my father's voice, "Miss, I think you might be lost."

I shake my head. "I'm not lost."

I can hear confusion in my father's voice. "Alexis? What... what are you doing here?"

I can't say anything, I don't have an answer for him. I pull my hair forward trying to cover the scars on my face. Hopefully he hasn't looked down at my legs yet.

Before I turn around I hear my mother walk out of the kitchen and say, "Did you say Alexis?" She pauses for a moment then I feel her hands on me. "Alexis, honey, did you use your gift to get away from the Elites?"

I shake my head then slowly turn to look at my parents. My mother takes me in her arms and holds me tight. I tell her, "I missed you."

She squeezes me a little tighter and says, "We missed you too."

They must be too excited to notice the scars, the dark

circles from no sleep under my eyes, and Zander's shirt. Keeping her arm around me, she ushers me into the kitchen and pulls a chair out for me. Quickly I sit down and pull the chair up to the table to hide my legs underneath it. I make sure to keep my head tilted so my hair continues to cover the horrid scars on my face.

After a moment my father clears his throat and says, "Do you want to tell us what happened?"

I deliberate for a moment, lift my head, and put my hair behind my ear. Both of them react as if they have been punched in the stomach. I take a deep breath and say, "They think I'm Inept. Apparently when I shut my own gift off my DNA doesn't even show it." Then I roll up the sleeves of Zander's shirt and add, "Because nothing showed on the results of the first test an evil, horrible man thinks I'm an Inept trying to *seduce* an Elite. All because I was following Zander around the physical test, he took me out and *taught me some respect.*"

After they get a good look at my scars, I unroll the sleeves of Zander's shirt and try to stay calm, because I can see the anxiety on both of my parents' faces. We sit in silence for a moment when I blurt out, "I saw Tara... without the haze... she's pregnant."

My mother's face lights up. "That's wonderful! Maybe someday we will get to meet him or her."

I shake my head. "No, you won't... everything is messed up since I'm here and not an Elite."

My father laughs, "You have no confidence in yourself... you never have! It's almost better that you're here, it will be easier to *recruit* people. If they are here, you can remove the haze and they will be more willing to help you. They will be surrounded by familiar faces, and know that their families are somewhere in our region. They gave you the upper hand!"

"You're missing one key element," I tell him. "A boy named Noah was with us, he's Elite now. He can enhance abilities, so he has the opposite effect that I do. I'm positive Thyn will use him to make his gift more powerful."

Then my father shakes his head, saying, "You'll still be more powerful. Your gift surfaced years before signs normally start and you fooled their high-tech tests. The only thing holding you back is yourself."

I don't respond to him, because I know he might be right. I start to look down again, avoiding eye contract with my father. Then my mother says, "Do you mind telling us everything that happened? Just so we have an idea of why you look so defeated and broken."

I nod and start from the beginning. I tell them about everything, every detail. When I get to my *extra test* my mother can't hold back her tears. It's nice to get everything off my chest. By the time I finish my story, it's late. My father heads to bed and my mother and I sit in the family room.

I look into her tired eyes and tell her, "You can go to bed... I'll be okay."

"You look like you're the one who needs to be getting to bed."

"I guess, but I probably won't sleep," I confess.

I don't want to be a burden on my mother, so I get up and start heading up the stairs with her following behind me. I enter my room, shut the door, and lean back on it. Slowly I slide down it until I am sitting at the base of my door. Finally I am alone and I let go, letting my tears flow.

Once my tears dry up, I get into bed. Without pulling back the blankets I lie down, curl up, and close my eyes. A few minutes later, *I see Axel... he is in my room. I start to panic, crying for help, but no one comes. He's getting closer to me, pulling different tools out of a bag. He finds the one he used on me before and I can feel the tip of it start to cut me,* then I wake up. My mother is shaking me with a concerned look on her face.

When she notices my eyes are open she stops and says,

"It's okay, it was only a bad dream." She sits down next to me and pulls me into her arms. "I'm so sorry... you're okay now... you're home."

I don't say anything, I just let her hold me. *It was a dream, he doesn't know I live here. He won't leave the Elite Region.* I try to convince myself it wasn't real, but it felt too real. It felt like it did in the Medical Center, then I start to panic again. Quickly I sit up and start to look at my arms and legs, making sure I don't have any new cuts... just in case.

My mother watches me and asks, "What are you doing?"

I look up at her. "I'm making sure... I know it seems crazy, but some weird things happened to us over there. So I need to check, to make sure I wasn't drugged again or something."

She looks angry. "They can't treat people this way... you're just a kid! You're all just kids! Their methods were never this sadistic when your father and I went to the Elite Region."

"Not everyone is... the tests aren't even that bad. Commander Avery, Thyn, and Axel are the sadistic ones. They're the ones who treat us like dirt."

Her anger fades back into concern. "You're right. Would you like me to stay with you tonight?"

I shake my head. "No, I think I'll be alright now."

My mother leaves my room and I lie back down. I know I'll be alright, because I know I won't be sleeping anymore tonight.

# CHAPTER ELEVEN

I lie in my bed while my room becomes brighter with the rising sun. I'm sure that the Elites expect me at work today, but it's not happening. I would much rather lie here all day than be a slave for the rest of my life. As I debate about staying in my room all day there is a quiet knock on my door, so I sit up and say, "Come in."

The door slowly opens and to my surprise it's Mya. "Hey… I hope you don't mind—I got up early this morning and started asking around to find out where you live," she tells me.

I smile. "Nah, it's alright. I was wondering how I would find you again. How far from here is your place?"

She walks across the room and sits down next to me. "It's not too far. I live on the other side of the clearing where the wall opens—about the same distance as it is from there to your place."

I nod to let her know I understand. "Mya… if you don't mind me asking, why did you come here?"

She shrugs. "I missed you, and it's not the same here anymore. I feel like I lost a part of me in the Elite Region and you're the only person I connected with over there."

I let out a little laugh. "I feel exactly the same, only

they took more than a part of me. They took my sister... my..." I clear my throat. "My other half... and I feel like they took my spirit. I was really starting to believe my ability is worth something, that I possess it for a reason... for a bigger cause than being an Elite. They took that hope and shattered it, all the confidence I had built up... that Zander helped me build up, is gone. I can barely even look my parents in the eye because they don't even look at me the same. They didn't only kill my spirit, they tampered with my appearance, so every day I will be reminded that I'm *nothing*."

Mya takes my hand in hers. "Alexis... you are so much more than nothing. Don't you see that those are the reasons you need to fight? To prove to them you are worth something, that we deserve better. If you give up... Zander and Tara are gone *forever*. I believe if you can pull yourself back together you can do anything you set your mind to." She pauses for a moment and looks away from me. "I'm nothing special, I don't have any abilities, but I will help you however I can. I believe in you."

I wish I can accept what she said, but I'm so lost that I can't. "I appreciate that you believe in me. I hope someday I will be able to put myself back together, but I'm not sure if I can. Are you going to work today?"

She shakes her head. "No, I'm going to ditch it as long as they don't come and get me. Why do you ask?"

"Because I'm not going... I won't go. Do you want to spend the day with me?" She nods, so I get up. "I'm going to get cleaned up, and I'll meet you downstairs." She smiles and leaves my room.

Carefully I take off Zander's shirt, fold it up, and set it on my bed. Then I grab my light pants and grey shirt. It's the most casual thing I have even though it's for work. I take a quick shower, put on the clothes, and start to comb out my hair. Mya lifted my mood, but as soon as I see myself in the mirror I'm feeling defeated again. *If I can't even save myself from a sadistic privileged Inept, how can I do anything?* I try to shake off the feeling of being worthless but it's too hard. So quickly I put my hair up and make my way downstairs to meet Mya.

When I get to the bottom of the stairs I can hear my father talking, "She's been through a lot, it's completely understandable for her to be cautious and feel insignificant. We just need to keep reminding her that she's worth something to all of us. That examiner took her innocence from her and shook her confidence. Once she realizes what she is capable of, she will use her pain to her advantage."

*He doesn't understand how I feel. I have already failed. I would be an Elite right now if I was capable of anything.* I take a deep breath and try to act like I didn't hear what my father said as I step into the kitchen.

My parents are sitting down across from Mya and they all look up when I enter the room. Then my mother gets up and wraps her arms around me. She says, "Hey sweetheart, were you able to get any sleep last night?" I don't say anything, I shrug while shaking my head, and she says. "I'm sorry... what are your plans with Mya today?"

I sigh. "I don't know. I would like to be outside, though. We were cooped up for a week." Slowly I remove my mother's arms from around me and sit at the table next to Mya. My mother sets a bowl of oatmeal in front of me and returns to her seat. I begin to absentmindedly stir it, never taking a bite.

After a while my parents go to their jobs for the day. I'm not sure where they're working today; since I was gone I have no idea what their schedule is anymore. Then Mya says, "You're not going to eat anything, are you?"

I shake my head. "No, let's just go."

She doesn't protest and follows me out the door. At the end of the path I stop and try to decide where to go. I don't want to go to the pond, I will only sulk on memories there. Just as I am about to decide on a direction to take, I'm startled so bad that if Mya hadn't been behind me I would have fallen over.

"Orion, are you trying to give me a heart attack?" I ask.

He doesn't say anything because he is too busy laughing at me. As I regain my balance I notice Mya looks like she is in shock. I tell her, "Mya, this is Orion... Zander's little brother. As you can see, he's been practicing his ability."

She rubs her eyes. "You can turn invisible?"

Her question sends Orion into another round of hysterical laughing. "No, but that would be even more awesome! I have a mental ability, I can make people think I'm not here. It's hard to explain, basically I can hide out in the open and I can do it on certain people or on everyone. Would you like me to show you?"

Mya nods and Orion grins so wide it looks like his teeth will pop out of his face. Then he grabs Mya's hand and they are gone. I'm a little jealous of how much control he has of his gift, I wish I could get mine to work that well. Finally I grow impatient and snap, "Okay, Orion, I think she gets it."

They come back into view a few feet in front of me. Mya is laughing and looking amazed. I catch up to them and we continue walking. I can hear them talking to each other but I'm not listening. I am focused on finding Zander, I'm sure he has to be here somewhere. They wouldn't keep a physical gift like his cooped up behind the walls.

Then Mya jolts me out of my thoughts when she says, "Alexis, where are we going?"

"Nowhere, really. I was hoping to run into Zander but I haven't seen him yet."

Mya picks up her pace, passes me, and stops. "Are you sure that's a good idea? Are you ready to see him as an Elite?"

It is nice of her to be concerned for me. "I'm sure. I

can't explain it but I feel like I *need* to see him." She doesn't say anything else and moves out of my way. Orion picks up their conversation where he had left off and I begin my search again.

We reach the clearing where the wall opens. With no sign of Zander anywhere, I decide to keep going. After a while I think I hear Mya say something about her home, but I'm still stuck in my mind. I'm starting to think I'm hallucinating, because almost out of nowhere I see him. I freeze, not sure what to do now, not knowing if it's really him or a figment of my imagination. He looks like he is patrolling the region, but his movements aren't candid, he looks awkward moving under Thyn's control—although I have to admit, he looks *really* good in the Core uniform. It hugs his body, showing his muscles, and it makes his presence seem more powerful.

I feel a hand touch my back. Mya says, "Go and talk to him, maybe you can turn his haze off."

I shake my head. "I can't... Thyn has Noah now, he's probably using him."

Then Orion raises his voice at me. "What is wrong with you? This is Zander we're talking about! You have known him your whole life, what are you scared of?"

I look at him shocked. "You're right... I am scared. I'm scared he's not the same person. I'm scared that they paired him with another Elite already. Most of all I'm scared that he doesn't love me anymore."

Mya says with frustration, "Alexis, I've seen you two together, he will never forget you. Besides it's only been two days."

*She's right... he loves me.* I start walking toward him, taking deep breaths, and trying to keep calm. I'm a few feet from him when he changes direction and begins walking toward me.

Finally I reach him and look into his clouded eyes. I keep staring as he says to me, "Inept worker, you need to get back to your job!"

My heart starts to race as I say, "Zander... please..." I keep staring trying to get him to come back to me when I remember it always worked when he was touching me. So I reach forward and grab his hand. Slowly the haze dissolves from his eyes and he focuses on me. I can't hold back anymore and quickly wrap my arms around him, not sure how long this will last.

He holds me tight, exclaiming, "Alexis, I've missed you so much!" Then he kisses the top of my head and says, "I love you."

"I love you too. I'm glad my ability still works with you!"

He says, "But you need to be careful. Remember Thyn can see what I see. He probably saw you before he lost control of me."

I lay my head back on his chest. "You're right, I'll be more careful next time... how long do you think this will last?"

"It doesn't matter, you're with me now and that's all I care about."

I look back and see that Mya and Orion are gone, either hiding or somewhere else, they must think we need a moment alone. I take his hand in mine but he pulls it away, grabs my arm, and starts dragging me along with him. "Zander, what's going on? You're hurting me!"

His voice sounds cold. "I am taking you back to your job."

Slowly I look up and my heart sinks when I see the haze is back in his eyes. *NO, not yet!* Suddenly I'm angry. Everything from the past week finally boils over. This is the last straw. I yank my arm away from him and yell, "I'm not going! You can't treat me this way... Thyn, I'm talking to you! I'm done being mistreated by you—every time an Elite hurts one of us, it's you!"

Before Thyn can make Zander grab me again I run as

fast as I can away from him. I don't slow down until I can't see him anymore over my shoulder. Then I stop, trying to catch my breath. I look up to see Orion and Mya in front of me looking nervously at me.

Mya points, saying, "He's coming, and he's not alone." I turn to see Titen jogging next to Zander and I begin to panic.

Orion grabs one of my hands and one of Mya's, saying, "I've never tried this with more than one person but it's our only shot. You have to stay quiet."

I try to control my breathing so they can't hear me gasping for air. All three of us stand motionless trying not to make any noise. Orion's gift must be working because they run right past us without even glancing in our direction. As soon as they are out of sight I let out the breath I was holding and sit on the ground.

Mya looks over at me. "What happened?"

I start to draw circles in the dirt with my finger. "I forgot that Thyn can see who the Elites are around. I forgot that he would know Zander was with someone. I don't know how I'll ever be able to do it again, as soon as he sees me he'll probably attack me... *oh no*... they know where I live!"

Orion drops to the ground and says, "I don't know if I can hide everyone."

Then I get an idea. "Orion, I just thought of how your gift will be useful! They should leave my family alone if I'm not there, so we will figure out what to do about our families later. I know how I can remove the haze from Zander without Thyn seeing anyone. I will need you to hide me and once I get Zander back to normal you can stop so he can see us. I don't know why I never thought of this before! We wouldn't need to hide all the time, only when Elites are around. Orion, do you think you can help me with this?"

"I'll try anything to get my brother back," he says.

"We probably shouldn't push our luck today, though."

"You're right. When do you think it will be safe for me to go home?"

He shrugs. "I could always hide you until we are sure they aren't there."

Mya says, "I wish there was something I could do to help."

I get up and hug her. "You did help... if you didn't come to my home today I wouldn't have left my room."

We spend the day walking around the region. Orion and Mya talk and laugh all day, while I spend time with my thoughts. As the sun is starting to set, we decide to go back home. On our way we stop at Mya's to let her parents know she's going to come stay with me tonight. We're all in a pretty good mood now that there is some sort of plan in place. As we get to the clearing where the wall opens to the Elite Region, Orion stops. "Shhh!" he orders.

Mya and I stop right behind him and watch as the wall opens up. Orion quickly reaches back to touch us, to make sure he can hide us. I've never seen the Elites switching out before. A group including Zander and Titen enter the Elite Region and another group comes into our region. Patiently we wait for the new group of Elites to pass and then quickly run through the clearing to the other side.

"That was close," I say, panting. "We would have been in trouble with that many Elites."

Orion and Mya nod in agreement and we continue walking until we reach my house. When we walk up the path, I notice the front door to my home is wide open. "That's weird, my parents never leave the door open." Then panic shoots through me and I sprint into my home to find both of my parents lying on the floor in our kitchen.

In shock I can't move. *This is my fault, I should have come straight home.* Mya pushes past me and kneels next to them, pressing her fingers to their necks.

She looks up at me and says, "They're still alive! Orion, run to your home and get your parents, we'll need their help." He nods and is out the door. "Alexis, it's okay... they will be fine."

My anger overpowers me and I begin throwing dishes around the kitchen. "*THEY CAN'T DO THIS!* We're not their possessions, we are living, breathing human beings. This has to stop... I will do anything I can to stop them!"

Moments later Orion comes in followed by his parents, who run straight toward mine. Carefully, Orion and Mr. Rane move my parents onto their backs to check their wounds. It looks like they have both been knocked out and have some broken bones. My father's arm is bent in an unnatural way and my mother's hand is contorted. Cautiously, Mr. and Mrs. Rane snap their bones back into place and tightly wrap them up in towels so they can set correctly. Luckily the Elites teach us how to tend to different wounds, since we don't have medication as powerful as theirs that heals us instantly.

Once they are done tending to them, they very carefully move my parents into our family room. I run upstairs and grab some pillows and blankets. When I get back downstairs my mother is awake and says, "Oh, Alexis, I'm so glad you're okay."

I drop the blankets and pillows and sit next to my mother. "I'm so sorry... this is all my fault. I saw Zander today, I removed his haze but I wasn't thinking."

She reaches up with her good hand, wipes the tears from my cheeks, and says, "Don't be sorry." Then her hand drops and her eyes close.

Nervously I try to shake my mother. "What's wrong with her?"

Mr. Rane pulls me back and says, "She's probably in a lot of pain, we will have to get some painkillers for her. For now it's better if she sleeps through it."

I fight my way out of his grasp and pick up the pillows

and blankets I dropped. Carefully I lift their heads and place a pillow under them. Then I drape a blanket over each of my parents and sit at their feet.

After a while I can't sit here anymore so I get up and go outside. I drop to the ground taking my anger out on it, ripping out the grass and hitting it. It's one thing to put myself in danger, but how can I be stupid enough to get my family hurt? If they die it will be my fault. If Tara is ever free from the Elite Region, she will never forgive me.

I let out a scream at the top of my lungs trying to get rid of my rage. I must have frightened Mya, because she hurriedly comes outside. "What's wrong?"

"Nothing. I just needed to let go for a moment. I'm fine now."

"No, you're not." She shakes her head. "You're mad and you deserve to be. Instead of taking it out on your yard and your lungs, take it out on Thyn. He's the one who did this, he's the one who controls the Elites, and he the one who lets Axel hurt Inept children."

I get up and Mya wraps her arms around me. I'm not in the mood to be comforted but I let her so I don't hurt her feelings. Once she lets me go, I go back inside and sit in the family room. It's crowded with all of us in here, but I'm not leaving.

Suddenly my father's breathing quickens but his eyes are still closed. I ask, "What's happening to him?"

Mr. Rane kneels beside him and start speaking to my father, telling him, "Try to take deep breaths... I know you can hear me! You need to slow your breathing down." My father still isn't responding and his breathing becomes even faster. Mr. Rane is shaking him, trying to get him to come to, when suddenly his breathing stops.

"NO!" I scream. "*Do* something!"

Quickly Mr. Rane starts to push on my father's chest, trying to get his heart pumping, then he breathes into his mouth to try to get him to breathe. He repeats this over and over again for what seems like forever, to no avail. He sits back with his head hung low. "I'm so sorry Alexis... he's gone."

I stare down at my father. "He can't be... they have already taken too much from me. He's not gone, keep trying!" When Mr. Rane doesn't move I throw myself down next to him and start to pump my father's chest, trying to get his heart to beat again. "DAD! You can't leave me! You can't leave Mom! We need you! Please... *Daddy*... please open your eyes... *please*, you can't die."

When he doesn't open his eyes, I collapse onto his chest and weep. No one bothers me while I mourn my father. I lie here for hours with my ear pressed hard against his chest, hoping that somehow his heart will beat again. Finally I slowly sit up, kiss his forehead, and pull the blanket up to cover his face. "I will make you proud, Dad. I will stop them. I love you."

Then I get up, head outside, and grab a shovel. The Inept Region doesn't have a graveyard, we aren't *privileged* enough for one, so I begin digging a grave in the yard. My hands begin to blister, but I kept digging. I need the distraction.

"Let me help you." I look up to see Orion standing next to the grave. I hand him the shovel and start to examine the blisters on my hands.

I watch as he digs deeper and deeper until the hole is long enough for my father to fit in. Then he crawls out of the grave and goes back into my house. Moments later he appears with Mr. Rane carrying my father. They are about to lower him into the grave, but I stop them, pleading, "Wait... *please*. I need to say goodbye. My mother needs..." my voice gives out as a new wave of tears overcome me.

They carry him back inside and set him in the kitchen. I stand in the doorway between the family room and kitchen, looking back and forth from my mother to my father. I can't stand being here anymore, so I go straight up the stairs. Getting into the shower without undressing, I sit on the floor letting the water run over me. *I won't let them get away with this! I will succeed in tearing the walls down... I will make my father proud!*

A knock on the door makes me jump. "What?"

"Alexis... your mother is asking for you." I can hear Mya's voice crack. She's been crying.

I hear her walk away, so I get out of the shower and go to my bedroom to change out of my wet clothes. I put on some different work pants, then I unfold Zander's shirt, slide my arms into the sleeves, and button it up. Even though it's too big, it makes me feel some comfort. Hopefully it will help me keep my composure with my mother.

As I go down the stairs, I notice the sun has been up for a while. I hadn't even realized we were up all night, too much had happened. I enter the family room and sit next to my mother.

She takes my hand and says, "We'll be okay... we still have each other." I nod. "Alexis, please don't blame yourself. They don't care who they hurt or... kill. They only care about being obeyed and they don't care who they have to demoralize to get it."

I can see that my mother has been crying, but is trying to put on a brave face for me. I run my fingers through her hair. "Mom... I love you."

"And I love you."

"We need to say goodbye. Do you think you can come outside?"

My mother says, "Yes. For this, I have to."

Mr. and Mrs. Rane help her up and slowly take her outside. I stand next to her, and Zander's father drapes my mother's arm over my shoulders. He and Orion return to the house and carry out my father. They place him in his grave and my mother can't hold back her tears. She's never going to see the man she loves again. She lost the love of her life, and I can't imagine what that feels like.

My mother looks over to me and asks, "Do you want to start?"

I pause before saying, "Daddy, I love you. I'm so sorry... I..." I'm at a loss for words; nothing can explain the pain I'm feeling. The worst part is I only want him to comfort me.

My mother sighs and says, "Grant... oh my wonderful, caring, joyful Grant. We had a good run, you gave me more than I ever expected. All I ever wanted... *needed*, was your love. Our love will never die, and my heart is forever yours. You will always be my soul mate, my lifeline, my friend, and I love you... so much."

Once my mother is finished, the Ranes' say something, but I'm so numb I don't hear a word of it. As Orion begins to bury my father, we take my mother back inside and I sit next to her again. Trying to distract myself, I touch her hair and she smiles up at me. "It will be okay."

I'm trying to figure out what to say, but I'm coming up blank, so I continue to play with her hair, until I finally say, "Rest... get better... I will be back later." She nods, I get up, and walk out of my home past my father's grave.

Orion and Mya aren't far behind me—I knew they would follow me. I go to the pond so we can strategize.

# CHAPTER TWELVE

Once we reach the pond I sit at the edge, take my shoes off, and submerge my feet in the water. Mya sits next to me with Orion on her other side and they both do the same. I'm enjoying watching Orion and Mya act their ages by splashing each other and giggling. Orion pushes Mya into the water and she retaliates by pulling him in with her. I want to be able to laugh and join in their fun, but I have too much weighing on my mind.

*I need to free Zander from Thyn... but if he stays in the Elite Region we will have someone on the inside... Thyn will eventually figure out something is going on if he keeps losing sight of Zander.*

Mya gets out of the water and says, "Alexis, what are you thinking about so hard?" She puts her arm around me and gives me kind of a half hug. While I go through my thoughts one more time, Orion gets back out of the water and sits next to Mya again.

I look over at them. "I'm stuck... I want Zander here with us, and I know you do too. But it might be better to keep someone on the inside," I say, looking at Orion. "Since he's in the Core he may be able to tell us valuable information that will help free all of us. Then there are our

families to worry about… maybe all of our families should stay in one place so we can protect each other."

Mya looks out over the water and says, "I don't think my family will come. They don't mind being Inept, my mother always told me if we follow their rules they will let us live in peace. I don't feel the same way, though, I don't see how working to exhaustion without the medical care they have and worthless food is living in peace." She sighs. "I will stay with you, but I won't be able to convince my family to."

"My family already decided last night to stay with you and your mother since she's hurt and your dad's…" Orion doesn't finish what he was going to say, he doesn't have to. I can see tears building up in his eyes. "Do you think we can really do this? That we can overtake a bunch of Elites?"

I nod. "We don't need to take over all of the Elites. We already have some of them on our side, and I don't think it will be very hard to convince others. A lot of them are from here, not all of the Elite feel disgust toward us. We even have a couple that were born in the Elite Region on our side."

Orion says, "So what do we do first?"

I get up and put my shoes back on. "We find Zander and fill him in."

I'm not sure where to start looking so I head back toward my house. I'm assuming Thyn will want to see the aftermath of what he did to my family last night. I can only assume he made Titen and Zander do it. "Mya, do you think Thyn knows I'm gifted? I tried to tell him but they didn't believe me… why else would he hurt my family?"

"I don't think he knows that," she responds. "I think he's upset that you keep undermining him. Honestly I think he's getting nervous because if a fifteen-year-old girl isn't afraid of him, who would be? Plus they messed up by letting Axel hurt you, it will only make people want to stand against them even more; then again, he might get a kick out of making someone's life miserable. He's probably too full of himself to see what's going on right in front of him. It's hard to say."

The entire way to my house I don't see Titen or Zander. I don't think anything of it because they're probably supervising a different area of the Inept Region today. When we finally reach my crooked little home I'm surprised to see Orion's parents still here. "Mr. Rane, shouldn't you both be working?" I ask him. "I don't want them to hurt you too."

He shakes his head. "We will not be working for them ever again. What they did to Evalyn and Grant will not be condoned. Your parents are wonderful people and they never deserved this." Then he wraps his arms around me and says, "Can you do me a favor?"

"Yes."

"Quit calling us Mr. and Mrs. Rane—it makes me feel old! There is no need to be that formal with us."

"I can do that Mr. Rane... I mean, Lucca," I say, turning a bit red in the face.

I walk into the family room to check on my mother. "Mrs. Rane... sorry, Kora, how is she doing?" It's going to take me awhile to get use to calling Zander's parents by their first names, it's a little weird.

She smiles. "Better, but still weak. She's been sleeping most of the day, which is good—it will give her body time to heal."

I go over, kiss my mother on her cheek, and leave the room to join Mya and Orion again. We are sitting in the kitchen with Lucca when we hear the door slam open. Lucca whispers, "The three of you get against that wall over there, and I will see what's going on." We do as he says and watch him walk out of the room.

He isn't gone for long—it looks like he flew across the doorway and we hear a hard thud as he hits the wall. I'm not sure how I can help, but my body seems to be doing its own thing, and I start to head for the door. I step out of the kitchen to see Titen and Zander in the entryway. "Stop!" I command them. "Why are you doing this?"

Titen is too busy concentrating on Lucca so Zander addresses me, "Because you apparently haven't learned your lesson. I will not be belittled by a pathetic, Inept, little girl. Until you take your rightful place and show the Elites some respect, this will continue to happen. Using two people you care about to destroy your family is more... *fun*... than I thought it would be. The look on your face, while you watch your sister's husband and the boy you wish you were good enough for, kill your other loved ones, is priceless. You and I both know they have no idea what's going on. Poor Zander will never know Titen slowly squeezed the life out of his father... and how he *killed* your father!"

I can't hold back my tears. "Why don't you kill me instead? I'm the one who is defying you!"

Before Thyn uses Zander to answer me, his expression changes—he looks confused and stares past me. I look behind me to see that Lucca is no longer there. *Orion!* I know exactly what happened, but the looks on Titen and Zander's faces show me they have no idea where he went. "Do you think because I lost focus with Titen for a few minutes that there aren't other ways I can hurt you?"

I laugh. "You've already taken everything from me. I've been tortured and I've been broken. I would say there isn't anything you can do that hasn't been done."

A sly smile crosses Zander's face as he says, "I know of one thing... I saw you and this boy at the Inept Testing Facilities. You might want to know he's been placed. I actually have her coming here right now so you can meet her. She was born in the Elite Region and is quite a beauty if I do say so myself."

"It doesn't matter, he will never forget about me, he

will never love her."

No one responds, so we just stand here. If another Inept were to walk into my home right now they would think I'm crazy. I 'm standing my ground against two very powerful Elites. I'm starting to feel uneasy with Titen and Zander staring at me with their clouded eyes, but then I see her come through the door of my home.

Thyn starts to use Zander to talk again and he says, "This is Azaria."

I look at her trying not to show how I feel. She is the most beautiful person I have ever seen. She is tall and slim with flawless dark skin. Her black hair flows straight down to the middle of her back and she holds herself like my mother does. Even if she wasn't so stunning, her composure would still make her more attractive than me. "What can she do?"

Laughing, he says, "She has a very unique mental gift... I'll show you." Suddenly my mind is filled with what looks like memories of her and Zander being... *intimate*.

I ask, "Memories?"

"Could be, but she can implant any image in your mind she wants to. I will let you decide if that was real or not."

I can't think of anything to say. I'm afraid if I try to speak he will see he got under my skin. Then something I never thought I would witness happens. Zander kisses her and I lose it, shouting, "No! He would never do this to me, he's only doing it because you're controlling him." I can't watch anymore so I quickly run to the family room only to see that everyone is gone.

I try to keep my voice down as I whisper, "Orion... Orion where are you?" I almost jump out of my skin when I feel someone touch me but don't see anyone. Slowly everyone starts to reappear and I say, "Orion... you did great! How did you hide so many people?"

With his forehead creased in concentration, he says, "I

don't know, but we're still hidden... I just hid you with us now... maybe you can remove their haze now?"

I shake my head and say, "They have another Elite here, she was born in the Elite Region, and might not want to be on our side."

Orion looks upset and says, "We might as well try to get her on our side!"

Before I can think about what he said, Azaria, Titen, and Zander come into the family room looking for me. Now's my chance while everyone is distracted. I take a deep breath and concentrate on the thoughts that always seem to help me use my ability. I think of a world with no walls, being equals with the Elites, and having all of my loved ones with me.

Orion nudges me and says, "Its working! Look!"

I look into their eyes and watch the haze fade from all of them. "Orion, you can stop now but as soon as we see any sign of them getting controlled again you have to be quick. Don't doubt yourself, I know you can do it." He nods and I watch as Zander's eyes meet mine.

He embraces me and is about to say something but is interrupted by Azaria. "What's going on? Why am I here?"

Zander lets go of me, walks over to her, and says, "Remember all those things I told you about? About Thyn, Axel, and the Commander?" She nods. "You're here because he made you come here and I'm assuming he did it for one reason." Turning to me, he says, "Nothing has happened between us, she knows how I feel about you. In fact she would much rather be with someone else too."

I stare at the ground and nod. I am trying to believe him but it's hard. Then I notice Titen looking past me and he walks over to my mother, who is sitting against the wall. He starts to approach her and she begins to panic, shouting, "No! Stay away from me!"

I join my mother and tell her, "It's okay... it wasn't really them... don't forget he's Tara's husband, he won't hurt you."

Titen says, "Why do you think I will hurt you?"

She looks at me, and I smile in an attempt to encourage her. Timidly, she starts to explain, "Yesterday you and Zander came here. We tried to handle things calmly, but you weren't in the mood to listen. You kept asking us where Alexis was but we hadn't seen her since before we left for work. You didn't believe us... you held us suspended in the air while... while Zander broke our bones. Then you let me drop but continued to hold Grant up, and you both kept beating him and now he's *dead*."

When she's finished with her story Titen looks like he might be sick. He says to her, "Mrs. Gander, I know nothing I can say will change what happened, but I swear to you I am no monster. I don't want to kill anyone... I don't choose to have Thyn control me. I'm sorry— please don't be afraid of me."

She looks at me and I tell her, "It's okay... he saved my life, remember? If he was a murderer, he would have let Axel kill me."

Slowly my mother stands up and walks toward Titen. She hugs him and he returns it with tears running down his cheeks. I glance at Zander to see him on the floor with his knees pulled up to his chest. His parents are trying to comfort him but it doesn't look like it's working. "Zander..."

He raises his head and I've never seen him so broken before. Quickly I get up and sit right in front of him. I put my hands on either side of his face and look hard straight into his eyes. "This wasn't your fault! I *know* you, and I know you would never hurt anyone."

He unfolds and wraps his arms around me. "They've turned me into someone I don't even know anymore."

I hold him tightly and say, "No, they didn't, you are the same person you have always been. He just uses you, he's not changing you. The fact that you're this upset proves it."

Then Azaria says, "She's right... all you ever do is talk about her and your families. You have a good soul that they will never be able to change." Then she takes a deep breath and says, "Alexis, I would like to stay here with all of you, I don't want the *privilege* of being an Elite. I was born into that region, and all I've ever wanted was to be out of it."

"That's not going to be easy," I tell her.

"I know."

I let go of Zander. "Can you come with me for a moment?" I get up and hold my hand out to him. He takes it and follows me in silence. I lead him through my home and up to my room.

I sit on my bed and say, "I just wanted a minute alone with you so we could talk more privately."

He sits next to me and I wait for him to say something but he doesn't. I am about to when he leans over and kisses me. He places his hand on the side of my neck under my jaw line, and almost automatically I lean back, and without breaking our kiss, he follows. I'm lying on my back, and he is on his side holding himself up so he is leaning over me. This is a new feeling for me, we have never been this passionate before, and I'm surprised it happens so naturally. My heart begins to race as I reach up, place my hand on the back of his head, and pull him down closer to me.

He moves his hand from my neck onto my side, and starts lifting my shirt. I let go of the back of his neck, push him away a little, and break our kiss. He sits up looking a little hurt and says, "I'm sorry, I don't know what came over me."

I smile. "Don't be sorry, I only stopped because I used to lose control of my gift when we kissed, and I don't think I could have controlled it much longer." I can feel my face getting warm as I start to blush.

He chuckles a little and says, "I've missed everything

about you. I don't like being away from you."

I lean against his shoulder. "I don't like it either, but I think it's best right now."

He gets up. "What do you mean?" I shouldn't have said anything, I was enjoying being with him like he had never left.

"We need people on the inside to find their weakness," I tell him.

He walks over to my door and places his hands on it. "I don't want to see anything over there anymore... I've only been there a few days, and I already have nightmares about the things I've seen. They don't have it much better in the Elite Region. They get fancy stuff, good food, and high-tech medical treatment, but it's not safe. If you're Elite and have an Elite child, they leave you alone, but... they have testing for their kids too, it's not as aggressive as ours is, but it's just as effective. Some of the kids that are Inept don't get to stay."

I walk over to him. I have so many questions but I can only get one out, "What do you mean?"

"They have a big show for the entire region to see which kids become part of the Elite Core and who is deemed Inept. Once they are separated, they choose a few from the Inept to keep—but only the ones that have *potential*, like Axel. He's Inept and he got to stay because he showed promise in understanding medicine. Last night was their ceremony. There were four Inept children, but only one was kept. The other three were killed right in front of us, by Titen. I don't think he knows... he was one of the few Elites who had the haze at the ceremony since Thyn and Commander Avery don't come to it in person. Alexis, they kill innocent kids, then expect the Elite to get married and have children. What's worse is you can tell which Elites are born there because it doesn't upset them, they let their children die! It's just like here, you hope you have an Elite kid so they can live a better life. Then there's the fact that even in the Elite Region they have no choices in love or life. Look at Azaria, she was born there with an amazing gift but she's treated like us. The worst part of it all is not having control over your own mind and body. Alexis, I helped kill your father! I can't go back. I don't want to hurt anyone else that I care about."

I duck under his arm and slide between him and the door. "Then don't, as long as you are with me it seems like I can keep the haze away, but we need to fill Titen in."

We leave the room and find Titen sitting on the floor next to the door. "You don't need to tell me anything, I was coming to make sure Zander was still himself and I heard everything. Did I really kill some kids?"

Zander nods. "It wasn't you, though. Maybe none of us need to go back... why can't we all stay here?"

I can't leave Tara there alone," he says. Then I have an idea—I'm not sure if it will work, but it's something.

"What if we can get her out? Orion can make it like we aren't even there, we can sneak into the Elite Region when the groups switch out and we can get her." I look back and forth from Titen to Zander as the idea sinks in.

Titen's eyes fill with hope as he says, "Can you keep the haze off of us?"

"I think so. Do you know how Thyn's ability works?"

"Kind of," he says. "I'm pretty sure he needs to know where we are. Before we come here we all have to meet by the opening in the wall, and up until we go in, we are in our own control. Kind of like at the Testing Facilities, when we were together before he started to control us, he knew we were in your living quarters. I'm pretty sure as long as we aren't seen by someone under his control he won't be able to find us. But if we do stay in the Inept Region we should find a place he won't come looking." He gets up off the floor and starts to go downstairs, then says, "I will let them know what's going on."

I turn to look at Zander. There are so many things I

want to say to him. I want to tell him how happy I am that he will be with me, and how much I love him. Chuckling, he says, "Why are you wearing my shirt?"

I look down at it. "It's dumb, but it made me feel like you were with me. I was out of it when I first got back, I still think I'm a bit lost now. I almost don't believe you're standing here with me."

"It's not dumb, and let me prove to you I'm real." He runs his fingers through my hair and softly moves them along my jaw line under my chin. I begin to get nervous as he lifts my chin. I can feel myself shake with anticipation, but can't make myself move. Then he leans over and kisses me softly, each kiss becoming more intense with each passing second.

Every time he kisses me I feel a surge of energy run through my body. It makes me feel like I can take on the world, like I'm as strong as he is. At some point we moved, because I'm using the wall to support me. My knees have gone weak and my breathing faster.

Someone clears their throat but neither of us are paying attention, so they do it again louder. This time we stop and look down the stairs to see Zander's father looking up at us. I can feel my face start to burn as I blush, and Zander has a huge grin on his face. "Do you two feel like joining us?" his father asks.

Zander sighs. "Yeah, we'll be there in a minute." I look back and forth between Zander and his father, and I'm about to run down the stairs but Zander stops me, saying, "Wait... please."

I watch as Lucca walks away and I turn back to Zander. He kisses my forehead. "Alexis, I love you—do you believe I'm real now?"

"I love you too, and yes, I do. I'm not sure if you felt the way I did before your father... um... interrupted us, but I have no doubt that you're really here with me."

"He has some really bad timing." He frowns. We both

laugh as we head to the kitchen.

Everyone is sitting around the table, even my mother. Zander and I stand against the wall as Titen continues to explain our plan. "We are only going to do this if Orion thinks he can handle it. Zander, Alexis, Orion, and I will go into the Elite Region and get Tara out. This is the only plan we have so far, but things are coming together, and as we develop our plans we will keep you informed. Before we leave to go into the Elite Region, we need to find a safe place for everyone."

It's too bad Titen doesn't have my ability, he would use it better. Even if I tried my hardest, I'm no leader. I need some fresh air, so I go out to my yard and sit next to my father's grave. I miss him so much that I start to bellow. "I can't do this," I tell him. "I barely have confidence in myself. How am I supposed to expect people to follow me, to *fight* with me?" I sigh. "I wish you were still here, I wish I would have come straight home... maybe you would still be alive. I promise I will make you proud. I will tear the walls down and do what you believed I could do."

Mya squats down next to me and says, "We decided to go see if my family will let us stay there, maybe we can talk them into helping us. If not, we will figure something else out." Getting up she says, "Oh and, Alexis, I believe in you... we all do."

I turn to see everyone standing a couple feet away from me. I can't help but smile. "Let's get going, we'll have to be quick to get to Mya's with enough time to get to the Elite Region." I look over to Orion and say, "You can do this, your control is a gift in itself." He smiles and we head to Mya's home.

It's taking us a while to get there because my mother is still weak. It takes a long time for me to convince her to let Zander carry her. "He won't hurt you, he couldn't even if he wanted to because I'm here."

She finally gives in, and Zander carefully picks her up saying, "Mrs. Gander, you will never know how sorry I am." My mother doesn't respond to him, and I can see the pain on Zander's face. Finally we reach Mya's house. She enters it with Titen while Orion keeps the rest of us hidden.

"It's taking too long, we need to get going before we miss our chance to get Tara," I tell everyone. I start to pace when Titen comes back outside.

"We are welcome to stay here, they still aren't fully with us but they will help." He looks at the others and says, "Mr. Rane, if at any moment Azaria gets the haze, get her out of the house. She doesn't have a physical gift so it will be easy. We just can't have Thyn see where we're staying." Zander's father nods and disappears into the house with everyone except for Titen, me, Zander, and Orion.

"We will have to spend the night in the Elite Region, the wall won't open again until the groups switch out. Is there a safe place we can stay?" I ask, turning to Titen.

"We'll figure something out."

Nervously we head to the clearing where the wall opens, when Orion stops and says, "I can't do this. If I get scared I don't know if I can keep using my gift."

Zander places his hands on Orion's shoulders and says, "You have more control over your gift than I do, and I've known about mine for a few years. I know you can do this, and I will be here every step of the way."

"Okay, I'll do it."

Shortly after, we reach the clearing and wait along the edge for the groups to change out. I can't believe we're actually doing this, that our plans are falling into place. I have Zander back and soon I'll have Tara back too. "Why doesn't she come here anymore?"

Titen explains, "That's the only good thing about the Elite Region—pregnant women don't have to be in Thyn's control. The only reason she was with you for your testing was because she had already been scheduled for it last year.

Anyway, she should be at our home waiting for me to get back."

"Do you really love her? Or are you just with her because that's where you were placed?"

"I actually love her... very much."

"Good." I'm relieved that my sister is really happy.

Then Orion shushes us and points at the group of Elites coming up to the wall. "We need to get close to them to slip into the Elite Region, but we have to be quiet. I can hide us physically but they can hear anything we say, and they can feel us if we touch them."

Quickly we join up with the group moving toward the Elite Region. It's a bit unnerving being around all of them with their clouded eyes. We're careful not to say anything or touch anyone, but it is difficult. Then the wall opens and we file into the Elite Region.

# CHAPTER THIRTEEN

Carefully we weave in and out of the Elites that are entering their region. I think at one point I bumped into someone, but luckily they didn't notice. After everyone has crossed the wall, I turn to watch it close. When I can't see into the Inept Region anymore my nerves start to act up. *Stay calm, don't affect Orion's gift.* It would be extremely bad for us if we appeared out of thin air without the haze.

Titen and Zander stop moving at the same time as the group of Elites. If I hadn't noticed, Orion and I would have kept walking away from them. It must be habit for them to wait, but it would be better for us to get going before the rest of them do, so I move quickly and grab Zander's hand and he snaps out of it. He nudges Titen and we join up with Orion again.

When we are out of hearing distance I whisper, "What was that all about? Why did you guys stop?"

The look on Zander's face is full of terror, but it is Titen who answers me, "When we first become Elites we get *trained* to do certain things. If we go against it... well, it's not good."

"But you didn't have the haze? How do they train you to stay there?"

"They train us without the haze. I'm not sure if you noticed, but as soon as that wall closed their haze was gone. We aren't allowed to leave the area until there is a signal that the other Elites are in their places. If something were to go wrong and we have to reenter to Inept Region, it's easier if we're waiting there so Thyn knows where we are… Alexis, there are Elites here with scarier gifts than Zander and I have. There is one Elite that has a gift so intimidating that it makes mine look pathetic. When he touches someone, it sends a pain through them. It's so intense that the person he is touching thinks they're dying."

I wrap my arms around Zander and say, "I'm so sorry, did he ever use it on you?" He returns my embrace, but doesn't answer me, which makes me think that it's something he's experienced.

I turn my attention back to Titen, asking, "Where do we go from here?"

He says, "I'll lead you guys. Tara will be happy to see you."

We walk down the main path and past about ten houses, then Titen turns left down an alley and past five more houses. He stops in front of a large white house with silver trim around the windows and door. "We need to figure out a way to check to make sure no one's here before we go in. Let's try around back, she normally waits in the family room, so she won't hear us come in back there."

We nod and follow him around his home. Carefully he opens the door, only far enough for each of us to slip in. Quietly we walk through their kitchen, which is more beautiful than the one at the Testing Facilities. Titen peeks around into the hall and waves us along. Then he turns into another room and stops in the doorway. So softly that I can barely hear, he whispers, "Orion, she doesn't have the haze, you can either hide her with us or show us to her—it's up to you."

Orion nods and says, "I need to rest, so I'll show us to

her." He concentrates for a moment then says, "Okay, she should be able to see you now."

Titen straightens up and walks into their family room. He says, "Tara... there's someone here to see you."

She laughs and says, "Oh, Titen... you startled me. You never come in the back door. Wait, what do you mean, someone's here to see me?"

I step out into the doorway, but as soon as she sees me she gets an angry look on her face and says, "What are you doing here? Are you trying to get yourself killed? Titen! How dare you bring her here?"

I cross the room and hug her. "We need to go, and you need to come with us. I'm actually surprised you're still here... that you're still you."

"What are you talking about?" she asks, looking confused.

I pull away from her and plead, "Tara, can you just trust me? And trust that Titen wouldn't endanger me and Orion by bringing us here if it wasn't important? We will explain everything once we are in a safer place." She nods and takes Titen's hand.

I cross the room and look out the window. Aron is coming toward the house. I yell, "Orion... you need to hide us—now!"

He steps into the center of the room and says, "I need everyone to touch me, to be safe it's working on you." Quickly, we all place one of our hands on him as the door bursts open.

I feel sick when I see Aron come into the room. Zander and I both look at each other and start to push everyone toward the back of the house. Once we're outside, I whisper, "We need to get far away from here... they have Aron in there, he can read minds. It doesn't matter how quiet we are, he will know we are here."

No one argues with me and we quickly weave in and out of houses trying to put as much space between us and

Aron as we can. We move back to the main road, close to the wall. I ask, "Titen, where should we go?"

"We might have to camp by the wall," he says. "I can't think of any place to go that they won't search. If we're out in the open, at least we will be able to see them coming and we can get away before Aron can hear us."

Once we reach the wall, we sit along it close to where it opens so we can get back easily. I sit between Tara and Zander. I hold his hand and lean on her shoulder. "Tara, I need to tell you something."

She brushes my hair out of my face like our mother always does. "What is it?"

"Please stay calm and don't blame anyone but me. Mom is hurt and Dad is... *gone.*"

She gasps and tears start to roll down her cheeks. A moment passes before she says, "Is Mom going to be okay?"

"She should be... she's been recovering well."

Tara turns towards Titen and does her best to be quiet as she breaks down. As she grieves for our father, Titen gently rubs her back, and says, "I'm so sorry."

She glances up at Titen, wipes her tears, and looks straight at me. "I'm guessing you want all of the blame because my husband and Zander had something to do with it?" Her voice cracks.

I straighten up, and insist, "No... Thyn had everything to do with it, and I want the blame because I deserve it. If I wasn't so stubborn I would have gone to work or I would have gone home right away. Maybe then he would have taken his anger out on me instead."

"No," Zander says, squeezing my hand. "He wouldn't have. He probably would have made you watch me beat your father and leave him for dead."

I reach up and brush the tears off his face. "You didn't do anything, and you would never hurt anyone."

It's starting to get dark, but none of us will be sleeping

tonight. We scoot closer to each other and Tara breaks the silence. "So, can you tell me what's going on now?"

Taking a deep breath, I begin, "I'm not sure where to start but I've decided to go against Thyn and Commander Avery. For some reason Thyn enjoys trying to break me, and he has, over and over again. He just doesn't realize that the more pain he causes me the more determined I am to change things. We don't need to live in separate worlds, we don't need to live in fear, and we don't need to lose the ones we love. Dad always believed I have my ability for a reason, and I want to make him proud. I'm not sure if Thyn knows I'm gifted, or if he thinks I'm some brat who won't listen. All I know is that I can't sit back and let him hurt anyone anymore in any way."

Tara pats my knee and says, "I always knew you would do great things."

"I haven't done anything yet, I've just pissed off the wrong guy. I can tell you one thing, though, I *can't wait* to see the look on Thyn's face when he sees that I beat his tests without trying, that I'm gifted."

Laughing, Zander says, "Speaking of your gift, I see that it's grown."

"What?"

He runs his hand along my arm and says, "You're joking, right?"

"No, I have no idea what you're talking about." I shake my head.

He chuckles, the lovely little chuckle that I love. "Well... earlier today you held off Thyn's ability from mine and Titen's minds..."

"Yeah, so I've done that before."

"Let me finish," he says. "While you did that you were also able to turn my gift off so I could carry your mother without hurting her... you did both of those, but at the same time left Orion's gift alone. Alexis, you really have no idea what you're capable of. Your father said your gift was always there, you didn't have to grow into it like everyone else. I wouldn't doubt it if your ability is stronger than Thyn's. He has Noah by his side 24/7 and you still shut him out. You're truly amazing."

I take in everything he has said then reach over and tap Orion, since it's so dark now that I can barely see him. "Are you still hiding us?" I ask him.

"Yes, I haven't stopped."

Suddenly I want to test Zander's theory. "I wish it wasn't so dark, I would love to see if I can purposely stop someone's gift and not another's."

Through the darkness I can see a shadow in front of me move. It's Titen. He says, "I can help you, and I promise I won't hurt you."

I don't see anything wrong with this, and I have Zander here to protect me if needed. "Let's do it."

He holds out his hand and helps me up. "I'm going to stand close to you. I need to make sure I can see you, otherwise I can't use my gift." Without saying anything I step closer, and can make out Titen's face. "Okay, Orion, if at any moment you can feel your ability shut off, let me know and we will stop." Orion agrees and Titen continues, "Okay, Alexis, I'm going to lift you up and I want you to stop me without shutting Orion's gift off."

I nod then remember it's dark. "Okay, I'm ready." Slowly I feel my feet leave the ground. It's a different feeling than the other times, it's like I can sense that his intentions are friendly, unlike when he's in Thyn's control. I clear my mind. I want to be able to do this without having to think of specific things. I want to be able to control my gift like I do with Zander. I take a deep breath and use my senses. I can feel a few different things. I feel protected, a sense of strength, gracefulness, and control. I filter through each one—I'm positive the protection is coming from Orion's gift, the strength obviously from Zander's, and the gracefulness can only be from my sister and her ability to glide through the air.

That only leaves the feeling of control, so I focus on that one, knowing it's coming from Titen. I take the feeling, push it from my mind, and my feet touch the ground. I look down to make sure I'm not imagining it, and sure enough, I'm back on the ground. "I did it!" I exclaim. "Orion, did you feel like you lost control of your ability?"

Sounding amazed, he says, "No, it didn't even weaken."

Excitedly I tap Titen and say, "Let's do it again... only this time I want you to try harder to keep me in the air. I've felt your ability at full strength before, and I know you weren't trying very hard."

He laughs and says, "Okay... let's try it another way then. Zander, could you come and stand next to Alexis so I can see you?" He agrees and stands next to me facing Titen. "Okay, I'm going to lift both of you... Alexis, I want you to stop me from using it not only on yourself but also on Zander. And don't forget to leave Orion's gift alone."

"I will do my best," I vow. Slowly I can feel my body lift into the air. I try to look over at Zander but Titen isn't holding back. He has me completely ridged, the feeling is bringing back my day with Axel. *How is Titen holding me so still without hurting me?* I can feel my heart start to pound harder and my breath shorten. *He's not going to hurt me... I have a powerful ability.* I'm able to calm myself down and begin to focus on Titen's gift. As I push the feeling of control out of my mind, I can feel my limbs freeing up, and soon I am back on the ground. I look to my left to see Zander still in the air, so I focus more on sensing Titen's gift. I can feel it concentrating around Zander and Titen, so I get an idea... instead of removing Titen's gift from around Zander, I focus on suppressing his ability—I think that's what I do with Zander all the time. I don't turn it off... I suppress it.

Once I figure that out, I watch as Zander drops, then I

turn to Titen and say, "I think I figured something out... try to lift one of us again." He looks at me and then at Zander, his face creased in concentration.

"Can't do it, can you?" I boast.

"How are you doing that?" he asks with a baffled look on his face.

"I figured out that I don't shut gifts off... I think I suppress them. When I clear my mind I can *sense* everyone's abilities around me. They give off different feelings, like Orion's gives off a feeling of protection. So I focused on yours and restrained it in your own mind, so you couldn't project it."

Zander grabs my shoulders and looking into my eyes says, "You are incredible!" Then he kisses me so passionately that I start to wish we were alone so we could stay like this forever.

Titen clears his throat and says, "We should probably stop practicing and keep a better look-out—we don't want a controlled Elite to find us. The sun should be coming up soon and we need to get through the wall with the rest of them... quickly."

We all sit back down, and I keep my mind cleared, trying to concentrate on feeling the abilities of Elites who aren't part of our group. Suddenly I get overwhelmed, there are so many different senses coming at me. I put my hands over my ears, trying to fill my mind with something else to distract myself. "There's too many!" I say, panicking, and start to rock, feeling like my brain is going to explode. I can feel the tears running down my face. "I can't suppress all of them! I can't even get enough of them out of my mind!"

I feel someone pick me up and move me. Then Zander says, "Orion, keep using your ability, they're coming to switch groups." I open my eyes to see that Zander's carrying me and the sky is starting to lighten up. He says, "It's okay, you can keep your eyes shut, we'll be fine."

"This didn't happen yesterday." I say, pressing my

hands against my head as hard as I can.

Zander says, "Your gift is growing, the more you work with it, the more it's going to open up. You're learning to understand how it works, and that leaves you vulnerable. Once you gain more control, you'll be able to sort through every gifted person in both regions."

That was the last thing I remember happening in the Elite Region. I'm not sure how long I was out, but I wake up lying on the ground with my head on Zander's lap. Running his fingers through my hair, he says, "Welcome back."

I try to sit up, but my head is spinning, "What happened? Where are we?"

"You blacked out... everyone's abilities all at once were too much for you, but you will be able to control that, you've done so many amazing things already. We are at the pond, I didn't want to take you to Mya's home and worry everyone. I know how much you love it here, so I convinced them to stop here until you woke up."

Finally I'm able to sit up and look behind Zander. I see Tara, Titen, and Orion sitting by the path, I'm assuming to keep a look-out. Zander is staring out over the water. "Do you think it will ever be like this all the time? I mean peaceful, where you and I can be together and sit at any pond we choose, not just inside these walls?"

"I hope so. I could sit here for days with you." I climb onto his lap and put my hands behind his neck. "I'm just happy that you're here with me."

"I don't want to be anywhere else," he says. Then he wraps his arms around my back and kisses me. I never get tired of his lips against mine. When he kisses me it makes me feel like nothing in the world matters but us. I push myself against him and he falls backward.

I place my hands on the ground on either side of his head, and hold myself up. "Zander... I love you. I don't know what I would do without you in my life."

"You don't have to worry about that, I'm not going anywhere."

I kiss him and say, "Promise you'll stay with me?"

"Forever."

I roll off him, get up, and take his hand. We walk together and join the others. Looking at me concerned, Tara asks, "Are you feeling better?"

"Much better," I say, nodding. "Let's get to Mya's." Titen, Tara, and Orion walk ahead of me and Zander. The house is going to be crowded, and we won't get much alone time when we're there.

It is interesting to walk right by the Elites without them seeing us, until I see Aron in the distance and whisper, "STOP! We need to go a different way."

They all look up, and quickly we head down a side street, hoping his ability isn't strong enough to reach us. But, like usual, I'm wrong... suddenly Aron comes running down the street toward us with a confused look on his face.

Zander challenges me, "You can do this... make it so he can't read our minds."

Clearing my mind, I can feel Aron's ability, and it feels intrusive. I focus on restraining it so he can't hear us. He stops running and begins looking around. It must be working, because he turns and walks away. Quickly we run toward Mya's home, not wanting to chance Aron finding us again.

We reach the door of her house and hurry inside. They are all waiting in the family room for us. My mother gets up and takes both Tara and me in her arms, and Zander's parents do the same with him and Orion. I look over to Titen, grab his hand, and pull him into our hug. My mother lets go of me and Tara. She wraps her arms around Titen and says, "Thank you for bringing my daughters back." He returns her embrace and nods.

She lets go of Titen and turns to Tara, placing her hands on my sister's stomach. My mother smiles and says,

"How far along are you?"

"Almost five months. She's going to be beautiful."

Tears of joy fill my mother's eyes. "It's a girl?" Tara nods and they embrace each other again.

I look around but don't see Mya anywhere and ask, "Where's Mya?"

Lucca sighs and says, "She's upstairs... when you guys didn't come back right away she got upset."

I run up the stairs and knock on her bedroom door. "Mya... can I come in?"

"Yes."

I open the door to find her sitting on her bed staring out the window. "I didn't think you guys were coming back... I thought they caught you."

"I'm sorry, but I had an issue with my gift. I am learning how to expand it so I can use it on more than one Elite; when the Elites gathered at the wall my mind became overwhelmed, and I blacked out. They didn't want to bring me back here until I came to, so I wouldn't upset anyone."

Finally Mya stops looking out the window and says to me, "I'm glad you're okay. Did you find your sister?"

I nod and sit next to her. "I'll always come back. Besides Zander, you're the only friend I have."

Smiling, she says, "We should probably get downstairs with everyone else."

We get up and rejoin everyone in the crowded family room. I walk in and look around for Zander. When I find him my heart sinks a little. He's smiling at Azaria and she's blushing. I know he loves me, but it's hard for me to see them together. They were placed together, so they are bound to have a connection. How could he not feel something for her while they were living together... alone. She is so flawless and I'm the complete opposite. Even before Axel scarred me, I was no beauty.

Zander looks up and makes eye contact with me from across the room. I try to smile, but I'm too busy beating myself up. He looks at Azaria and his smile fades; he can probably guess what I am thinking.

My stomach starts to hurt, so I leave the room and go to the kitchen. *He loves me, I have bigger things to worry about.* I cross my arms on the table and bury my face in them. I hear another chair slide out, someone has joined me. I keep my head down and say, "I'm fine, I'm just not feeling the greatest."

Someone touches my arm. So I lift my head to see Azaria sitting next to me and ask, "What do you want?"

She says, "I want to let you know you have nothing to worry about. Zander is like a brother to me, I have no romantic feelings toward him."

"That's hard to believe knowing you two lived together."

"We *never* stayed in the same room. He let me have the bedroom and he slept on the couch. I wasn't lying when I said you were all he talked about. You're all he cares about, and I know you care about him, otherwise my presence wouldn't upset you."

I lay my head back down. "I believe everything you're telling me, but it doesn't change what I saw... what *you* showed me."

She gives me a confused look. "I don't know what you're talking about."

"That's why you're here... to torture me with your gift. Thyn used your ability on me, I saw what looked like a memory of you and Zander being more intimate than we have ever been. I saw a picture of you two that broke my heart. I always thought we would be with each other... only each other."

She blushes. "That never happened, my ability is tricky. I can put fake images into your mind, or real ones. Do you want to see one of my real memories?"

I nod and she takes a deep breath. Suddenly I see an image of her sitting in a home with Zander. He is sitting in a chair looking miserably out a window. She is trying to comfort him but he never responds to her. Then it jumps to another memory of them sitting at their kitchen table together and she says, "Tell me about her."

He sighs. "She's wonderful. I've known her my entire life, and I was too afraid to tell her how I felt. We've only been together for a couple months and I wish I would have told her before, so I would have had more of a chance to be with her. I've loved her for years but was too chicken to say anything about it. I know we're supposed to have a happy little life together, but I will never betray her trust. I will always love her and I can't build a family with you... even in ten years I will still be sleeping on that couch."

Then the memory fades and looking down, I ask, "Did that really happen?"

"Yes, every word of it is true. He never once looked at me like I was anything except his roommate." She grabs my hand. "He is a good guy, I truly believe we both could have lived in that house until we died and would have never been more than friends."

I give her a weak smile. "Thank you for showing me the truth. And thank you for not pushing the boundaries and trying to get him to love you."

"I wouldn't be able to, because I understand how he feels."

"I'm glad he had you... that he wasn't alone." She looks at the door and drops my hand. I turn around in my chair to see Zander standing in the doorway. "How long have you been there?"

"Long enough... I wish I could figure out what it is about you that makes Thyn enjoy ripping you apart so much." Discreetly, Azaria gets up and leaves the room.

"I don't know... maybe it's because I upset Axel, and they think I'm Inept and don't deserve someone like you. Even though I'm gifted, I *don't* deserve you."

"Alexis, when will you understand I want no one but

you? I love you and you are more than good enough for me." Out of habit I touch the scars on my face and glance toward the family room. He pulls my hand away from my face and says, "That doesn't matter, you are still the most beautiful girl in the world."

I smile and complain, "It's too bad there are so many people here. It makes it tough to get time with you alone."

"I almost don't even care what they think," he says. He leans over, kisses me, and like it's a signal, someone joins us in the kitchen.

I pull back from Zander to see Titen and Tara sitting across from us and sarcastically ask, "Is there something I can do for you two?"

Titen gives me a skeptical look and says, "We need to figure out what to do next. We need to get more people from the Inept Region on our side. We can't accomplish anything with only four of us, because I *will not* let my pregnant wife do anything to endanger herself or our daughter's life."

"I don't even know where to begin," I say.

He thinks for a minute. "We start with my family, and move onto the families who lost their children. There has to be some smart people here that can help us build weapons, drugs, or *something* to help us."

"Do you think we could use some of my DNA or blood or whatever it is that the Elite use in a drug or weapon so we can suppress their abilities even temporarily? It would help, wouldn't it?"

The look on Titen's face makes me think I'm brilliant, and he says, "That's a great idea… we just need to find the people here who can help us."

"There isn't anything we can do about it today," I say. "Let's start tomorrow morning."

Both Tara and Titen agree and leave the kitchen. Zander stares at me and runs the back of his fingers across my cheek to my hair, saying mischievously, "Now where were we?" He smiles and picks up our kiss where we left off.

# CHAPTER FOURTEEN

There really isn't much space for anyone to sleep in Mya's small house. Mya, Orion, Zander, and I are in her room. Her parents let Mr. and Mrs. Rane sleep in their room with them, and everyone else is spread out between her siblings' room and the family room. Mya offers to let me sleep in her bed, but I am fine with sleeping on the floor—that way Zander can be next to me.

We're lying around in Mya's room when she leans over her bed and asks, "So what's the plan for tomorrow?"

"We're going to go meet Titen's family, he thinks they will help us. Then we are going to search for other families who lost their kids to the Elite Region. I'm not sure if anyone will really want to stand against the Elite with us, but we have to try."

"Can I come with?"

I hesitate for a moment. "Sure... it might help convince them that even if they aren't gifted, they can play a part in this," but Orion complains it might not be safe for her.

"Maybe you should stay here," he says.

Looking hurt, Mya says, "Why? Just because I can't do anything special doesn't mean I can't handle myself. I'm going."

Orion rolls over to his side, turning his back to everyone. *That's odd... he never seemed concerned before... maybe he's afraid he can't hide everyone.*

I'm trying not to worry about tomorrow, or anything at all. I am happy to be with Zander. He is lying on his back so I lay my head on his chest up by his shoulder. Then he kisses my forehead and says, "I love you."

I smile. "I love you too."

Surprisingly, I drift off to sleep easily like nothing has happened to any of us, like our first night in the Elite Region, the night before our tour. Despite falling asleep easily, however, I wake up in the middle of the night full of anxiety, softly crying and shaking. Slowly I sit up trying not to disturb Zander and I try to remember my dream.

I wish I hadn't searched my mind for it—I am only torturing myself, because I remember seeing the same memory Azaria had planted in my head when she had the haze. My dream gave me a front row seat to it, and to make matters worse I notice that while they were being passionate *they both had the haze.* I've never thought of that before—what if they refuse to be together but are *made* to? If Thyn takes the time to place each Elite with someone who they can create an even more powerful Elite with, why wouldn't he make sure that happens?

Quickly I get up, run out of the room, down the stairs, and outside. I start to heave, but I have nothing to throw up. I can't even remember the last time I ate anything. I drop to my knees, place my hands on the ground, and shake my head trying to get rid of the image. *No, no, no... that's crossing a line even for someone as sadistic as Thyn.* Pushing myself back, I sit on the ground. *It never happened, this is his way of getting to me. It's not true... I hope.*

The sun starts to come up so I go back inside before anyone can see me. It looks like Titen is the only one awake so far, so I join him in the kitchen and ask, "Couldn't sleep?"

He shakes his head. "I've had trouble sleeping ever since I found out I've been used to do Thyn's dirty work. I'll never know how many people I've hurt... or killed."

"That wasn't you, though," I remind him. "Once people understand how Thyn's ability works, how he takes someone over completely, no one will think badly of you."

"Maybe. I take it since you were outside and I didn't see you come downstairs, that you had trouble sleeping too?" I look down but don't answer him. "Do you want to tell me about it?"

I take in a deep breath to hold back my tears, "I have a question. You told me when Thyn controls you that you lose pieces of time. Have you ever lost part of your day when you were at your home?"

Thinking for a moment, Titen replies, "It's hard to tell sometimes, because after a while you start to get used to chunks of your day missing. But I think maybe once or twice it happened when I was first placed. I'm pretty sure that's only because I wasn't doing a great job of listening to their rules."

"Which rules?"

He laughs. "Most of them, but I hated being controlled, so I wouldn't go meet at the wall like we were supposed to."

Struggling to spit the words out, I continue, "So... he never... um, he never made you *do* anything with..." I bury my face in my hands and I can't finish my question.

"*OH*," he says, looking a bit red. "Not that I can recall... unless he went to great lengths to cover it up. Something like that wouldn't be easy to hide—the people involved intimately would figure it out pretty quickly."

I mumble, "I'm sorry... I know it sounds stupid. I just had a bad dream is all."

"About what?" Zander's voice startles me as he enters

the room. "I got worried when you weren't upstairs... are you okay?"

"I'm fine... it was nothing," I say, trying to smile.

He doesn't look convinced but changes the subject and says, "So how much longer are we going to let the other two sleep before we go?"

Looking at him confused, Titen says, "Two?"

I nod and explain, "Mya wants to come with. She was with me and Orion all the time before; I think she'll be fine."

He looks concerned but keeps it to himself since Mya just entered the kitchen followed by Orion. She sits down next to me and asks us if we want anything to eat

"I'm not hungry," I say, "but you guys can go ahead and eat."

She gets up and starts making some eggs for her and the boys. Then Zander can't hold back his questions anymore. "Will you please tell me about your dream? I can't stand not knowing what's bothering you, and don't say it's nothing. You never eat anything when you're upset."

I'm trying to figure out what to say when Titen says, "Zander... do you mind coming with me for a moment? It's important."

Zander doesn't take his eyes off me when he gets up, and Titen points him toward the stairs. Titen looks back at me and I mouth, "Thank you," to him and they both leave the room.

At first I'm relieved but then I'm filled with doubt. *He's going to think I'm an idiot.* I'm starting to get mad at myself, because supposedly I have this amazing mental gift but I can't even act like a sane person half the time.

The smell of the eggs is making me feel sick again. I can't focus on anything except that stupid dream I had. I wish Thyn would have hurt me physically, because I will *never* get that image out of my mind.

After a few minutes Mya sets out four plates and starts to dish the food she made. I lean back in my chair with my arms crossed in front of me and wait nervously for Titen and Zander to come back. I watch as Orion scarfs down two helpings of eggs then they finally return. They sit down and begin to eat like they never left.

I look over to Zander and his eyes are sad, but he looks troubled at the same time. *I need to learn to keep my mouth shut.* I keep hurting the people I love because they worry too much about me, but I don't help the situation any by overreacting all the time.

Once they are finished eating we all say goodbye to our loved ones, just in case. Then Titen says, "Okay, Orion, are you ready?"

He nods and says, "We can leave now... no one should be able to see us."

Titen peeks out the door to make sure no one is there so it doesn't look suspicious that a door is opening but no one is coming out. "Let's go, it's going to take us a while to get there, they live past the cornfields."

I say, "So we'll be walking past our homes." It's more of a statement filled with disappointment than a question.

He says, "It's quickest that way... it would take too long to go around in the opposite direction."

When we're on the street, Zander takes my hand in his and I can feel his heart racing through his veins. "Are you nervous?"

"Kind of, but not for the reason you think. I can probably take on anyone who challenges me as long as I don't have the haze."

"Then why?"

Instead of answering me, he says, "Orion, how far can we separate and still be hidden?"

Thinking for a moment, Orion says, "I'm not sure, stop walking and I'll let you know when it starts to feel weak around you two."

We stop and when they are about two houses away, Orion calls out to us, "I can't separate from you much further, I can control this space but I don't want to chance separating anymore."

Zander nods and we start to walk at the same pace as Orion, Titen, and Mya, which keeps us at the same distance behind them. "Alexis, Titen told me about your dream."

I can feel my heart beating faster and my face burning. "I'm sorry... please don't worry about it. I'm fine."

Squeezing my hand, he says, "I'm going to worry about it, because I never thought of that... and... I don't... *know*, I can't tell you you're wrong."

As soon as the words leave his mouth I feel nauseous again. "I wish you could."

"I need to talk to Azaria when we get back, to make sure. I don't think that happened, but I want to be sure before I say it's not true. I'm sorry..."

I take in a couple of deep breaths trying to hold myself together and say, "Don't be... if it's true, it's not your fault." The thought of it possibly being true is tearing me apart inside, but I can't let Zander see it. We need to focus on the plan for the day; if it is true we will get past it... somehow.

Looking up at him, I reassure him, "Please don't worry about it. I know where your heart is. I know you would never willingly hurt me in that way."

He rubs his eye, and his forehead creases as he says, "Alexis, I will *never* forgive myself if it's true. I promised you that no matter how much they controlled me that I wouldn't hurt you. If he made us sleep together... then I broke my promise."

"No, please don't think that way. I love you and nothing will change that."

"You have no idea how important you are to me." He drops my hand. "Thyn is trying to drive a wedge between us. I don't think he liked the idea of an Elite being in love with someone he thinks is Inept. I *need* you to know that if it happened it means *nothing* to me, it won't change anything."

"I won't let it change anything." Looking at Titen, Orion, and Mya, I notice they're waiting in front of a house. I hadn't even noticed we passed our own homes already.

Zander and I hurry to catch up with them. Titen is standing in front of the path without moving. I nudge him and say, "Titen, it's still early, they probably haven't left for the day yet. I'm sure they'll be happy to see you."

He nods, walks forward, and looks through a window. "They are in the kitchen. It doesn't look like they're worried, so I don't think anyone is in there with them, but let's check another window to make sure before we show ourselves."

We look into the family room window, and no one is there, so we gather by the door. Titen looks hard at Orion and says, "I need for you to show only me—I don't want to overwhelm them or chance them seeing anyone else until we are inside."

Orion nods and Titen knocks on the door. His father opens it and his mouth falls open as he says, "Titen! What are you doing here?"

"Can I come in?" His father opens the door and we all follow him into his home. "Are you guys alone, are there any Elites here?"

"No, we are alone," his father says, looking at him anxiously.

Titen enters the kitchen and his mother gets up from her chair with a look on her face like she's seeing a ghost. "Titen... why aren't your eyes clouded?" she asks.

"That's what I'm here to talk to you two about." Before he can say anything else, both his parents wrap him in their arms and his mother begins to sob.

He hugs them back and says, "I have some friends with

me, and one of them is very gifted. He can hide himself and others from someone's mind. I'm going to have him stop using his ability, just know that we are not going to hurt either of you in anyway." They both nod and Titen turns around and says, "It's okay, Orion, you can stop now."

Normally it's hard to tell when Orion stops using his gift, but the look on Titen's parents' faces tells us they know we're here. Slowly they back up, sit down at their table, and listen as Titen explains everything to them. When they find out he murdered people, it's hard for me to keep listening. I know I am going to come into the story soon and I start to feel self-conscious. Why should someone risk their life for a stubborn fifteen-year-old girl?

Titen's parents never say anything while he is explaining, and looking defeated, he asks, "Will you help us?"

For the longest time they stare at each other, then his father says, "I know someone who might be able to help you with the weapons or drugs you were talking about trying to make... I only have one question. Why should we believe that this young lady is gifted at all? They sent her back."

"We'll show you," Titen says.

I look at him nervously and watch as a slew of different objects begin to lift off of the kitchen shelves of their own accord. "Okay, Alexis, you can do it," he says.

Clearing my mind I search for Titen's gift and can feel it throughout the entire room. So I concentrate, push it back into his own mind, and everything drops. Thankfully Titen didn't levitate anything breakable. His parents look at me in amazement and his father says to me, "I have wanted things to be different my entire life. I have never seen anything like your ability. The time has finally come, and we will do whatever we can to help."

I smile and say, "Thank you, we will need you to come with us. We are staying somewhere safe, and I don't want to risk Thyn sending someone after you two. He seems to enjoy tearing people apart anyway he can." They both agree and go upstairs to pack a few things.

"So where to now? Or should we go back and start again tomorrow?" I ask Titen.

He says, "If you don't mind, can we wait until tomorrow? I haven't seen them in years, and would like a chance to catch up."

"Of course, it's not like Thyn is going anywhere we can't find him."

Titen's parents are finally ready to leave, so Titen asks Orion, "Can you do this with two extra people?"

"Yes, but we will need to stay close to each other," Orion says. "We can leave whenever you're ready."

Titen slowly opens the door and quickly shuts it again. "Hurry to the back of the house!"

Nervously we all rush into the family room and he slides a window open. "There isn't a back door, but we need to get out of here. Aron is out front!"

Quickly Orion climbs through the window followed by Mya. Titen's parents are next. They aren't as small and agile as the rest of us, so it takes them a couple minutes to get through the window.

"Go... get outside," Zander says as he starts to push me toward the window, but it is too late—Aron has entered the family room.

I try to empty my mind so he can't read it, but he says, "Interesting... I know there are a few of you here, but I can't see you." Then he's thrown through the air and up against the wall.

Titen looks at me and Zander, and whispers, "Go, I'll hold him off. I'll be right behind you."

Aron lets out a creepy laugh and says, "That's what you think... I have a few of my friends coming this way, they are just as powerful as you, Titen."

As fast as I can, I climb through the window and call

out, "Titen, come on, you can hold him back at the same time. We need to go!"

Titen is through the window before I can blink and all seven of us are making a run for it. Titen says angrily, "Alexis, why didn't you suppress his gift?"

I'm a little upset that he's mad and explain, "Because I didn't know which one to suppress, and by the time I decided it was too late!"

Finally we stop running and while he's trying to catch his breath, Titen asks, "What do you mean, which one?"

"Aron is a good kid!" I say. "I wanted to take him with us, but I wasn't sure how many of us Orion could hide. But then I decided it didn't matter, all I wanted was to save him, but I was too slow... I'm sorry. If I would have removed the haze from Aron before I climbed out of the window, we would have had another person on our side. At the Testing Facilities, he became a good friend of mine!"

"No, I'm sorry, I know how hard it is to see people you care about like that... anyway, we need to get going before he catches up."

More quickly than before, we hurry back to Mya's house. This time I don't have a conversation with Zander to distract me when we reach my home. I hesitate, wishing I could go speak to my father at his grave. I start to walk toward my home when Zander grabs my arm and says, "We don't have time..." I sigh and rejoin everyone.

Once we reach Mya's home, everyone welcomes Titen's parents with open arms. I sit in the kitchen watching as they meet my sister and find out about their grandchild. For that moment I'm happy, knowing that what we're doing is making a difference.

Zander pulls out the chair next to me and sits down. "I wanted to let you know I'm going to go speak with Azaria. I'll be right back and tell you everything. I love you." He kisses me and then he and Azaria go upstairs.

A momentary pang of jealousy fills me even though I

know he's talking to her for my benefit, but it passes when I realize I'm starving, so I grab a roll and start eating. Tara comes into the kitchen and asks, "How are you?"

"I'm fine... I'm just disappointed that I hesitated and couldn't save Aron."

"You've always cared about others before yourself. You have gone through some pretty traumatic things, but you haven't let that stop you from helping other people."

I tell her, "It bothers me, but ever since they took you away I've learned to brush things off. That's probably why Thyn hates me so much."

She hugs me then goes and joins her husband. It's kind of nice to sit in the kitchen alone. I feel like I haven't had a moment to myself since all this started, but I'm glad they are all with me.

I look up to see Azaria join the others in the living room, but Zander hasn't come down stairs. I start to worry, so I go up to check on him. He is standing in the hallway, facing the wall and leaning his head on it. "Zander... what's wrong?"

When he turns around he doesn't have to say anything—the look on his face says it all. Suddenly I feel so angry that I think I'm going to scream at him, but I don't. I turn and run down the stairs into the family room, screaming at Azaria, "YOU LYING LITTLE... AH! You knew this whole time that it wasn't fake! YOU KNEW! How *dare* you lie to me! We have done nothing but take you in and keep you safe! And you decide it's *okay* to lie through your teeth!" She smirks at me and I lose it. I lunge at her but bounce back and I yell, "Titen, let me go!"

My anger helps me control my gift more and I'm on the move again. Then Titen wraps his arms around me from behind. "UGH! Stop! She deserves worse than me strangling her."

"Not until you've calmed down," he struggles to say as I kick and scream.

"*Calm down?*" I yell. "Would you if someone else slept with Tara and then lied to your face about it?" Everyone in the room gasps. "Titen, LET ME GO! *NOW.*" I'm trying to fight him off, but he's stronger than I am.

"No... it's not her fault."

His words make me even angrier, "You're right, it's not. But does that mean I deserve to be lied to? Just let me go! Look at her... she's happy about it!"

Before anyone has a chance to see it, Azaria wipes the smirk off her face, stands up, and says, "Alexis... I'm sorry. I wanted to believe that it didn't happen, that Thyn didn't violate Zander and me in that way. I shouldn't have lied, I knew what happened right away. He didn't because when Thyn quit controlling us he was sleeping, so I made it look like any other day. He was already on the couch, so I tried to hide it. I *never* wanted this to happen. I'm in love with someone else and Thyn had left us alone until almost a week ago."

I ask her, "So around the time my parents were hurt?"

"I think so... please forgive me."

"I wish it was that easy. Titen, please let me go... I don't want to be in here anymore."

He lets go and I walk out of the room. I head back upstairs to find Zander sitting on the hallway floor. He's more upset than I've ever seen him before. "Zander..."

Looking up at me, he says, "It's okay if you hate me... right now I hate myself."

I sigh and sit down next to him. "I could never hate you, and you shouldn't hate yourself. Thyn is a monster, he violated both of you... it's my fault. If I would have come back here and done what I was supposed to, none of this would have happened. He would have never forced you to sleep with Azaria."

"You have to be messing with me," he says, laughing. "*You're* taking the blame for this?"

"Yes, because I deserve it. Like Axel and Thyn both

said, if I had just learned some respect for them, this wouldn't have happened."

"Please... Please don't blame yourself, it makes it worse." He shakes his head. "I am sorrier than anyone will ever know. I wanted... I wanted to share that moment with you someday, but now it will never be the same."

"It could be," I say. "You didn't even know that happened with you and Azaria. Can't we pretend it didn't?"

"How can you be so forgiving?" he asks. "With everything that you've been through, I was sure you were never going to want to touch me again."

"That will never happen... I love you too much." I lean over and kiss him.

I put my head back against the wall and ask, "Zander... do you trust her?"

"I guess... she was the only one I ever really saw once we were placed together. Why?"

"When I went down there and was upset, she had a stupid smile on her face. It was like she was happy with the way I reacted... and what do you mean? You two weren't placed together right away?" I turn to look him in the eyes.

"I had the home to myself until after the first time I saw you while I was an Elite. Then they placed her with me, and I was actually surprised she wasn't already placed... she's almost seventeen."

I clench my fists, fighting the urge to attack her again. "Zander, I don't trust her. You can't tell me it's a coincidence that she was placed with you only *after* I removed your haze the first time. He did it to break me... he knows her ability, he must have planned to bring both of you in front of me like that day in my home. Only he didn't know that I would suppress his ability and that Orion would hide you and Titen."

"Why would she stay then?"

"I have no idea," I say. "Maybe to spy on us?"

"Well, let's be careful around her until we can talk to

Titen about it. I shared so much with her about the people I care about—I hope she's not playing us."

I get up and go into Mya's room. Shortly after Zander follows me. I put my arms around him and lay my head against his chest, and he holds me tight. I look up at him and ask, "Can I tell you something?"

"Anything."

"I don't know how much more I can handle..." There is more I want to say but I start crying uncontrollably. I back away from him and sink to the ground. "I get that he's after me, but why does he have to do unthinkable things to you? Zander... I don't know if I can do this anymore."

He sits in front of me and grabs my shoulders. "Alexis, you don't have to... we could figure out a way to hide from him for long enough that he will forget about us."

I shake my head. "I can't do that to Orion, or anyone else down there." Suddenly I have a picture blocking my mind—another image of Zander and Azaria. I place my hands over my ears and scream, "NO! Stop!" I start to pound on my head trying to get the picture of them wrapped up together out of my head.

Zander grabs my hands. "Alexis, what is it?"

"No... ple... please." I try to free my hands so I can press them against my head but Zander won't let me.

He wraps his arms around me. "Just tell me what's happening."

"Azaria..."

Zander picks me up and stands up in one motion, then heads downstairs. He hands me to his father and I try to pound the image out of my head again.

Then I hear Zander yelling, "DO YOU THINK THIS IS SOME *SICK* JOKE?

I look up to see him confronting Azaria, and she gives him the same sly smirk she gave me. Suddenly she is against the wall with his hand grasped around her throat. "Give me one good reason not to crush your windpipe."

A new image starts to swirl in my head and I yell, "Zander! Stop!" He turns to look at me and lets her drop. "Lucca, put me down, please," I ask Zander's father. He slowly sets me down and I walk over to Azaria. "You're lying."

She smiles and says, "Am I?"

# CHAPTER FIFTEEN

I stare at her while my anger grows. "It's not possible!"

Laughing, she says, "How would you know?"

I don't want to give her the satisfaction of arguing with me so I turn to walk away. As soon as my back is to her, she places the new image into my mind again. I stop walking and take a deep breath, trying to relax. I'm trying to suppress her gift, but I'm too upset.

She begins to laugh at me again and says, "You are way too easy to get to! Axel never told me it would be this easy! Then again, I didn't think I'd have this chance, but I guess Thyn thought it would be a good idea to leave us here since he quit controlling us. Normally he will tell me what he wants me to do, but this time he didn't. It took me a while to piece together everything. I was beginning to think he abandoned me, but when you told me about the image he had me place in your mind I knew. He must have wanted me to figure it out for myself. I'm here for one specific reason... *you.*"

*She doesn't know I removed their haze, she thinks Thyn did.* I turn to look at her and she gives me that annoying smile again.

"Are you finally going to fight your own battle instead of having your boy toy do it for you?" she taunts me. "I do wish Thyn wouldn't have controlled me... the *first* time. He's very handsome, I'm not even sure how he notices your existence."

Zander starts to go after her but Titen holds him back with, "Zander, don't... you don't like being a murderer *with* the haze, how do you think you would feel if you did it willingly?" Zander stops and backs away from Azaria.

Azaria is looking pretty confident in herself now that she knows Zander won't hurt her. "So, Alexis... I know you've seen it, but I could give you some pointers... I know what he likes." She looks over to Zander and winks. I take a step forward but she raises her hand and waves her finger. "Uh-huh... do I need to show you again?"

She doesn't wait for an answer and the image that she played in my mind to get Zander to stop choking her replays over and over again in my head. I stop and start to pound on my temple, trying to knock it out of my mind. Of course this amuses her and she says, "Axel didn't tell me it would be this *fun* to watch you squirm... he said that when he was cutting you that you *begged* him to stop. Hmm... let's see if I can make you beg."

New images run through my head of her and Zander sitting at their kitchen table without the haze. He is telling her how he only pretended to love me so he wouldn't hurt my feelings... that he knew he would be an Elite and wouldn't have to deal with me much longer. Then it escalates into the image of them being intimate without the haze.

My breathing starts to quicken and I can feel my heart breaking. "It's not true... it can't be true!"

She laughs. "Only I know the truth, and I don't think I'll be telling you any time soon."

Azaria plays the images over and over, isolating Zander repeating the words, "... *pretended to love her.*" I can't hold my tears back anymore and they run down my face. I look around, and everyone is watching this happen... letting it happen. "I'm not going to beg you to do anything... I just wish everyone would leave the room."

Azaria sighs and says, "Oh, honey, it won't matter, they are *all* watching what I'm showing you. Oh, I just remembered I haven't shown anyone else but you one thing... let's see how they react."

I see the image she showed me earlier and watch as Zander turns and punches a hole straight through the wall. My sister looks at her skeptically and then says to me, "If she's lying we'll be able to tell soon. It isn't easy to fake being pregnant."

I hadn't thought of her as *pregnant*—all I thought about was the small child running around in my mind with lovely dark skin and hair. If the little boy hadn't turned around to show me his eyes—Zander's eyes—I would have never known why she showed it to me. I can hear Zander crying and he says, "If I beg you to stop, will you?"

She considers it for a moment then says, "No, but I would for a kiss."

He yells out, "Never!"

"Why not?" she says, smiling. "It's not like you haven't before... and you enjoyed it."

I can't take it anymore and shout, "STOP! Just shut up!"

She laughs and is about to say something again but I don't let her. I'm so angry that I throw her to the ground and hold her down. "How's this for fighting my own battle?"

I raise my hand and slap her across her annoyingly perfect face. It feels good to hit her so I pull my arm back again and ball my hand into a fist. I hit her over and over until someone pulls me off kicking and screaming. I fight whoever it is all the way up the stairs, screaming, "She deserves it! I want her *dead!*"

I am pulled into Mya's room and I turn to see Zander—no wonder I couldn't fight him off even with my anger. As soon as I look into his eyes my anger fades, and the pain from my heart breaking comes back. I dive forward and start hitting his chest. "How *could* you! I love you and you're with me out of pity!"

He wraps his arms around me and pulls me tight to him so I can't hit him anymore. I start to struggle trying to get away. I manage to say, "Let... me... GO!"

Holding me tighter, he says, "No... I will never let you go. You asked me if I would stay with you and I promised you forever... I told you I would never leave you. Alexis, I know seeing those images can be compelling, but I never said those things, and I never *willingly* had sex with her. You are the one I love, that I want to grow old with, and when you calm down you'll know that I'm telling you the truth, that I love you."

I let his words sink in. I want to believe them but I don't know if I can. If she really is pregnant, I don't know how I could live with that. I say, "You're going to be a wonderful father."

He lets me go and sits on Mya's bed. "I hope I am someday... to *our* children. Alexis, please don't believe her... I couldn't stand to lose you."

I stand here and stare at him. "You won't lose me," I say. "But it's hard not to believe her, the images are so realistic." I sit next to him. "Zander, I love you."

He looks at me and slides his fingers through my hair, saying, "I love you... so much." He leans over and starts to kiss me. Almost instantly my worries are gone and I know he never said those horrible things. He leans back, pulling me with him, never breaking our kiss. He begins kissing me more passionately so I push myself up and say, "I'm sorry."

"For what?" he says, brushing the back of his fingers along my check.

"I'm sorry because I can't. I'm not ready... especially

not as an act to prove anything... I want it to be normal...
innocent."

"There's no reason to be sorry, and that wasn't my
intention," he says. "I just can't get enough of your lips."

I confess, "I was thinking that the other day about
yours!" He sits up and presses his lips against mine. Just as
my anxiety starts to subside I see a flash of him with
Azaria. Quickly I get up and cross the room.

"What is it?"

"It's nothing... she's messing with me again, and I
can't kiss you while I have images of you with her in my
head."

"We need to get rid of her," he says. "It seems like she
has no idea that you're gifted... we could find an Elite and
give her to them."

"We can't... she knows too much—she knows about
Orion... about the plan... and about where we are. Can't I
just hit her again?"

Wrapping his arms around me, Zander says, "I don't
believe that you want to hurt her."

I shrug. "I do... but I know I couldn't. We should..."

Turning me around, he says, "We should what?"

I try to look up at Zander but I'm too upset.

He starts to shake me and demands, "Alexis! What's
going on?? Answer me!"

I become limp and Zander catches me. I don't lose
consciousness but I have already lost so much more than
that—the chance at a normal happy life, my father, almost
all my trust for Zander, and worst of all my sanity.

Zander carries me downstairs and lies me down in the
family room. I can see everyone standing around me as
different pictures flash through my mind, alternating
between Zander and Azaria being intimate, and my family
and friends—dead. I sit up trying to find Azaria but I can't
see her. "Where..." I can't finish my sentence with the next
round of different images in my head. It's disorienting and

I plead, "Titen... help me... please." I can hear Azaria laughing in the other room. Her laugh turns into a scream of pain, then she is silent and the images are gone. I roll over onto my side and curl up into a ball, waiting for it to hit me again, but it doesn't. Even though the pictures aren't as vivid I will never be able to erase them from my mind. I start pressing my palms against my head in a lame attempt to remove the images from my mind.

Someone touches my shoulder and I push myself away as fast as I can and say, "No... I'm sorry, don't cut me... *please.*"

Zander says, "Alexis, what's going on?"

I cover my ears, saying, "No. No. No... *no!* Get out of my head..."

I scoot back to the wall and start to bang my head against it. "Get out... get out... get out."

I turn around when I feel my hair move out of my face. Tara is looking down at me as she says, "Ale... she can't be in your head anymore... she's dead."

Shaking my head, I insist, "Don't let *him* hurt me."

Tara squats down and looks straight into my eyes. "Who?"

I start to scratch at my scars, breaking some of them open, then my body goes rigid and I scream, "NOOO! Titen, don't help him... please! He'll kill me this time!"

Tara grabs my face. "Alexis! We are not going to hurt you... Axel isn't here and Azaria is gone! Snap out of it!"

I can feel tears running down my face as I say, "Stop... just let me go... Tara, make them let me go!!" She shakes her head *no.*

I scream, "WHY? Zander, where are you! Help me!"

He comes into my view and says, "Alexis, please calm down... Titen will let you go if you relax... I'm right here."

I nod and can feel my body become more relaxed. As soon as I can feel Titen stop, I shoot up off the ground, and make a run for the door. "I won't let him hurt me... not again."

I feel someone grab me, I fight and scream, but before I can figure out who isn't letting me escape, my head fills with the same sensation I had during my test with Thyn. The pressure keeps building until I pass out.

*I see myself lying on Mya's bed with Zander right next to it, holding my hand. He whispers, "Please, Alexis, wake up. It's been days since I've seen your full, bright smile. I need to hear your voice, your laugh, to know you're okay. Please... please." His voice is strained, and I can tell he's hurting.*

*A noise by the door doesn't even stir Zander. Lucca runs his hands through his hair as he asks, "Any changes?"*

*Hanging his head lower, Zander replies, "No... Dad, what's happening? Why is she like this?"*

*"I don't know. We've been discussing it, and we think maybe it's her mind protecting itself. Sort of how her tests came up negative. Zander, you have to realize, tampering with someone's mind is a dangerous thing. I'm not sure how long she will be out, but she needs time to heal."*

*Zander doesn't respond, he slightly touches my face, and sighing, Lucca says, "Zander... there's one more thing."*

*"What?"*

*"She might not be the same Alexis she used to be. She was already struggling with what Axel did to her, then she lost her father, and now this. She might be... unstable." The tone of his voice sends a shiver through me.*

*This is just a dream, a really weird dream, I'll be fine. I just wish I would wake up.*

*Again, Zander says nothing to his father, so Lucca leaves. For some reason I feel compelled to follow him. I venture out of Mya's room, down the stairs, and to the kitchen.*

*My mother is sitting at the table, with Mya next to her.*

*When my mother sees Lucca she asks, "How is she?"*

*"The same."*

*She looks defeated, but Tara encourages her, "Mom, she's strong. She will get through this. I know it would be nice to know what's happening, but I know she will wake up, and she will be okay."*

*I decide I don't want to be around them, looking at their sad faces, so I make my way back up the stairs.*

*I sit on the floor in Mya's room, against the wall staring at Zander, who's staring at me, lying in Mya's bed. This is where I stay for so many days I lose track. I didn't even know time could pass like this in a dream. The entire time Zander never leaves, and barely eats when someone brings him food.*

*Frustration overtakes me and I shout at myself, "Wake up! Wake up! Wake up!" Ugh, why can't I get out of this nightmare! Suddenly I feel another weird sensation, only instead of pressure, it almost feels like I'm becoming weaker. Panic moves through me as I wonder if I'm dying. I can't be dying! This is just a dream, that's all, nothing more! Soon my surroundings become blurry, and eventually all I see is darkness.*

When I come to I'm on Mya's bed facing the wall. I roll over to see Zander sitting in a chair next to the bed. He has his elbows on his knees and his face in his hands. "Zan..." I try to say, but my voice gives out. He looks up, places his hands on either side of my face, and kisses me. When he pulls away he gazes at me for the longest moment. I can tell he hasn't slept much, his eyes look heavy, his hair is messy, and I can feel him shaking.

"Hey there... welcome back," Zander says softly.

I smile, clear my throat, and ask, "What are you talking about? Did I black out again?"

He nods. "I'm not sure what happened, but you kind of snapped and... I don't even know how to explain it... I've been so worried."

"Why? I'm sure I was only out for a few minutes."

Slowly Zander shakes his head and says, "Try a few *weeks*... your health never deteriorated, but it was like you were in a coma. I was starting to get scared that you weren't coming back to me."

I sit up and begin to look around nervously. "Where's Azaria?"

"She's dead... Titen snapped her neck before you blacked out. She was causing you to lose your mind. I don't think he could stand by and watch you get hurt again... like he had to with Axel."

My heart starts racing. "What does Axel have to do with this?"

"When you broke down you were acting like he was here. Your mother said it happened once, when you first came back from testing, but it was in a dream."

"I remember that dream... why can't I remember anything that happened before I blacked out?"

"I'm not sure... but we have an idea about why you were comatose."

I move to the edge of the bed, dangling my legs off it. "What's your idea?"

"Well, we think your mind suppressed itself... in order to block out any pain you were having. We don't know what your gift is fully capable of, and it's done something like that a few times now... during the medical test, when you were with Axel, in the Elite Region when everyone's gifts were overwhelming you, and a few weeks ago."

I squeeze his fingers. "I'm okay now... you don't need to look so sad."

"Alexis, they brought you to your breaking point. You were losing it. You were banging your head against a wall, screaming at anyone who touched you, and begging Titen to save you from Axel. I knew you've been through too much, more than any person should have to handle."

While Zander starts to look me over again, I begin to

remember the dream I had. For a minute I debate telling him about it, but I decide against it. He will only worry about me more.

Leaning over I kiss him and say, "I feel better than I have in a long time... please don't worry, I can do this... I have to do this so they can't hurt anyone else... Zander?"

"Yes?"

I touch my stomach as it growls at me. "Can we go eat something? I'm starving!"

"Of course." He laughs.

He picks me up and holds me in his arms but I say, "I'm pretty sure I can walk."

"I know, I just enjoy you being in my arms full of life!"

He carries me all the way down the stairs then lets me walk. I'm a little unstable so he keeps one of his arms around me to help me stay balanced. I turn into the kitchen and everyone's faces light up. My mother and Tara almost knock me over with their hugs. Then Mya squeezes me as tight as she can. Looking around, I ask, "Where's Titen?"

Zander points toward the family room. "He's explaining everything that's happened, in more detail, to some new people who have joined us."

I smile and go into the other room. There are six more people in there that I've never met before. Titen looks up, sees me, and springs out of his chair. He wraps his arms around me, and says, "I'm so glad you're okay! I hope you don't mind that I continued to gather more help while you were... umm... out."

"Besides being hungry, I feel pretty great," I say. "How did you find all these people?"

"My father knows a few of them, and then they brought friends. It looks like more people than we could have ever imagined feel the same way. Before we get more help we need to find a bigger place to stay, but everything is falling into place." I smile at him, wave to everyone sitting around him, and rejoin Zander in the kitchen. I'm almost skipping as I cross the room to him. He hands me a plate with a sandwich on it, so I kiss him on the cheek and say, "Thank you."

I sit down next to Mya and begin to inhale the sandwich Zander made me. She keeps staring at me and it's making me feel a little uncomfortable. Finally I ask her, "What?"

"Nothing, I'm just happy to see your eyes open."

I smile as I take the last bite of my sandwich, and notice that it doesn't bother me that Titen killed Azaria... and that scares me a little. I get up, head back to the family room, and stand in the doorway waiting for Titen to finish his story. When he's done I walk in, and ask, "Titen... can we talk?"

He excuses himself and leads me out of the family room. We join everyone else in the kitchen, and I take a minute to gather my thoughts. "Why did you kill her?"

"I knew you would ask me that. I had to... I was watching you fall apart and you asked me to help you. I started to remember the day Axel tortured you. I remembered how I felt having to watch you suffer, and I was just standing there because I was too afraid to do anything. I wasn't going to do that again. I'm not going to be afraid of them anymore. They kill people just because it's fun for them... I did it because I care about you, about everyone who has ever been on the bad side of Thyn and his henchmen."

"Thank you."

He looks at me like I'm about to go crazy again and asks, "What?"

I hug him. "Thank you for helping me... both times."

He smiles and rejoins our guests in the family room.

I look at Zander and say, "I wish we could go outside."

"You missed a lot while you were sleeping," he says, flashing his crooked smile at me.

"What did I miss?"

Nodding toward Orion, he says, "Seeing what was happening affected him differently than you. No one can even see this house right now or the people inside it. We figured out he sort of makes a mirage in someone's mind. It looks like a home is here, but if they think about approaching it, the thought kind of dissipates, and they forget about it and move on. Which is good, considering the Elites have been on a manhunt lately. They have been searching *everywhere*."

"How far away from the house can we go?" I ask.

Orion smiles. "I have it out to the road, and no one will even see the path leading up to the house."

"What the heck, Orion? I get traumatized, become comatose, and you get all the best effects from it!" I smile at him.

"That's because I'm more awesome than you are!" he teases me.

I shake my head as I walk toward the door and tell him, "You wish!"

When we are standing by the front door I stare at it and Zander touches my shoulder, saying, "It's okay."

"I know, I'm just confused about what happened before I blacked out."

He leans past me and opens the door. "Well, let's go talk about it." I walk outside not realizing it had snowed. I turn to go back in but Zander is behind me with a couple blankets. "This should help keep us warm."

He makes me so happy I can't believe I ever thought he didn't care about me. He folds one blanket, sets it on the path, and we sit down. Then he wraps the other one around his shoulders and put his arms around me. "So what are you confused about?"

"I have a question first... did anyone ever find out if she really was *pregnant*?"

Zander takes in a long, sharp breath, and says, "She

wasn't... my mother took it upon herself to... *check*... after Azaria was dead. I don't think my mom liked the idea any more than either of us."

"That's a relief."

"Anything else?"

"Zander, I'm sorry... I shouldn't have taken my anger out on you, you didn't deserve it because you did nothing wrong."

"Don't be sorry. I understand."

"Is something wrong?"

"No," he says, shaking his head. "I'm just trying to take in this moment. I wish we could go to the pond, alone, and sit like this."

"Me too." I stare out into our snowy region. "Zander... what were you thinking when I lost control?"

He looks like he's trying to hold back tears when he coughs a little and says, "I don't really know... I've seen you sad and angry before, but it was like you had lost the time from when Axel hurt you to now. You didn't respond to anyone except me and Tara. I never knew how screwing with someone's mind can really mess a person up. When you begged Titen for help, he looked like he was going to be sick and Azaria set him off by laughing at your pain... mostly I was afraid that you were gone, that you would never be the same again. Like I've said before, I can't lose you... I won't. You are my... everything, and nothing will change that. Even if you would have been like that for the rest of your life I would have never left your side."

I look up into his beautiful eyes but am interrupted by an intrusive feeling. A look of panic must have crossed my face, because Zander starts to look around and says, "What is it?"

I whisper, "I can sense Aron's gift... should I save him?"

Zander nods and says, "Yes! I'll be right back." He runs into the house and I can sense Aron getting closer. The closer he gets the more I can feel... what I think is Thyn's gift—a strong sense of control... stronger than the feeling I get from Titen.

I start to focus on Thyn's ability trying to remove his control away from Aron's mind. Zander returns with Titen and Orion. Zander asks, "Where is he?"

"I'm not sure but it feels like he's almost here." I keep pushing back Thyn's gift more and more as Aron gets closer.

Finally he comes into view with a huge grin on his face. "I am growing rather fond of this boy's ability. It's so nice being able to know exactly where you are even if I can't see you," Thyn says, speaking through Aron.

I focus harder and concentrate on freeing Aron's mind. I close my eyes and keep shoving the feeling of Thyn's gift away, removing it from the air around Aron. "Hide him!"

As Aron's eyes clear I can feel Orion's gift surrounding all of us. Once the haze is completely gone from his eyes he looks right at us and says, "How did I get here?"

"You were patrolling under Thyn's control... you happened to walk by while we were outside," I say.

He runs his hand through his hair. "You removed my haze?"

"Yes... why does it seem like you didn't want me to?"

"Don't get me wrong, I am happy to be back on this side of the wall, but I was trying to build a resistance in the Elite Region. It's pretty easy when the liars can't control their thoughts."

I look back to Titen and say, "Maybe we can go and get them?"

Titen says, "We can once we find a bigger location. We don't fit very well in this house the way it is."

Aron seems pleased and says, "Good!" We go back inside and introduce Aron to everyone.

We are all gathering in the family room, and I see that

part of the wall is dented. I stare at it as flashes of my breakdown come back to me. I remember sitting there trying to knock the images out of my head. As I look at the wall I hear a soft voice in the background say, "Alexis?" I ignore it as Azaria's laugh and scream replays in my head.

I jump when Zander grabs my arm. "Alexis? Are you okay?"

I gasp. "I'm fine."

I look up to see Aron looking at me worried. *Aron... it's nothing... you don't need to worry about me.* He looks at me disbelievingly but rejoins the conversation he is having.

I look back at the dent and more pieces come rushing back. Quickly I turn to leave and Zander says, "Where are you going?"

"I need to get out of here," I say. My head starts to spin and I stumble out of the family room. I trip over my own feet and fall to my hands and knees. *Breathe... I'm fine... I'm not going crazy... I can handle this.*

Helping me up, Zander says, "Alexis, you're not fine."

"I am," I insist. "I got a little dizzy, that's all."

He pulls me into his arms and kisses my forehead.

I look toward the family room to see that Aron has followed Zander and me out of it. "So if it's nothing, why do you think you're going crazy?" he says.

I give him an irritated look, "I don't think that I am..."

Laughing a little, Aron says, "Really? You want to try to lie to me?"

I bury my face in Zander's chest and he says, "I'm sure you saw whatever went through her head before she left the room."

Aron nods, "A few bits and pieces, but I'm not sure if I want to know more. It seems pretty intense, so we should probably find a place to stay sooner than later."

I want to be far away from that room, but it is too cold outside, so I pull away from Zander and walk up to Mya's room. I shut the door and throw myself down on her bed, letting my tears fall onto it.

Zander slowly opens the door. "Do you want to be alone?"

I shake my head and he comes in. He sits next to me and softly rubs my back as I cry.

Once my eyes dry up I look up at Zander and say, "You said I was *sleeping* for three weeks, right?"

"Yeah, why?"

"How am I so tired then?"

"I'm not sure, but if you want I can leave so you can sleep."

"Don't go."

"I won't."

Zander moves across the bed and lies down. I curl up, lay my head on his chest, and close my eyes.

# CHAPTER SIXTEEN

When I get up the next day I'm alone in Mya's room. Slowly I sit up and decide to take a few minutes to myself, so I cross the hallway to the bathroom and run myself a warm bath. The water is relaxing, but my mind is still moving at a hundred miles an hour, jumping from bad memories to happy ones of rescuing my loved ones from Thyn's control.

The water starts to cool off so I get out. The only clothes I have are the pair of work pants that I was already wearing and Zander's button-down shirt. After I get dressed I look in the mirror and notice for the first time how large Zander's shirt really is on me. I'll have to remember to ask Mya to take it in for me since she's so good at sewing. I brush out my hair and put it in my bun. The way I put it up makes it look messy, but that's one of the reasons I always do it this way.

I head down the stairs and join everyone in the family room. No one looks up as I enter—they are all listening to Titen say, "Today we are going to go search for an abandoned building big enough to fit a large number of people. We are going to need all the help we can get to take on Thyn and his Elite followers. Orion's gift is strong, so we will all be traveling together. You have to remember to stay quiet and do not touch anyone that walks near us. It isn't safe for us to leave a group here and come back for them. Thyn knows the general location where Aron's haze was removed and could come back at any minute... I don't want to scare anyone but you need to know. There are Elites that are quite a bit stronger than Zander and me, who can do things mentally and physically that will make you wish you were dead."

*That's nothing new for me.* Aron shifts his weight and his eyes become sad; I keep forgetting he knows what I'm thinking. I stop listening to Titen ramble on about safety, go to the kitchen, and search the cupboards for something to eat. I find some dry crackers, sit at the table, and begin to eat one at a time. I'm glad every time new people joined us that they brought as much food as they could carry. As I eat I stare out a window and see snow lightly falling, with the sun peeking through the clouds. *Oh no, it's snowing... that's not good.*

I run to the family room and say, "Titen... it's snowing, they will be able to see our tracks!"

"I can move the snow around to cover them... we will be fine," he insists.

Zander smiles, crosses the room, and placing his arm around me says, "You were out cold for a while there!"

Nervously I ask, "How long?"

"You fell asleep before the sun set last night, and now it's about mid-morning. Everyone's been up for a few hours. We're getting ready to leave Mya's and find a bigger place."

I sigh in relief. "Good... I don't know how much longer I can stay here. I get anxious just standing in this doorway."

Before Zander can say anything Titen raises his voice so everyone can hear him say, "Okay, let's start gathering what we will be needing and head out. You all have five minutes to grab what you think will be useful to us."

Zander takes my hand and leads me up the stairs. We start grabbing all the blankets and pillows that we can and shove them into a large box. He carries it and we move onto the bathroom. He shoves towels into the box and grabs all the medicine and first aid supplies. Once he has gathered everything he thinks we need we join the others downstairs.

About half our group has their arms full of supplies, waiting for Titen to give the go-ahead. He looks at Orion and says, "Are you ready?"

Orion says, "I'm ready, just remember we all need to stay together. If you step out of the... *dome*... that I am creating around us, and don't tell me, you will be seen. If that happens, do not panic because you will draw attention to us. Everyone nods and we walk out the door into the snow.

Immediately the cold hits us and everyone begins to shiver, so one by one Zander hands out the blankets. People have to share, which isn't a big deal, but I am a little surprised by one pair. Mya and Orion are bundled up together, he has his arm around her trying to keep her warm. I look up at Zander and ask, "What's going on there?"

"I think he has a crush on her," he whispers, "but he hasn't really acted on it. The only thing that shows it is his instinct to protect her. Kind of like when he didn't want her to come with us to get Titen's parents."

"I'm glad some good can come out of all of this." He nods in agreement and turns his attention to the surrounding buildings. I start to look too—the sooner we are out of the cold, the better. As we pass houses they begin to thin out and we are crossing through our market place. The little money we get from working goes to food and necessities. I stare at the different places—our food supply building is practically falling down, and our medical supply building is standing strong, but it has broken windows and doors. The sight of everything falling apart makes me angry. If they treated us like humans, all of this probably wouldn't have happened.

We make our way across the Inept Region in the opposite direction of the fields, and our old homes. I can see the factories coming into view and begin to get nervous. This is where the entire region will be working right now since nothing can be done with the fields in the winter, which means all the Elites assigned to supervise the workers will be in one area.

Carefully we walk between the buildings, moving as quietly as we can with this number of people. One of the newer members of our group points to an old run-down factory just a few blocks in front of us. Titen starts to head for it to see if it is a place that we could stay in. It's the farthest building from the main factories and it is huge. If it's really abandoned, it will be perfect. We'll be close enough to all the workers to get them to join us, but far enough away that the Elites won't catch on to us.

Suddenly I feel a rush of different abilities and fall to my knees. "Titen, wait... there are so many!"

Zander is trying to help me up just as fifteen Elites come toward us. I almost think they can see us, but then they turn and go down another path. I look up at Titen and he's waving us all forward. Quickly we all meet up with him and he whispers, "Wait for me here, I'm going to go in and see if it's empty."

Tara grabs his hand and says, "You'll be seen if someone is in there."

Kissing her softly, he says, "Better me than all of you—I'll be right back." Then he disappears through the door.

I hate waiting, I wish he would have taken me with him so I could help. I unwrap from the blanket Zander and I are sharing and start to pace. *I have to help him... I owe him.*

Without consulting anyone, I run for the door. Zander notices too late and grabs at the air, trying to hold me back. I get past everyone and enter the building. It's dark and cold—nothing a little fire can't fix. I start searching the lower level. "Titen... where are you?" but I can't find him, so I climb up some stairs to search the upper level for him.

I reach the top of the stairs and see someone walking down the hall toward me. Slowly I back into a room, but someone grabs me from behind and covers my mouth. I turn my head to see Titen looking anxiously out of the room. When the person walks by I can see that it is an Elite man. He is wearing the Core uniform and looks to be smaller than Titen but much larger than myself.

Titen carefully uses his ability to lift a large brick off the ground and hits the Elite in the back of his head. The Elite falls unconscious, so Titen opens a window and quickly moves him out of it. Using his ability, Titen sets him on the ground gently. "Alexis, what are you doing in here?"

"I wanted to help you," I say. "I needed to help you."

"Well, it's too late to send you back," he says. "I just have the rest of this hallway to search, then we can get everyone." I nod and follow him down the hallway. He turns into each room, searching each corner and closet to make sure no more Elites are in here.

Finally we reach the end of the hall and there is no one else in the building, so we run down to the front door and wave everyone in. Then Titen turns to Orion and says, "Can you hide this entire building? There was one Elite roaming the halls, but I knocked him out from behind so Thyn shouldn't know we are here."

"Of course I can," he says, looking smug.

While everyone's getting settled, I explore the old factory to try and find some debris we can use as firewood. I search a few rooms upstairs and start piling some brick up in the hallway that we can use for a fire pit so we don't burn the whole place down. I also find some old papers and some wood that has fallen off of the walls, so I add them to my pile, when I look up I see Zander standing against a wall.

"Hey, I was about to come get you so you could help me carry all this brick downstairs... we can use it to build a pit for a fire."

He comes over to me. "Please don't run off like that again. I can't lose you!" He takes my hands in his.

"I had to," I say. "I owe Titen my life."

He lets his hands drop. "If you go and get yourself killed, it was all for nothing! It wouldn't matter that he saved your life."

"You're right. I'll try to be more careful... now will you help me with this stuff?"

Without saying anything he holds out his arms and I start to stack the bricks on them against his body. When all the bricks are in his arms, I grab the rest of the debris, and we go downstairs. We set everything in the middle of the largest room and I begin to pile the bricks in the shape of a square, leaving the middle empty. I stack them until the pit reaches my shins and I begin to build a fire for us.

Luckily someone grabbed a box of matches from Mya's home that I use to light the fire, and everyone gathers around it. I get a little anxious when there is a large number of people in such a small space, so I grab a blanket and go upstairs. I turn into one of the rooms and cross it to the window. I clean the window off and gaze out of it. I've always thought the Inept Region is beautiful in a unique way; if we had some resources from the Elite Region it would be even better.

I clear my mind and try to escape it for a moment. I want to be able to sense multiple abilities without feeling overwhelmed. I stare out the window toward a group of Elites but all I can feel is a sense of intrusion and I say,

"Hey, Aron."

He steps up to the window next to me, asking, "How did you know I was here?"

I give him a one-sided smile. "You mean you don't know?"

"I can read minds, but you cleared yours so well that it wasn't giving away anything."

"I've been learning more about my gift to strengthen it. I can sort of *feel* other people's abilities. Yours has its own distinct feel to it."

He doesn't say anything as he looks out the window and I know something is bothering him. *What's wrong?*

"Nothing... you must have missed being able to communicate without stumbling over your words."

"I know something's bothering you... you can tell me."

"Alexis... I haven't thanked you yet, I lied before. My plan wasn't going well in the Elite Region, I was alone. Thyn has Noah under his control all day every day, and Fatima wants nothing to do with a fight."

I say, "I don't want that either, I'm hoping if I can suppress Thyn's gift it won't come to a fight."

Looking at me skeptically, he says, "Then what are the drugs they want to make for?"

I can feel myself starting to blush as I think, *it's because I'm not strong enough... mentally or emotionally.* "They are going to infuse my DNA with a drug to temporarily suppress the Elites' gifts who come against us, because I can't do it."

Aron looks straight at me, takes my hand, and says, "Alexis, you can do it... you've done so much already. Zander's right, you really have no idea what you're capable of. The fact that you're standing here and not off drooling in a corner from everything that you've been through, proves that!"

I pull my hand away and shake my head. *I'm not so*

*sure.*

He turns back to the window and says, "How is anyone supposed to have faith in us, and join us, if you don't believe in your own ability?"

"Everyone else's gifts will compel them. Orion's gift alone would be enough to convince me that it's possible... Aron, you can't tell me that there aren't people doubting me."

"I can't... but I wish I could. It's extremely frustrating to see them act a certain way in front of you, but their thoughts are the complete opposite."

I walk away from the window and sit on an old broken-down desk. "Would you be willing to tell me who does that?"

"No... it wouldn't help anything... you just need to prove to them that they're wrong about you."

I can feel tears building up in my eyes but do everything in my power not to let them fall.

"It's okay to cry," Aron says. "It doesn't make you weak, it shows that you care."

I look away from him and force my tears back. "It makes me look vulnerable," I say. "I'm an easy target. Thyn and Axel know they can get to me by involving the people I love." A flash of Azaria with Zander crosses my mind. "I'm sorry, the thoughts just come into my head. It's hard to get rid of them."

He comes over and hugs me. "Don't be sorry... when someone thinks of a memory, I can sometimes feel the pain in them. Your heart's been broken and that is *nothing* to apologize for."

I can't hold my tears back and begin to sob into Aron's chest. Once my tears stop, I raise my head to see Zander standing in the doorway, so I pull away from Aron.

He starts to leave the room, but Aron says, "Zander... trust me, it's not what you're thinking." Aron's forehead creases as he says, "Well then, if you don't trust me... trust her. She was upset, so I gave her a friendly hug to comfort her. Alexis is like a sister to me... nothing more."

Confused, I get up and ask, "Zander, what is he talking about?"

"Nothing... I'm overreacting."

Looking angry, Aron says, "Do you really think she would do that? That she would inflict the pain she felt on you?"

"STOP! Stop acting like I'm not even here!" I complain. "Zander, tell me what's going on right now!" I cross the room to him and look angrily into his eyes.

Zander tucks a loose strand of my hair behind my ear. "I'm *jealous*, and Aron's right... I shouldn't be."

Sighing, I think, *Aron... can you give me a moment alone with Zander please?* Without acknowledging my thought, he leaves the room.

"Why on Earth are you jealous?"

"I walked into the room to see you in another guy's arms and I don't know, I just got jealous and wanted to rip his limbs from his body."

I place my hands on either side of his head. "Zander, I love you... only you. You saw the pain that Azaria put me through, making me think you would rather be with her. Why would I do that to you?"

"I know... you wouldn't. I wasn't even thinking right when I came in here. I've just never seen you that emotionally exposed with anyone but myself and your family."

I push myself up onto the tips of my toes and softly kiss him. "I'm sorry I made you jealous. He's only a friend... I swear."

He leans down and kisses me, holding my face in his hands. As he is kissing me he lifts me into his arms, sits on an old chair, and rests me in his lap. "Alexis... I..."

I interrupt him with another kiss. I run my fingers through his hair, stopping at the back of his head. I curl my fingers around a chunk of his hair, and pull him closer to me. He begins to kiss me more intensely, and of course like it's a signal, someone clears their throat. I pull back from him and huff.

"I'm sorry to interrupt, but we may have a problem." I look behind me to see Orion and Mya standing in the doorway.

I push myself off Zander and stand up. "What?" I ask.

Mya says, "My parents don't want to be here. They took my siblings and went home... Aron said they are thinking about telling the Elite where we are... I'm sorry."

I give a worried look to Zander and run past Orion and Mya down the stairs. "Aron! Did they really think that? Could you tell how serious about it they were?"

"They weren't just thinking it, her father is planning it. I'm sure there will be multiple Elites here in a matter of minutes."

I start to panic and say, "We need to get everyone out of here!"

Titen comes out of a group of people. "Where would we take them? We will have to fight the Elite off... *you* will have to remove the haze from them all."

I shake my head and say, "I... I can't."

Zander, Orion, and Mya come downstairs and join everyone. Then Zander says, "You can... I believe in you."

I glance up at Aron and he nods. At least it's not Zander who thinks I am incapable of gaining control of my ability.

Titen walks toward the door. "Orion, stay in here and make sure the building stays hidden." Orion nods, grabs Mya's hand, and pulls her along with him to join the others. "Alexis and Zander, I need you to come with me."

Quickly we follow Titen out the door into the cold. My breathing becomes harder with the increased abilities I can feel. "There are a lot of them coming... more than I've dealt with before."

Titen says to me, "Now is the time to show what you can do… if you don't remove their haze they are bound to find all of us, including Mya, Tara, and Orion."

He's right, I can't let Thyn get them… they're innocent.

Titen stands a little in front of me on my left, and Zander does the same on my right. Instantly I know their plan—they are going to hold them off until I can remove the haze; if I can't they'll be taken.

I don't have much time to sort through the different abilities in my mind. The massive group of hazy-eyed Elites have just rounded the corner and are coming straight at us. I take a deep breath, focusing on the different abilities filling the air, and then I feel it. Thyn's gift gives off a creepy sense of control. I focus on it and can feel that it is surrounding the group of Elites. I close my eyes and try to free their minds.

I open them to see a few Elites stop in their tracks and turn to watch the others walk right past them. Some of them run, while others stay with the group. I close my eyes again then open them to focus on the Elites who still have the haze. As I watch them I see that just over half of them are free of the haze. More run off while others stand there confused.

I look toward the Elites leading the pack and push Thyn's gift from their minds. When they stop walking the Elites still in control almost walk right over them. There are too many of them. There are still at least twenty Elites being controlled by Thyn and I don't know if I'm strong enough to stop them. As they come within ten feet of us, Titen starts to push and throw a few of them back, but they get back up and start coming at us again.

I refocus and remove the haze from more of them. Now there are only ten left in Thyn's control. Titen is busy holding off five of them, and when I look toward Zander I see that they are almost in his reach. I stare at them and I'm able to remove the haze from two more. Then Zander grabs one and throws him into the others, knocking them all down.

I start to panic when they get back up. I can no longer determine whose ability is whose. Titen turns to me and screams, "ALEXIS! Get rid of the haze NOW!" So I close my eyes tight and push every ability I can feel away. When I open my eyes I realize what I have done—they can see us, and none of them have the haze, but Zander and Titen can't defend us.

Quickly I stop using my ability and see Titen throw a few more of them around. *"Aron... they can see us! Get everyone out of here! Have Orion hide all of you!"* I hope he heard me and that they are leaving through the back.

I look up to see about fifteen Elites with their haze back are heading straight for us. I notice out of the corner of my eye that Titen has stopped using his ability and turns toward me. I gasp when I see his clouded eyes and yell, "Zander, we need to go!" but it is too late—he also has the haze. I try to focus on Zander to free his mind, but it's no use. I'm too upset to do anything, so I look into Zander's eyes and say, "Thyn... I'm the one you're looking for... take me and leave them alone!"

A horrid laugh comes from Zander and he says, "Why would I lose two of my best Elites? I think I'll keep all of you." Then Zander comes at me, lifts me up, and folds me over his shoulder. As he turns to go back to the Elite region, I place my hands on his back and push myself up. I see Aron and Orion watching from around the corner of the building.

*Aron! Please keep them safe...*

# EPILOGUE

I watch as the Elites take her away, this can't be happening. What can *I* do to keep everyone here safe? All I can do is hear their thoughts. Panic roars behind me, and I turn just in time to grab Tara. "TITEN! ALEXIS!" she screams. "Aron, let me go! I need to get to them! I need to stop Thyn from taking them!"

Keeping my hold on her I try to sound calm as I tell her, "Tara, you need to think of your baby. If you don't calm down she might suffer from it. We will figure something out, but running after them will only get you captured."

She finally quits fighting me, and folds herself around me. *I can't do this without him... how am I supposed to raise a baby alone and homeless... oh no... what are they going to do to Alexis!* Tara's thoughts fill my mind as she breaks down in my arms. After a couple of minutes while she is still heavily crying, Titen's parents pry her off of me and try to comfort her.

*What did she do to deserve a life like this? If Grant was still here, he would have never let this happen! She should still be here!* I don't recognize this voice in my head, but I put the pieces together and realize it's Mrs. Gander's.

I find her sitting in the snow, against the back of the factory. I tell her, "Alexis will be okay. She's strong. Strong enough that she had to be carried away; Thyn couldn't control her mind."

Mrs. Gander stands without acknowledging me, goes over to Tara, and embraces her. Together they cry, and everyone's thoughts are swirling in my mind. No one knows what to do, and everyone is in full-on panic. So I gather what little confidence I have and raise my voice loud enough for everyone to hear: "Everyone, please calm down. I know you are all scared, we lost our three strongest Elites today, but more than that we lost three people we love. As Alexis was being carried away she asked me to keep all of you safe. Honestly I don't know why she thinks I can, but I have to try. Don't give up on this yet. I know her... I know her mind, and she will not go down like this. We will get them back, and we will still accomplish what we've been working on. In the meantime, we need to find a place to stay. We also need to continue to gather help here in the Inept Region, and we need to start creating drugs. That way when we get them back we will be ready."

Surprisingly, everyone's thoughts become more positive, which makes me more confident. *Maybe I can do this... for her.*

Lucca steps forward and says, "Aron is right, we can't stop working. My son was taken today, and I won't let them win. We will get them back, and be ready. First we need to find a place to stay. I know it's cold and it's not ideal to be outside right now, but we can't stay here."

Quickly, everyone gathers all of our supplies from inside and we begin our search for a new safe house. I've never been past the factories so I don't know what we will find, but hopefully we can find something. As we walk, I have the feeling like I'm being watched. I search my mind and go through everyone's thoughts, until I hear the most beautiful voice my mind has ever allowed me to listen to: *He has no idea how powerful his gift is. Even if it's not physical, or able to suppress gifts, he can hear anyone coming. Alexis was right to tell him to keep us safe... he's the only one who can.*

I slightly turn my head, not making it obvious that I'm trying to see her, and I'm able to glance at her. Her eyes are focused on me, and the snow that has started to fall gently lands in her hair. The contrast of the white of the snow and the blazing red of her hair is stunning. Her eyes meet mine, so I quickly look away, trying not to make it too apparent that I was watching her.

"Mya, are you cold?" Orion asks.

I can't help but feel a little jealous and a little annoyed... *Ugh, this kid never backs off. I swear he can't take a hint.*

"A little, but I'm fine," she says, her voice shuddering. I'm not sure if it's from grief or because she really is cold.

"Here, you're shaking," Orion says. I slightly turn again and see that he has a blanket wrapped around himself, and cloaks her in his arms. This kid is infuriating! When will he realize she doesn't see him that way?

Mya's eyes meet mine once more and she blushes as she thinks, *Oh no... he probably thinks there's something going on between Orion and me. Well, I guess it doesn't matter anyway. At least not until all of this is over. We need to focus on getting Alexis, Zander, and Titen back, then on destroying the regions.* I chuckle a little, trying to keep my attention on the task at hand. I'm relieved that she's thinking this but I try not to let on that I know. I try to refocus, we need to find a place to stay.

It feels like we've been walking for days when finally there is an old rundown building in the distance. "Aron, can you hear any thoughts coming from there?" Lucca asks without turning to look at me.

Carefully I shuffle through the different thoughts from our group, trying to detect any unfamiliar ones. I get slightly distracted by Mya's thoughts, but I'm able to push myself past them. "No. There are no other thoughts besides our group," I answer him confidently. Feeling pretty proud of myself I turn around to see Mya's reaction. She has her head down, her eyes on the ground, and Orion is staring at her.

Quickly I scan her mind, hearing: *I hope she's okay... I miss her already. I don't think she understands how much we all care about her.*

Without even thinking about it, I walk over to her and pull her away from Orion's arms. At first she hesitates when I take her hand, but soon enough she hides her face on my shoulder along my neck. "We have to get them back," she mumbles.

"We will. If I have to, I will go into the Elite Region and get her myself."

"No! You can't!" she cries out.

Then Orion interrupts us and says to her, "We can, because I can hide us. They won't even know we're there. Then I'm sure Aron can piece their thoughts together and find her."

I close my eyes and roll them, so he can't see my frustration. Suddenly Mya pulls away from me and embraces him. His thoughts are cocky, but he has no idea. He doesn't know that from the day we met, she hasn't been able to keep me off her mind.

Once Lucca is finished checking out the building we all make our way into it, and begin to make it our home. When everyone is settled, I gather them all together and tell them Orion's idea. "I'm not very good at this leading thing, but I am going to do my best. Especially because Alexis asked it of me." I look over to Lucca and say, "I'm sure you will help me, and I am more than willing to accept the help, but Orion and I have an idea. We will go in and out of the Elite Region, and I will listen to the Elites' thoughts until we can figure out where they are keeping Alexis, Zander, and Titen."

No one says anything until Tara speaks up, "I want to go too."

"No, at least not until your baby is born," I protest.

"Fine, but if you haven't found them by the time I have this baby, I'm coming with you!"

"Fair enough."

Over the next couple of months, Orion and I venture into the Elite Region at least once a week. At first everyone was talking and thinking about Alexis, mostly because Thyn and Axel were boasting that they captured her. Now, the thoughts are few and far between, and it makes me worry. Eventually they even stop completely, making us all fear the worst, but we never give up.

Orion and I stop going across the wall as often, until one day while we are on a run. I decide to walk close to the wall in order to hear across it. *Did you hear the drug isn't working on her? They have to have one of the kids kept at the facilities use his ability. Then when she's out they test different amounts of the drug on her, so she doesn't come out of it. I heard they almost overdosed her once!*

I stop and the supply run group stares at me. "Alexis…"

"What about her?" Mya asks, unable to contain the hope in her voice.

"They're having a conversation about her! I can hear what one Elite is saying to another, through their thoughts," I say wishing I could hop over the wall right now. "I know where she is! I don't know why we never thought about it before."

"Where is she?" Tara asks anxiously.

"The Inept Testing Facilities."

# ABOUT THE AUTHOR

Elizabeth C. Bauer lives in Minnesota with her loving husband, cat, and dog. She found her passion for writing at a young age, beginning with poetry and short stories. She began this series in February of 2014 with the hope of inspiring others to follow their dreams.

You can connect with her at:

Twitter: @ElizabethCBauer

www.facebook.com/authorelizabethcbauer

39306264R00150

Made in the USA
Lexington, KY
15 February 2015